Heart
BROKEN

THE GRITT FAMILY SERIES

Real, Raw, Romantic

Gabrielle G

GABRIELLE G.

Real ❤ Raw ❤ Romantic

I'VE AVOIDED MY HOMETOWN FOR TWENTY-SEVEN YEARS FOR ONE REASON.

AARON GRITT.

NOW THAT I'M BACK IN SPRINGS FALLS, I'VE DONE MY BEST TO NOT RUN INTO HIM.

BUT IF I HAPPEN TO, LET'S HOPE HE ISN'T AS HOT AS HE WAS AT EIGHTEEN.

BUT THE UNIVERSE IS FUNNY THAT WAY.

MY LIFE IS PROOF OF IT—SECRETS AND ALL.

SO, I'M NOT SURPRISED WHEN HE STANDS IN MY CLASSROOM BEFORE ME AS THE PARENT OF ONE OF MY STUDENTS. FORGIVING HIM WHEN HE WALKED AWAY HAD ALWAYS BEEN HARD, BUT NOT AS HARD AS IT IS TO FINALLY TELL HIM THE TRUTH.

CAN YOU FORGET YOUR FIRST LOVE?

I DIDN'T.

EVEN IF I DIDN'T RECOGNIZE HER RIGHT AWAY, THE GIRL WITH A STAR-SHAPED BIRTHMARK WAS ALWAYS SOMEWHERE ON MY MIND.

BUT SHE ISN'T THE COMPETITIVE AND DRIVEN SEVENTEEN-YEAR-OLD CAPTAIN OF THE GIRLS HOCKEY TEAM I LOVED ANYMORE.

I DON'T KNOW WHAT HAPPENED, BUT SHE HAS LOST HER FIRE AND NEVER MADE IT INTO THE PROS LIKE SHE DREAMT OF.

NOW I KNOW WHY, AND IT'S MY TURN TO DECIDE IF I CAN FORGIVE HER.

A SECOND-CHANCE, SMALL TOWN ROMANCE NOVEL YOU WON'T BE ABLE TO PUT DOWN.

Heartbroken Soundtrack

Brown-Eyed Girl – VAN MORISSON
Happy Together – THE TURTLES
Ironic - ALANIS MORISSETTE
Losing My Religion – R.E.M
No Diggity – CHET FAKER
Daughters – JOHN MAYER
Sinners – LAUREN AQUILINA
Nothing Compares to You – FREEDOM FRY
Take Me to Church - HOZIER
It Must Have Been Love – MARIA MENA
Someone Like You - ADELE
I Try – MACY GRAY
Faith – GEORGE MICHAEL
Perfect – ED SHERAN
Two Punks in Love – BÜLOW

DEDICATION: To those who believe it ain't over 'til it's over. (Thank you Lenny Kravitz.)

THEN - ALANE

"*H*ave you seen him, Al? Like seriously, he's the cutest on the hockey team."

It's been five weeks since we started high school, and my best friend Patricia can't shut up about her crush. He's all she talks about. All. The. Time. How he wears his jersey, how he sways his hips on the ice, how he never has girls hanging on to him like the other players, or how he's so smart that he's one year ahead. I'm wondering when I'll get the report on his bowel movements.

She doesn't care much about the team, but as the youngest captain our female hockey team has ever had, I do. I need to be focused one hundred percent at every practice, so I can prove to my parents that I can get into Bishop's Academy—the best hockey prep school in the state. I need to enroll for my last year of high school, so I can get my chance of becoming a professional hockey player. I don't know why, but hockey has always been my passion.

Ever since I learned to walk, I wanted to skate. Every

bounce of the puck fascinated me when I was two; still does at fifteen.

I'm the best on the ice.

When our captain had to step down because of an injury, the team voted for me to be captain, it was an odd vote of confidence, but it boosted my self-esteem even more. We could become an excellent team, if our players chased the actual puck more than the boys on the hockey team, who barely acknowledge us just like the rest of the school. The only one who's here at every practice, watching us and sometimes cheering for us is Patricia's crush, Luke Gritt, also known as one of the Coach's sons.

Of course, Patricia thinks he's here for her and he'll make his move any day now; I'm not so sure about that. Contrary to her wishful thinking, I really don't understand why he comes. Luke watches me, but not as if he's interested in me or wants to go out with me, more as if he's studying me. When my eyes meet his gaze, he acknowledges me with a nod of his head. Patricia is right; he's cute, if you like fourteen-year-old boys with whiskey eyes and dark blond hair.

"Did he nod at you or at me? Why would he nod at you? Do you know him or something? Can you introduce me?"

Lacing up my skates, I ignore her and hit the ice for warm up. I don't know Luke Gritt. We share a few classes, but that's it. I know his reputation as a hockey player, and from what I saw, he's good, even if it seems to me that he would prefer to be drawing. He always has his nose in a notebook. He's also the brother of Aaron Gritt, the goalie for the boys' team.

Aaron is the most handsome boy on that team, but he's a distraction I know my game can't afford. My brain needs to stay in my practices, in the game, not wrapped up in some good-looking, grumpy boy who apparently can't stand the human race.

That's the thing about the Gritt brothers.

If the youngest is all smiles and sunshine, the older one is a dark cloud around the school. For most girls, and especially my best friend, the sun shines right through the dark sky that Aaron is. For me, he blocks the sun every time with his sandy blond hair and blue eyes, or are they grey? I've never been close enough to see them clearly. Shaking my head, I try to focus on the practice, which is about to start.

Head in the game, Alane! Head in the game!

I go around the rink a few times before Coach calls out the drills of the day. It starts pretty easy with two equal lines in the middle of the ice. Coach passes the puck to the first person of one line, who then passes it to the next player in the opposite line. It's nothing exciting, and I'm restless, needing to do something else, to do more, to work harder. We are *not* five-year-old players. One of the girls passes way far off its mark and the others begin to giggle.

I sigh in frustration.

"Smith! Is there a problem?" Coach yells.

"No, Sir!" I reply as if I'm in the army.

"Come here a minute, Smith!" I skate toward Coach, my head down, knowing that a lecture is waiting for me. I've heard it from every coach since I started to play this game. I need to be more patient with my teammates, a real leader needs to keep their attitude in check, and I will never get to where I want to go without a team. It's killing me just thinking about it. Luke's eyes are on me again, and he raises his eyebrows in an amused manner. I'm sure he knows his father is about to chew my ass out, and he seems ready for the show.

"I'm sorry, Coach. I didn't mean to give you attitude. I just get frustrated when they giggle to get the boys' attention." Coach Gritt's eyes widen in surprise.

"Look, Smith, you seem like a sweet girl, and I know it can get frustrating. I'm not going to give you the speech of being better with your teammates. I know you do well; you're just not as interested in boys as they are. It's okay. I'm sure your father is happy about that. I called you here because I think it would be great if you'd train with my son. He could be in the nets, and you can do special drills with him. It will probably push you further. What do you think?" I look at Luke on the side. So that's why he comes to our practices. His dad certainly told him about his plan, and he wanted to be sure I was up to his standards. I've seen him play, and I know I can beat his ass on the ice. Luke is grinning now and seems really amused by all of this. I'm going to wipe that smile off his face, that's for sure.

"Say yes, Smith!" he shouts from the other side of the rink.

"Get ready, Gritt! I'm going to kick your ass!" I answer back, skating back to my team.

"You won't, Captain! Not a chance!" he yells back, jogging toward the lockers. Coach Gritt is behind me, also heading to the team to give his next instructions.

"Can you stay after practice today? I'll call your mother, so she won't worry."

"Yes, Sir."

"We'll make a schedule later. Now, back to practice."

Once practice ends, I'm not even sweaty. The girls go to the locker room, and I stay behind on the bench, readjusting my equipment. Patricia is pissed at me for some reason that undoubtedly has to do with Luke.

"Ready, Smith?" This voice is not the one of a fourteen-year-old. I raise my head slowly, appraising every part of the body belonging to the boy facing me. I can't make out his muscle tone under the equipment, but I know it's not Luke. As soon as my eyes find his, I feel myself blushing. Aaron. And his eyes are blue-grey, like the livid bruise I see on his cheek.

"What happened to Luke?"

Aaron looks at me confused. "He's there," he says, jerking his head in his brother's direction. "Certain to be drawing some shit, waiting for me to drive him home."

"Language, Son!" Coach Gritt says from behind him.

"Sorry, Dad," Aaron mumbles before skating away.

"Are you ready, Smith?"

"Can I have a minute?" Coach nods, and I skate towards Luke.

"I thought I was skating with you, Gritt," I tell Luke once in front of him. He's sitting on the bleachers, feet on the bench with a notebook on his lap and a pencil in his hand. He looks behind me, in the direction of his brother, but I don't dare look, too afraid I will meet his gaze again. If I can, I will avoid his eyes for the rest of practice.

"What gave you that impression?" Luke says, focusing back on his workbook.

Is he for real? "You told me to say yes."

"I did." He smiles. "I just never said it was with me."

"Smith!" Aaron says, "I don't have all day!"

I spend the next hour skating up and down the ice, trying to be faster and better than Aaron but failing every time. He's just quicker, stronger and more agile than me. As much as it frustrates me, it gives me the push I need to be better, but mainly, better than him. I work hard to play better than most of the boys my age, and I won't give up during my first practice with one.

"When is the next practice, Coach?" I ask a little out of breath.

"Every second day after the boys or girls' practice. So, three times a week. Afterwards, if the two of you want to add some more, I'm not against it," Coach Gritt answers with a strange glimmer in his eyes.

"Fine by me." I remove my helmet and untie my soaked blonde hair from the tight ponytail giving me a headache. "Gritt?" I say turning to Aaron.

"Hmm?" He seems to be daydreaming or brooding again. "What?"

"You good to practice three times a week with Smith and I, and alone with her on weekends, if needed?" Coach repeats to his son.

"Whatever you need, Dad. It's my punishment, after all."

"Punishment?" I'm a little startled by what I just heard. Training with me is a punishment for him. Nice, jerk! Aaron points at his shiner on his cheekbone.

"Don't take it personally, Smith," Coach says. "Aaron is at my beck and call for a little while. I knew you needed help to excel, so I asked him to assist."

"What did you do?" I ask Aaron, who's glaring at me with annoyance.

"Nothing," he mumbles, taking a sip from his water bottle before turning around and skating away off the rink. Definitely a jerk.

"Do you need a ride, Captain?" Luke screams.

"I'm good. Thanks, I'll call my mother!"

"Don't bother her. Aaron and I can drive you home!"

"Help me, God," I hear Coach mumbling behind me while packing his things.

"Come on, Captain!" Luke insists. I can imagine the discussion that will come up with my mother, if not one but two boys drop me off at home. There is no way in hell the ride is worth the trouble. I shake my head to refuse once again.

"You can use the phone in my office, Alane," Coach says before walking away.

"Your loss." Luke shrugs, making his way towards the lockers as well. I stay inside the rink alone, enjoying the silence and solitude while I untie my skates.

That's why I arrive first at practice and always leave last. I love being on my own in the arena. It makes me feel important somehow, as if my dreams are tangible. I stay a few minutes more, lying down on the bench, raised on my elbows with my head tilted back, and I inhale deeply with the smell of sweat floating around, letting the cool air of the arena bring my temperature down. Every time Aaron looked at me, my heart raced. I feel ridiculous for the mini-crush I have on a guy who's clearly not interested in the least. Luke seems more interested in me than his brother, but I'll never get close to my best friend's crush. I'm not that kind of friend.

Head in the game, Alane! I repeat to myself to chase Aaron from my mind.

When I've taken it all in and feel ready to go home, I sit up and open my eyes, only to find a set of blue eyes watching me intensively. Aaron is on the other side of the arena, looking shocked as if he saw a leprechaun on the ice. He's looking straight at me, and I'm not sure why. He seems mesmerized, but I know it can't be from seeing me. I feel him gazing at me from head to toe and my body begins to feel warm. His gaze is like a thermostat, building the heat in me in a way only he can turn on whenever he wants.

I can't move, I can't speak, I can't breathe.

As fast as he appeared, he backs away, his eyes still on me with his lips tight and his jaw clenched. I stay petrified until he disappears through the doors.

Luke's head pops in.

"Bye, Captain. See you tomorrow in science." He waves at me.

Closing my eyes again, I repeat the only words that can calm my pounding heart.

Head in the game, Alane! Head. In. The. Game.

2

NOW - ALANE

oken up by the ringtone of my phone with a number I don't recognize, I check the time. 9:45 P.M.

Still foggy from my accidental nap, I lift my head off my students' science homework and let the call go to voicemail. I stand up to get ready for bed. As soon as the phone stops blasting, remorse invades me.

What if it's an emergency? What if something happened to Adam? What kind of mother would I be letting an emergency call from my son go to voicemail? Oh my God, what if he got arrested and I'm his only call? What if he needs me? What if he's hurt? Or hurt someone? I need to calm down and set my head straight. I need to relax. He's safe. He's always safe. The scenarios are always in my head. It could be a wrong number for all I know.

Adam is all right.

Adam is safe.

Adam is well.

Adam's safety has always been a trigger for my anxiety

attacks, but I haven't had any in a while. Since being back in Springs Falls and leaving him behind in Phoenix, my anxiety has returned. I worry a lot about Adam. More than about my sick mother I take care of, the reason I came back here. I don't like being far away from him. I never liked it.

Fortunately, when I called my friend Patricia, she lined up a job for me at her private school in the city nearby. It had been my lucky day… or not. I was hoping, in a way, I wouldn't find a job and had an excuse not to stay long. I was hoping to only be here a few weeks and bring my mother home with me.

But I was lying to myself. I needed the job.

Not because I needed money—being the ex-wife of a plastic surgeon meant I was set for life—but because I'd have never been able to spend time so far away from my son if I had nothing to do all day but think about him and what kind of trouble he could get into.

Not that Adam is troublesome.

He's, in fact, a very responsible and lovely adult. He's just the most precious thing I have, and I can't stand anything happening to him. It has been so since his birth. Nobody could get near him but me. He was a gift from God, after all, and I needed to keep an eye on him at all times. It was him and me against the world. We had to let his father in at some point, but he was, and will always be, mine and only mine. Needing to know if he's fine and hoping he'll answer me so I can find sleep, I send him a text to calm my nerves. The nights he stays silent are the worst.

Me: Did you just call me, Adam?

Adam: Nope.

He knows that if I ask, it's because I'm worried. I never hid my mental health problem from my son. We don't hide things from each other; that isn't how it works between us.

Me: Alright then, good night, sweetie.
Adam: 'Night, Mom. I'll call you tomorrow.

Feeling calm, I get ready for bed and persuade myself that the call was a mistake. But my phone rings again, with the same number. I have no choice but to pick up, or I won't sleep tonight. I know the anxiety will eat me up until morning. I don't want to feed the monster inside me. As stressed as I am, I try to grasp what this could be about, not answering would be worse.

"Hello?" I'm not sure what else to say or who would call me at night. I'm way passed my prime. At forty-four, I don't get late-night calls. My ex-husband doesn't call me much anymore, and the few friends that I have are presently sharing a bed, even with the time-difference between Arizona and New York State.

"Captain?" A deep voice answers me. "Is that you, Smith?" Only one boy called me Captain my whole life. A stupid, annoying, mischievous boy I was friends with over twenty-five years ago! Just hearing the nickname sends me back to the first time he used it.

"Gritt? How did you get my number?"

"You don't talk to me for more than twenty-five fucking years, Alane, and the first thing you ask is how I got your number?"

"I...I..." It seems that Luke Gritt is not a little boy anymore. If I've lost most of my confidence, it seems he gained it all. So goes the universe. It needs balance.

"I heard you were in town," he interrupts my stuttering. "Meet me before I leave."

"I don't know, Luke. I don't want to be trouble for your

family." I never wanted to be. For the last twenty-seven years, I never went back home. My parents traveled a little to Arizona to visit, well, my mother did. I barely saw my father for all those years. When he died ten years ago, I came in for one day and tried to be as discreet as possible so nobody would know I was in town. Since then, I have asked my mother to move to Arizona, but she's as stubborn as a donkey, and you can't make her change the path she thinks God drew for her.

So, when she got sick, I'm the one who had to uproot my life and move back here. Coming back was hard, but I had to. I wasn't going to let my mother die alone. It took me over twenty-five years, but I put on my big-girl pants and flew to upstate New York. I flew back *home*. A strange feeling for a place that hasn't been mine for so long.

"He knows you're back. We spoke about it at supper." I register what he's saying, but I won't acknowledge it. I don't want to talk about his brother. Not now, not ever.

"So, you're not in LA being all big and mighty?" For years, I didn't know where Luke was or what he'd done with his life until his name was mentioned in a gossip magazine as the tattoo artist of celebrities, and the next thing I knew, I was looking him up. If it weren't for his roguish whiskey eyes, I would have never recognized him.

A full beard, styled dark hair, build like a guy who spends a lot of time at the gym and not enough time outside. Luke did not become what I thought he would. I imagined an art teacher with longish hair and a smooth face, and I had found the spitting image of a biker, with tattoos, piercings, facial hair and rings on his fingers. After this discovery, I needed to follow him on Instagram. Next step would have been to reach out, but I never could bring myself to do it. Contacting him meant explaining, and I still didn't know how to disentangle what had happened, even twenty-seven years later.

"You keeping tabs on me, Captain?"

"Kind of." Hearing his voice, even if he has a different tone than when we were kids, makes me feel things I haven't for years. The main one is safe. The other is home.

"Meet me before I leave. We need to catch up, and I want you to meet someone important to me."

"Okay," I whisper in the night. "But can you not…"

"You know the deal, Captain. I'll tell him I saw you, but if you don't want me to tell him anything that doesn't concern him, I won't say anything else." Luke always was the best at keeping my secrets, as long as they didn't involve his brother.

It's one of the reasons I left.

I couldn't talk to him about his brother breaking my heart. I couldn't talk to Patricia about the Gritt brothers. I couldn't talk to my parents, and I certainly couldn't speak to my Coach about his son.

So, I flew to Arizona, living with my Aunt Clarisse, a renowned writer and the least judgmental person on Earth.

Then I met Mark, married him and raised Adam. I completed a teaching degree and taught science for years. An easy life until Mark and I divorced a few years ago. He reproached me about not being enough in our relationship, not wanting the same things. And I didn't. Not anymore.

I had left a piece of my heart with a boy in New York State, and I needed it back.

Aaron Gritt and I had a dream, and he destroyed it, leaving me behind to bleed when he ripped my heart out and took it away on his way to Culinary School.

"Okay then," I tell Luke awkwardly.

"Want to meet at the rink?"

"No, better to grab a coffee."

Luke and I make some plans for the next day after school, and I hang up smiling at the memories of the boy I once knew.

Over the years, I've thought a lot about all the what-ifs my story with his brother held. What if I had stayed? What if I had followed Aaron? What if I had spoken up the day, he broke my heart? What if I saw him again? Aaron has always been my favorite what-if. But that's all he'll be, a what-if, a fantasy I could never have, a boy who changed the path of my life forever, who crushed my dream and shaped me into who I am today.

He was my first love, my first heartbreak, and my first disappointment.

And now, I just want to avoid him as best I can.

I know he is in town, I know he is a local celebrity, I know he owns the best restaurant in the state, I know he has two kids, and I even know he's a parent at the school where I teach. I pray hard I don't have to ever call him for a problem with his children.

There's no way I can face him again without reliving the most intense years of my life, but as experience had taught me, my fate is not a kind one. I am the queen of bad luck and unexplainable situations.

So, of course, I would have to see him, and soon.

I know it, God knows it, and the Universe knows it too.

And if I see him, I'll act like an adult, leaving the past behind and our history under wraps so we would be able to discuss the problem of one of his children. I just hope his wife will be there too. It would be awkward but salutary not to have to face him alone and wonder what would happen if he took me on my desk.

After all, Aaron was the boy I could never totally have, not because of other girls or because he wasn't mine, but because I came from a very religious family and there was no way we could have sex before marriage.

We both promised we would wait until he didn't.

We both thought it was a given, until it wasn't anymore.

We never had sex, and I really hope he grew bald and had gotten fat.

But again, I know with my luck that won't be the case.

3

THEN - AARON

"So, isn't she perfect?" my stupid brother asks, once again, after practice on our way back home.

"Shut up, Luke!" I grip the steering wheel.

"Aar, I'm telling you this girl is perfect for you. She is competitive, pretty, funny and smart. You should have listened to her hypothesis in science class today. It was incredible!"

"Why don't you go for her then?" I know why, and I'm an asshole to ask him.

Luke made his coming out to me this summer.

Not that he kissed a boy, but he's pretty sure he doesn't want to kiss a girl. That's how I got a shiner last week and became my father's servant for the next seven days.

My parents are hippies, totally against violence.

Because Luke asked me not to tell my dad what I fought for, I got punished for hitting a jerk homophobe who insulted my brother and had to practice with the beautiful brown-eyed captain of the girls' hockey team.

"That's why you need a girlfriend. To let me be and have a little fun," Luke says not fazed by my previous comment.

That's my brother, the happy, laid-back one and understanding of others. I'm more the asshole who distances himself from everyone.

The only one I want to know all about is Luke.

I want to be in his brain to understand how to be relaxed. I want to breathe happiness. I want the dark cloud over my head to dissipate. I've always been the miserable one, and he's always been the shiny one. My parents think it's because of all the maryjane they smoked when Mom was pregnant with me.

I was born a crier and they barely slept for a year because of it. So, when she learned she was pregnant again, Mom decided not to smoke during her pregnancy. Luke came into the world with a smile on his face. They didn't need more proof to see the cause and effect.

When they had two more kids ten years later, she didn't smoke joints either while being pregnant, and Salomé and Barnabas were born happy as clams, but just a little less happy than Luke. I've come to the conclusion that nobody can be as happy as Luke.

"I don't need a girlfriend, and I'm not even sure she likes me."

"But the question is, big bro. Do you like her?" I shrug for an answer. I know he has a plan. He has been studying her since school started because he claims he knows she's the one I should lose it to.

According to Luke, she's the perfect sweet, beautiful girl-friend my virgin self should fall in love with. He's a romantic. If he weren't gay, I'm pretty sure he'd be married at eighteen and have children by twenty. He wants to find the one true love, like in a Disney movie, and of course, he wants me to find mine as well.

"She's perfect, but she'd be even more perfect if she had a brother."

I chuckle a little. "What does your perfect man look like?"

He sighs. "I don't know, Aar, I guess for the moment, he looks a lot like Mark Wahlberg."

"New Kids on the Block, huh?"

"That's kind of how I knew I was gay, bro. I got hard looking at them dancing; the Wahlberg I like is the Marky Mark one."

"Gold chain and bandana?"

"And bare chest, don't forget the bare chest!"

I shove Luke nicely on the shoulder. Only he can make me laugh so naturally. That guy is everything to me.

"So, what are you going to do, Aar? I know you like her. Not only because I hear you masturbate at night, but also because you can't speak when you are next to her." Luke looks at me and grins knowingly. "Oh shit! I was saying this as a joke, but you did rub one out thinking of her. This is awesome. I'm a genius. I knew it!" the smug ass says.

"Don't tell Dad, or he'll bug me forever, or worse, he'll stop the practices."

"Not quite a punishment after all." Luke smiles.

We park in front of the house and run into the kitchen, each trying to arrive first at the fridge. We need sustenance before getting out there to help our father.

Our parents own a farm and grow vegetables. At the beginning, they just wanted to be able to feed us what they knew would be good for us. The farm grew, and they now have a few employees to help but still rely on us to give a hand. As they say, we should learn how to feed our future families.

What I like the most is cooking with mom.

I love to invent recipes and pair vegetables with meat. I'm

quite good at it, but that's not something I share with the world. I mean, I can't really tell the hockey team that I like to cook. Even if Chris, our captain, is my best friend, I'll get a roasting.

Sometimes, I wonder if I could become a chef, but that's a crazy idea. I think my father expects me to become a hockey player or take over the farm one day. So, I guess, I'll go into business anyway.

As I'm shoving whatever I can find to eat in my mouth, there is a light knock on the door. Luke pushes me towards it for me to go open it, so I humor him and do so.

Right in front of me with her magnificent brown eyes and beautiful long blonde hair in a tight ponytail stands Alane.

As usual, when my eyes meet hers, I'm transfixed.

My heart pounds, and the world disappears.

I do all I can during our practice sessions not to fall into her eyes, or even look at her. It's been this way since I saw her so relaxed the first time we practiced together.

She was lying on the bench, propped on her elbows, looking at the ceiling, and her hair was like a fall of spun gold. She compelled me that day. I had never seen a girl so laid-back.

Of course, Luke had told me how she wasn't much into gossip and drama. But seeing her so unperturbed had turned me upside down. And seeing her now, standing on our threshold, I'm spellbound again.

"Hey, Aaron." Her voice is sweet but firm, nothing like the nasal voice of most girls our age.

Trying to swallow my peanut butter sandwich to return her greeting, the bread gets stuck in my throat, and I choke on it, sending me in a fit of coughs right in front of the girl I want to impress.

Impressing Alane is impossible.

Everything I do at practice seems to be taken as a challenge to do better, and she does better every time. If she wanted, she could choke better than I'm doing right now. As I'm wondering if I'll die at her feet, Luke magically appears with a glass of milk for me to chug down, which helps the sandwich go down.

"Hey," he says with all his cool. "What are you doing here, Captain?" She seems horrified that I almost died in front of her. She blushes, and my cock stirs. I don't need more embarrassment, so I pray to Jesus, Mary, and Joseph not to get an erection in front of the girl I like, with my brother standing next to me and his arm around my shoulder.

"Hey, Gritt, you forgot your workbook on the bench. I thought I would bring it back to you," she tells my brother with a beautiful smile.

People tend to smile at Luke, and I'm used to it. Nevertheless, I want that smile to be mine, to be given to me. It illuminates her face and underlines her freckles. It makes her even more beautiful than she already is.

"Thanks, Captain. Look, I have to run and help my dad, but Aaron was just telling me a few ideas he had to improve some of your plays. He was going to talk to Dad about it, but since you're here, why don't you just come in. I'll go tell your mom that Dad will drive you home later, if that's okay with her."

I have no idea what he's talking about, but that's Luke, trying to get the girl for me. I didn't even have to tell him I liked the girl because he already knew I liked her. He runs outside toward Alane's mom's car, and as her mother looks in our direction, Alane waves to tell her it's okay, and her mother leaves. We're still facing each other on the threshold, and I feel like the cat got my tongue.

It's awkward seeing her standing here before me.

It's strange having all her attention.

I don't know where to look or what to say.

I throw my hands in my jeans pockets and wait for her to tell me something, to tell me what to say or what to do.

I'm at a loss for words.

That's when my six-year-old sister Salomé comes running into the room crying her head off, followed by my four-year-old brother Barnabas with the body of a Barbie in one hand and the head of the doll in the other.

"Aaaaaaaarooooooon." Shit, I forgot I was in charge of watching them today after practice so my mother could go help my dad with something in the garage. Salomé runs toward me, inconsolable, and cleans her nose on my jeans. I bend down to her level and wipe her tears with my hand.

"Hey, Sal, what happened?" My little sister is the cutest thing on earth, with her big brown eyes and long dark blonde hair, she looks more like Luke, but her eyes are much bigger, and she knows how to bat her eyelashes so we can't refuse her anything. Well, Mom does. Dad, Luke and I can't.

"Barnabas broke the doll, again," Barnabas imitates Salomé from behind her, and I hear Alane laugh at the declaration of my little brother. It's a cute laugh, like her. It's light and high pitched, and the way her shoulders rise and fall makes her breasts bounce incredibly in the thin tank top she's wearing.

I try to stay composed, but that's before I hear what the four-year-old next to me has to say.

"Aaron! You see the boobies. I want to kiss them." Out of

context, my little brother could easily sound like a pervert, but he has, in fact, been breastfed until recently, so "kissing the boobies" does mean putting them in his mouth but not for what I believe adults do.

"Oh my God!" Alane says mortified.

"I'm so sorry," I tell her at the same time. "He was breastfed for a long time, and he..." I stop in my tracks when I realize I'm about to share my mother's breastfeeding story, and as disturbing as that is for a son, it might be even worse for a stranger.

"I'm, well, maybe we can discuss the play another time?" She blushes and averts her eyes. Crouching down to the little asshole, I repeat what my mother has told him millions of times.

"Barn, you can't speak about ladies' boobies that way," I scold him.

"Are you Aaron's girlfriend?" Salomé asks. Alane shakes her head.

"Luke?" Alane shakes her head again.

"Mine?" Barnabas asks with love in his eyes.

"I could be your girlfriend, little man, but I don't know your name." She ruffles her hands through his hair.

"Little man," he answers totally enamored. She drops to his height and gives him a hug, and for the first time in four years, Barnabas is quiet. No laughter, no clownish behavior, no tantrum, no shenanigans, he wraps his arms around her neck and quiets down.

"One day, I will marry you," he whispers softly. Alane blushes again and lets the little bugger go.

"Well, you won't be able to marry her if Aaron does," Salomé says with all her sass.

"I'll share with Aar. I don't want to share with *you*!" He runs off again with the broken doll in his hand. Before running up the stairs, he turns back and sends Alane a kiss with the biggest theatrics I have ever seen. Alane giggles, her tits bouncing again, and I see Barnabas' eyes widen and his mouth opens to say something rude once more. Before he says anything, I intervene to save the situation, releasing Salomé from my arms.

"If you two go play nicely, I'll read *you* your princess book tonight, Sal, and the dragon story for *you*, Barn. If you don't, I'll tell Luke to get the tickle monster out." They both grin at me and run off to their shared bedroom, the same bedroom Luke and I used to share until Sal arrived. Dad decided to build an extension over the garage for Luke and I, to each have our own space and have more privacy.

"Do you want me to drive you home?" She nods and sends me a shy smile that seals the deal of melting away my heart and hardening my cock.

"Okay, let me tell Luke quickly, so he can take care of the two little people in the house, and I'll drive you." After finding Luke behind the barn doing nothing, I drive Alane home. The cab of my old truck smells like the rink with a hint of strawberry coming from her, and all I can think about is kissing Alane Smith. Silence falls between us, and it's the first time I'm uncomfortable saying nothing. I generally am the king of mute, but with her being in my truck, I don't want to miss a thing.

"I'm really sorry for Barn's comment. He's only four, and I think Luke and I are maybe a bad influence on him." I know it's undoubtedly not Luke. If Barn was commenting on dicks, it could be Luke's fault, but breasts, yeah, not Luke's doing, neither is it totally the breastfeeding.

"Um... It's okay. Let's forget about it," she says softly.

"Sure. It was pretty funny though. I think Barn is in love with you," I babble awkwardly because I can't shut up now that I started.

"Well he does want to marry me," she jokes.

"He doesn't have that much experience with girls."

"Because you do?" She cocks an eyebrow. It's my turn to blush and be embarrassed. "Oh my God, I'm sorry Aaron, it was supposed to be a joke, I didn't realize. Shit. I'm sorry." I nod, embarrassed by my blushing. The silence falls again.

"Well, Alane, I'm not sure where I'm going," I tell her after five minutes driving around town.

"Oh sorry, of course, you don't know where I live, you're not a creeper like your brother. It's not far, just behind the church." I laugh because Luke is a creeper with her. I'm not sure what his deal is, but he knows everything about her and keeps sharing pieces of information.

"You know, I think he forgot his workbook on purpose today, or because he wanted to have an excuse to talk to you tomorrow, maybe he even wanted you to come to our place. We weren't even talking about hockey before you got there. I have no idea why he's so obsessed with you." I tell her earnestly. Talking to her is easy. I like it a lot.

"My friend Patricia thinks he likes her, and he's trying to get to her through me."

"Doubtful." We arrive in front of the church and Alane tells me to stop there, not to come too close to her house.

"Ashamed of me already?" It's a joke but the way she pinches her eyebrows and bites her lip, I might be closer to the truth than I thought.

"Well, if my father sees a boy driving me home, I might not be able to get to practice for a while."

"Really, who are you? The pastor's daughter or something?"

"Indeed, Aaron, that's who I am," she whispers while opening the door. She jogs the rest of the way, her ponytail bouncing right and left while I imagine her breasts jumping up and down. I might have to fight my youngest brother, but I'm pretty sure, I want to marry that girl, too

4

NOW – AARON

"I'm not sure what I want to do with the farm," Barnabas says, drinking his beer.

We're on my parents' porch, talking about life and what the future holds. Well, I'm not speaking, Barnabas and Salomé are. I'm listening, and missing Luke, who left a few days ago with his boyfriend. I like the new boyfriend. Dex is a silent type. We had one short meaningful conversation, and I could see the guy wasn't a bullshitter. I would have never imagined my brother with a three-piece suit lawyer, but he's as quiet as I used to be, or still am.

"Look, Barn, if you want us to sell the farm, we sell the farm. It would be hard for my business as a wedding coordinator, but I'll survive. Or maybe we could turn it into a Bed and Breakfast or something? We are close enough to the mountains and the lake; we could do well in tourism. The bridal couples and families always ask if they could sleep here. Aar, what do you need from the farm?"

"The veggies mainly, but if that's not what Barn wants to do, I'll find another supplier." It will suck balls not to get my parents' veggies, but I'm not going to force my brother down a path he doesn't want. God knows, I didn't follow the way my father thought I would. Luke didn't either.

"I feel kind of obligated," he says, finishing his second beer.

"Barn, you're thirty-three and still live in the house you grew up in with our parents. "

"You do too, Sal," Barn shouts back defensively. Sal moved back a couple of years ago when her business in New York went up in smoke because her then-fiancé fucked her over with her partner and literally fucked the partner too, or something in that vein. Salomé never told us the whole story. Nevertheless, I thought Luke, Barn, Dad and I were going to kill the guy, but Sal and Mom implored us to behave.

Salomé's eyes fill with tears, and I'm sent back twenty years ago when I used to separate those two, who loved each other more than anything but would fight to death.

"Low blow, Barn!" I reproach him.

"Sorry, Sal!" She nods her forgiveness.

I sometimes wonder when my sister will get back on her feet. She withdrew a lot since this happened, it left her heart broken with some trust issues.

My wife of twenty years and I decided to divorce, and I'm not even heartbroken about it. I knew it wasn't working for years.

She had a job two hours away and never came home because she supposedly had no time. However, every opportunity she had, she left on vacations with friends and colleagues, yet I didn't.

I'm not dumb to think she was faithful.

We haven't had sex in almost two years, and the last time we were in the same bed, I was drunk. Jessica is way too beautiful not to have men running after her.

We met in Seattle the summer before I started culinary school. She had just gotten hurt as a young pro-athlete. I went out with the son of the people I was staying with, and she was one of his friends. We drank too much—me to forget the life I left behind, her I don't know why. Jess made her move. We rented a hotel room, and I lost my virginity to someone I thought was a one-night-stand. She looked for me the next night, and we ended up in the same bed again, and the night after, and the night after that.

When I went back home four years later, we were engaged.

Jessica wanted a family, but first, she wanted to travel the world. She did while I worked in different restaurants around town.

I didn't want to travel the world.

I wanted to be home in case Luke came back. He had left just after Alane, and I was missing him.

I was missing her too, but after having broken her heart, I wasn't allowed to want her to come home.

I didn't let myself think of her too much.

I didn't try to find her or reach out to her.

I was certain she was happy.

My mother had asked hers, and it seemed she had met someone and had a baby. Who was I to miss her? I was getting married to a beautiful, tall, doppelganger of Naomi Campbell, and I wanted her more than my teenage-self had wanted Alane. I wasn't a kid anymore, and the love I had for Jess was maybe a little less romantic, but it was tangible. Jess and I were strong.

When she came back, we made the decision that we would live close to my parents, I would open my own restaurant, and she would work as a sports reporter in the state. Again, we made it work, even if we were sometimes hours away. We had two kids, Hailey and Lawson, and despite her schedule and my crazy hours, we managed.

But after years of being apart, we were raising children but barely had a life together. She started to stay more and more in the city, which was an inconvenience for me. I couldn't stay at the restaurant as much as I needed and leave the kids home alone. So I compensated when she was home.

Step by step, we grew apart until we became just friends.

She left for Las Vegas last month, we are divorcing amicably, and even our kids don't seem to be missing her. So, Sal being hurt three years after the breakup is not something I can comprehend, but I know she still doesn't deserve Barn being an ass about it.

"Have you seen her?" Barnabas asks me with a glint in his eyes. I know whom he's asking about. How could I not know, when that's all my family is talking about these days. Forget the family, anybody who knew me in high school asks me. Even my friend Chris, who is now living in Miami, questioned me.

"I didn't, but Luke did before leaving," I tell my brother.

"I know that! He said she was even more beautiful than before but a little sadder, too." Barnabas feeds me information I don't want.

I didn't want to talk to Luke after he met with Alane, and I let him go back to LA without asking anything.

I don't want to know.

I don't want to see her.

I don't want to talk to her.

I did tell Dex, Luke's boyfriend, I would try to get a shot at my happiness if I could, but that was more of a fantasy than a reality.

I mistreated her, I lied to her, and I broke her heart. Why would she want to give me another shot at something I destroyed?

"Baaarn!" Salomé interjects.

"Don't be jealous, Sis," he says mockingly.

"I'm not."

"But you used to be," I tell her, reminiscing how she couldn't stand the time I spent with Alane. Salomé shrugs.

"Well, my three brothers were enamored with the same girl, and it wasn't me. Bite me for not liking not being the center of your attention when I was six."

"But you were never like that with Jess," I tell her.

"I had lost you by then. You left. Luke left. I only had Barn. Who you brought home did not matter anymore," Sal says with the same voice she had when she was younger. When she complains I still see her as a kid, the little sister I spoiled so much even at thirty-five.

"Dad!" Lawson, my fifteen-year-old son, comes in running, his sister on his heels.

"Hailey is in trouble!"

"I'm not. You're such a piece of shit, Law!"

"Language!" I say for the umpteenth time.

"It's true, Dad. The perfect student finally found a teacher who doesn't have their nose up her ass because she's the best athlete in the school!"

"You're jealous because you're a stupid dumbass!"

"Language!" I raise my voice, standing up to separate what I see will become a fight in the next few seconds.

"Sorry, you're not a stupid dumbass, Law, you're intellectu-ally challenged." Barn laughs behind Hailey. I would laugh too if they weren't my kids.

I turn to Hailey. "What is he talking about?"

"Nothing, this new teacher just doesn't know shit. She said if I failed another assignment she would talk to Principal Hardcore and reduce my practice time. She went on and on about having another plan and not gambling my whole life with something I love in high school. She sounded like Grandpa. She's so fucking annoying!"

"Language, Hailey, that's the last time, and it's not Principal Hardcore, it's Harbor, you know it. So, what I heard is that you failed, and you don't care?"

"Whatever, science sucks, I don't need it to play basketball!"

Hailey is a very competitive young athlete who loves her sport. Dad and I tried to get her into hockey, but she was all about the ball.

She's tall, with latte colored skin, brown eyes and curly light brown hair. She is beautiful and has no time for boyfriends, which is a salvation. I don't need a punk to try to get in her pants.

She is the polar opposite of her brother. Not physically, they look alike, except Lawson's skin is paler, and his hair darker, but their full lips, thin nose, and features are the same, yet that's where it stops.

He's an artist. Always with a notebook in his hand, doodling, creating, or drawing. He loathes sports but breathes art and technology. He's quiet and shy, while she's explosive and charming. She also likes to test me and push my boundaries; Law just follows my rules.

"So, what are you going to do?" I ask her.

"Well, you need to talk to the teacher and help me. That's what Mom would do."

"Oh boy," I hear Salomé say. I forgot we had an audience.

"Hailey, you know Mom wouldn't have done shit! Seriously, don't manipulate Dad because you can't get your way for once," Lawson says. I agree with him, Jess wouldn't have done shit, and when she did, she would have done everything to be the cool mom and get Hailey a pass, so she can be forgiven for not being around. I'm the bad cop. It's okay, I'm used to it.

"Dad, language!" Hailey says pointing at her brother.

"Hailey, that's enough," I tell her sternly. "If I meet with that teacher, what's his name?"

"Her name is Mrs. Smith," Lawson informs me.

"So, If I speak to Mrs. Smith, you realize it can go worse for you, right?

"Especially because she's her homeroom teacher as well," Lawson says proudly.

"Son," I say turning to him, "with all due respect, shut up. In fact, you three, let me speak with Hal alone. She doesn't need an audience to deal with her shit." Barnabas, Salomé, and Lawson go inside, while I stay on the porch with Hal.

"Hal." I motioned for her to sit down. "Is everything okay?" She shrugs, pouting. "Honey, look at me. You're normally a straight A student. What's the deal?" She keeps her eyes on the floor avoiding my eyes. "Talk to me, baby girl. I'm not a mind reader. Is it because your mom left?" She stays silent, tears falling along her nose. "Boy trouble?" *Please no, please no, please no*. She shrugs. "Friend problems?" She shrugs again. "Do you need to talk to Aunt Sal about it?"

I remember the first time Hal got her period, and of course, Jess was traveling. In the beginning, she refused to talk to me, and I had to call Sal for Hailey to articulate what the problem was and how I could help. I can't believe that was already three years ago.

"No, it's just… It's stupid, and you're going to tell me it's in my head like everybody else told me."

"So, you told everybody before me?" She shrugs again.

"Hailey, tell me," I insist. She sobs a little before taking a deep breath in.

"I think Mrs. Smith hates me. She's always on my case, always saying sports aren't enough, that it's not because I'm the captain of the basketball team that I don't have to work. The others all think like Lawson. They are saying that the other teachers were just giving me good grades I didn't deserve for years. I compared my copy to Madison's, and Mrs. Smith asked so much more from me than from Maddie. It's just not fair. I don't even know what I did to piss her off."

"Okay, do you need me to meet with her and discuss the issue then?"

"Well, if I continue getting bad grades in science, my GPA is going to tank, and I might not get scouted. I need it, Dad, I promise I'm working hard; I'm just..." She sighs. "Between Mom finally showing me I don't matter and the new teacher, it's a lot. And there is that new boy Maddie and I both like on the hockey team, but I don't want to lose my friend over a boy, and I told her so. Maddie doesn't really care about me, she said if she had the chance she would kiss him." That's the thing with teenage girls, there is always a lot to decipher, and it might take quite a lot of time to come to the root of the problem. I believe the boy drama is what is bothering my girl, but there is nothing I can do about that.

"So, we have a boy problem, a bestie problem, a school problem, and a parent problem. That's a lot of problems for one girl," I tell her, wrapping an arm around her shoulders.

"Yes," her voice trembles under the emotion.

"What would you say if I cooked your favorite meal tonight at the restaurant? You and I, for a date. We'll abandon Lawson here with Grandma and Grandpa."

"You're going to make duck confit and cheesecake just for me?"

"Of course, baby girl. You're my favorite daughter after all. I'll request a meeting with your teacher and try to see what I can do, but you need to work, Hailey. I'll also explain the situation to your mom. You can call her, you know, she certainly would like to hear from you."

"I don't really want to talk to her." I tilt my head inviting her to continue sharing her thoughts. "She left us, you know. Now it's only you, Lawson and me. Not that it wasn't before, but I always thought it was temporary. I feel stupid to miss her when she doesn't miss us. She never did." I'm not sure what to tell her because I have no clue if Jessica ever missed us. I thought she was family-oriented until we had a family, and then I realized she was more career-oriented than anything.

"Come on, let's go eat some duck, and stuff our faces with cheesecake."

"Thank you, Daddy. I'm glad you're the one who stayed," she says, giving me a hug.

"I would have never left, Hal. You and your brother are all that matters to me."

5

THEN – ALANE

"Hey." Aaron stops in the corridor to talk to me. I feel myself blushing inside and outside. It's the first time he acknowledges me at school, in front of everybody.

"Hey," I answer, letting my new bangs fall over my eyes.

"You changed your hair." He wipes my bangs from my eyes and tucks them behind my ears.

It's the first time he's touching me as well. It's a touch like a boyfriend would give his girlfriend. I still feel his fingers behind my ears, even when he removes his hand.

"Can I talk to you after school?" It feels like the world around me doesn't exist. All I can see are his eyes, his smile—him. I only see him.

"What about?"

"Well." He blushes. "I would really like to not have an audience to say what I have to say," he whispers. My eyes darting to the side to see that we have, in fact, spectators gawking at us. Chris is standing nearby, unquestionably waiting for him, as well as Chris' sister, Patricia, waiting for me. Luke is grinning not far away, and the rest of the student body are sending us side-glances, especially the girls. I've seen how they look at him.

I can't fault them. He's beautiful, tall, cute, and sporty. He would make the perfect first boyfriend, if I didn't have hockey to play and a strict dad.

"Okay," I answer, "I have practice though. Want to meet at the rink?"

"Mind if I watch practice with Luke?" he asks sweetly.

"Of course not."

"Okay then."

"Okay." We hold each other's gaze, smiling. For a guy who didn't speak much, Aaron has opened up to me a lot these past weeks.

He drives me home after practice, always dropping me off far from my father's sight, and we discuss hockey, his siblings, and the music we like. He fascinates me, and I hate the fact that I think so much about him all the time. I need to keep my head in the game.

Coach Gritt has intensified the practice for both of us, and there is something so appealing to be able to compete against him. He doesn't treat me like a girl, he doesn't let me win, but if I do, he high-fives me and sometimes even hugs me.

Luke is always there, watching us, and asking me how I am and how I feel. I think we're friends now. Of course, this has put some tension between Patricia and I because she was sure Luke wanted to ask her out. I tried to talk to him about it, but he didn't take the bait. I don't think he likes her.

I'm still looking deep into Aaron's eyes, smiling at him when Patricia tugs my arm.

"Come on, Alane! We're going to be late for science!"

"And us for English. Let's go, Romeo," Chris says pulling Aaron backward by the shoulders. Aaron winks at me and walks away with his buddy teasing him, turning a few times to look at me and smile. I look in the direction where Aaron disappeared hoping he would come back and smile at me again.

"Alane, we're going to be late," Luke says, bringing me back to Earth.

"Where is Patricia?"

"Who knows, she was scoffing and pouting, making her way to science." We start walking towards the lab when we see the principal.

"Gritt, Smith! In Class."

"Yes, sorry Sir. We were discussing hockey and lost track of time, we're going now," Luke excuses us as if his answer was ready.

"Chop-chop!"

"Yes, Sir," we answer, hurrying our step.

"She likes you, you know," I tell Luke speaking about Patricia.

"Oh, I know!" He laughs. "I'm not interested."

"Why? We could double date," I say shyly. His brows crease.

"So, you want to date Aar?" He smiles. I nod.

"But I have no time. I need to play hockey, and my father will never allow it," I answer, moving quickly to the last free table in the lab. Patricia didn't save me a seat, and that's okay, I much prefer to partner up with Luke. At least he knows what he's doing.

"We'll see..."

"So, if you're not interested in Patricia, why do you come to watch our practice so much?"

"For you, of course."

"Me? I'm confused, didn't you just smile when I said I wanted to date your brother?"

"I did, believe me. I want Aaron to date the perfect girl—a girl who can also be my friend, and I thought you were it. I just needed you both to cross paths." He shrugs.

"You don't even know if he wants to date me."

"You're funny, Captain!"

"Shhhh," Patricia turns around to scold us, her eyes filled with jealousy.

"Sorry," Luke mouths and winks. Patricia giggles, blushing. Once her back is to us, he rolls his eyes at her.

"Thank God her brother is cute because she's so annoying," he says with a smug attitude.

"You... You..." I gasp.

"Yep, only Aaron knows. Some others wonder."

"You like boys?" I murmur. He shrugs.

"So, now you see why Patricia and I can't work and why I need a new best friend?"

"Who was your best friend?" He nods in the direction of a guy I saw for the first time a few weeks ago when he came to school with a black eye. He had never been on my radar before, but rumor has it Aaron had beaten him up because of a girl. Nobody knows who the girl is though.

"The one Aaron beat up for a girl?"

Luke points his thumb toward himself. "Meet the girl," he says softly quoting the word girl.

"Oh my, you have to tell me what happened!"

"I will but you have to promise that everything I tell you will stay between us," He says pointing his chin in Patricia's direction. I nod quickly to reassure him.

"I would never—" I start whispering.

"Gritt! Smith! I didn't say anything when you were late, but can you keep your Show and Tell for after class?" The whole class is looking at us, some girls giggling, others shaking their heads. "Yes, Miss. Sorry for the interruption," Luke thunders. "I'll tell you later," he whispers back. The teacher is still looking at us, and I dive my head into the books to be sure I don't get distracted again.

The Gritt brothers are going to get me into some trouble I can't afford.

Patricia, Luke and I walk to the rink where Chris and Aaron are waiting for us. I feel like I'm flying to him. I might as well be flying; I'm walking so fast. Patricia is harping on about whatever to Luke, who is blissfully ignoring her.

Once I'm standing in front of Aaron, I lose track of everything else.

He's wearing a blue jacket with baggy pants and a T-shirt. It's simple but perfect, whatever he does is always perfect. I hear Chris telling Patricia to let Luke be. I also hear him complaining about his best friend falling for his sister's best friend, which means they can't double date. I hear Luke and Chris laugh at Patricia's suggestion to double date and Chris telling her it won't happen. I'm wondering if Chris knows about Luke, but I won't pry.

I'm lost in some livid-ocean colored eyes for now.

"Hey," Aaron says as he did in the corridor earlier in the day. "So, I wanted to ask you if you would like to go out some-time, just you and I without... them," he adds with a nod of his head in our friends' direction.

"I would love to, but my dad won't allow it." My eyes fall to the floor to hide my embarrassment.

"So... I went to see your father. He interrogated me for an hour and asked about my intentions towards you, and I had to promise no funny business before getting married, but he said that it was okay with him if you were okay with it, so..." I tilt my head up, my whole body jerking towards him.

"You asked my dad?"

"Well, yes, I mean, you're the Pastor's daughter. I don't think I can date you without his approval." He frowns.

I'm dumbfounded.

I never thought he would go so far as asking my father. I can only imagine how uncomfortable that must have been, especially for Aaron, who doesn't like to talk. My father surely asked him about his beliefs, intents, plans for the future, and why his parents never come to church.

"I'm sorry," I say hiding my face in my hands. Aaron peels my fingers off my face and keeps his hands on my cheeks.

"It's okay, Al. I just want to know what you think of us dating."

"Like boyfriend and girlfriend?" He nods. "I don't have much time on my hands, Aaron. I need to work extra hard to get the scholarship I want for Bishop Academy and to become a pro-hockey player. You know that, right?"

"If you want to date me, we can make time. I mean. We're already practicing together, I'm driving you home anyway, we just need to do homework together, run together, and spend Saturday nights together. We'll find a way," he says, taking my hand.

My brain is screaming yes, all I want is to be with him, but I'm worried he won't understand when I have to be home by eight thirty on Saturday nights and when I stay late to do more drills with his father.

"I already know about the early curfew and the crazy schedule. I also asked my father if he was okay with me dating one of his players. All you have to do is say yes, Al."

"Okay." I giggle stupidly.

"Okay," he repeats, looking into my eyes, grinning from ear to ear.

"I have to go?" I whisper.

"If this is a question, the answer is no." He leans in slowly, looking at my lips, wetting his. When he's so close that I think he's going to kiss me, I stop him.

"Not here." I point at Chris, Luke and Patricia watching us.

"Shit, sorry. When you're around, I tend to zone out of my surroundings." He blushes.

"Same for me." I laugh.

"Can I walk you to the rink?" He takes my hand.

"Of course. By the way, Aaron, boyfriend or not, I'm still going to kick your ass at practice." He laughs, tugging me forward so he can wrap his arm around my shoulders.

"I know, Al. I wouldn't have it any other way."

"Smith! Head in the game!" Coach Gritt yells. "If my dumbass sons and their friend are distracting you, I can tell them to leave!" Aaron's eyes are on me, and I can't focus on the puck.

That's exactly what I was worried about.

My teammates giggle, trying to get the attention of the boys, not knowing Aaron is mine or Luke is not interested. I believe they can solemnly focus on Chris. I repeat the drill from the start and still do it like shit. I start again, but I miss my slap shot, which I usually never miss. The girls are shaking their heads now, knowing I won't get a good shot in.

When I'm too much in my head, I'm no good.

No athlete is.

Head in the game, Smith!

I try again, and this time, the puck flies out of the rink, way too high from the net.

"Boys! Out!" Coach Gritt yells, and the three boys stand and leave. Aaron looks like his dad just told him he was grounded for life. Luke slaps his shoulders, and his brother shoves him hard, making Luke lose balance and fall on Chris. Note to self: don't poke the bear when he doesn't get what he wants.

Coach Gritt continues working my ass off as to make me forget his son, and it works. He even makes me stay a little longer. I've been here for an extra thirty minutes, and I'm sure Aaron has left by now.

I'm on my bench, relaxing and bringing my heart rate down after the hard practice and the stiff words Coach had for me for being distracted.

I'm trying to put every emotion in place in my head. If everything is in its place, I can stay focused, get the boyfriend, the grades.

My head needs to be in the game.

I can do it all; I just need to organize my thoughts to visualize the end game.

Once I open my eyes, Aaron is watching me from the other side of the rink. Like at the end of the first practice we had, his gaze is intense. He strolls in my direction, his eyes never leaving me.

"Hey, Al."

"Hey."

He sits next to me, his hand brushing mine on the bench.

"I was afraid I'd missed you, and you'd left," he says, his pinky looking for mine.

"Oh no, I was doing my little ritual." I share with him something I haven't told too many.

"Your ritual?" He flips a leg over the bench to straddle it. I do the same, to face him. My eyes fall on his lips. I bite mine.

"Yeah, I always visualize what I did wrong, what I should do better, how I can do it better and what went well. Then I repeat my mantra and try to relax before going home."

"What's your mantra?" he asks, moving my hair from my eyes.

"I want to kiss you."

"That's your mantra?" He blushes.

I shake my head. "Head in the game," I mumble.

"I want to kiss you is a better mantra." His mouth comes closer to me. I nod slightly for him to continue. His hands find mine, and he intertwines our fingers.

"Can I kiss you, Alane?" he whispers almost against my lips.

"Yes," I say before his mouth lands on mine.

It's my first kiss.

My heart is beating hard, and my whole body feels sweaty. His lips move slowly, massaging mine. It's kind of scary, a little awkward, and a lot of fabulous. I relax into him and slightly open my mouth. His opens too, and I feel the tip of his tongue caressing my bottom lip before he leans away.

Opening my eyes, I'm rewarded by the brightest smile I ever saw on his face. It feels magical. It feels like we just shared the biggest secret in the whole world.

"Sweets," he mumbles.

"What was that?"

"Whatever happens now, you'll always be my first kiss, Alane Smith."

We hold our gaze silently for another minute before Aaron declares he has to drive me home. All I can think about is how to categorize what just happened between us and still keep my head in the game, because surely now my head will be in the clouds repeating that kiss until we can kiss some more.

"And whatever happens, you'll always be mine, Aaron."

6

NOW – ALANE

*W*hen I started to work at Lake Academy, Patricia gave me my class lists. As she extended the paper to me, I saw the glint in her eyes and the smirk on her face. It didn't take me long to realize why.

The family name jumped off the page and tears sprung into my eyes.

Lawson and Hailey Gritt.

Two names Aaron's mother had discussed with me over and over.

Two names I thought I'd name my children.

Hailey because Mrs. Gritt thought it was my name for a while, Lawson because she always liked it. We used to laugh about her fictional grandchildren. She insisted we had time, but she could see it clearly. She also thought I was there to stay. Aaron's mom was free and loving, but she said she could see real love when it was in front of her, and Aaron and I were meant to be together forever.

I believed her.

How wrong she was?

How wrong was I?

Patricia knew the story. We discussed it, and laughed about it when we were kids, so I was surprised to see a hint of exaltation on her face when she saw my heart break all over again.

She had always been a little jealous of my relationship with Aaron. Not because she wanted to date him, but because, for a long time, she didn't understand why Luke wouldn't date her. The reason was easy, he preferred her brother, but she didn't know.

When Aaron and I were done, I knew she was happy.

It proved I wasn't better than her.

It showed that no Gritt wanted me, after all.

She knew Luke would choose his brother, and she wouldn't have to face his rejection anymore. She believed she would have me back, and the Gritt boys would be out of our lives. Little did she know, I hadn't planned to stay behind.

We barely stayed in touch over the years, and we're hardly close now, not like we were in middle school, before I dated Aaron. We never spoke about my ex-boyfriend, but I learnt he had children when she let it slip that her brother Chris had been asked to be the godfather of Aaron's youngest. Needless to say, I never knew Aaron's children's names, I was glad I hadn't because it felt like he continued our life without me.

It hurt in a way it hadn't hurt for a long time.

Calling Patricia to ask for a favor had been difficult. I didn't want to owe her anything.

Of course, Patricia knew Aaron's kids were attending the school—she is the principal, after all— but she assured me they were easy kids, and I wouldn't have to meet him. After seeing Luke and his boyfriend Dex, I wasn't sure if I wanted to see Aaron. Luke was amazingly sweet like he used to be when we were young but hotter now. I had concerns with the idea of seeing him, but as soon as I hugged him, the anxiety dissipated. He was Luke, my funny, easy-going, almost best friend. I've asked him not to speak about Aaron, and he didn't. We talked about his life in LA and my life in Arizona. I talked about Adam a little; he spoke about his tattoo parlor a lot.

We were reconnecting.

Unfortunately, his boyfriend hadn't promised not to speak about Aaron. When I protested, he threw in some lawyer jargon, and all I could figure out was that he had found a loophole. Dex was intense, and his blue eyes were equally as chilling to me as Luke's warm brown eyes were warming me up. It was a hard contrast sitting facing these two.

"So, you're the happiness he let go?" Dex had said out of the blue. "I can see it."

"Dex, don't be a dick!" Luke had chastised him. I was confused, but if my confusion was a sign that I had no idea what these two were talking about, it didn't stop Dex from going on.

"I'm sorry, are we supposed to shut up and let these two lose more time? Your brother says he doesn't want to hear about her, but then goes on and on to me about grabbing his happiness and if he has a chance, to not let Alane go again. Mrs. Smith here is trying hard not to bring up the subject, but every time she looks at you, she's dying to ask about him, and I'm supposed to shut up and see what happens?"

What surprised me the most was how accurate he was.

Was I so easy to read?

I did want to ask Luke who, what, when and where about Aaron, but I was trying not to. Knowing Aaron didn't want to hear about me hurt. Knowing he wanted a chance at happiness confused me even more.

"Babe, you can't fix this," Luke told his boyfriend.

"The hell I can't!" Dex said impatiently. In all that, I had one question. One simple question I knew I needed the answer to.

"Isn't Aaron married?"

Because if he was, why didn't he want to hear about me? What had I done that made him want to forget me? And how was I his lost happiness? He was married for more than twenty years, I believed with the girl he dated right after me, and when I say right after, I mean, a few weeks after dumping me and leaving town.

Luke winced at my question, and Dex laughed. How these two were dating was puzzling. One looked like the Ice King and the other like a Care Bear.

"Not for long," Dex said as Luke sent his elbow into his ribs.

"Beardy, I'm not against rough play, but not in public." I blushed at imagining these two having rough sex. God knows I'm not into that anymore.

We left things with a promise to keep in touch, but we both knew that ship had sailed when we were kids.

Aaron, though, is another story.

I don't want to face him, but I am curious. Who is Aaron Jax? Is he a good husband? Is he a good dad? Judging by his kids, he seems to be.

Lawson reminds me of Luke, always with a notebook in his hand, artsy, and loves science. He's a cute kid and girls are not immune to his charm.

Hailey, on the other hand, is the tough beautiful athlete, too perfect to be true, too competitive to have real friends, and too smart to put it all in sports. She and I are like oil and water, we don't get along, and I suspect Hailey has it easy because she is the star athlete.

I know the feeling, and I'm pretty sure she isn't giving a hundred percent.

It didn't surprise me when Patricia said Aaron wanted to meet with me to discuss Hailey, but I was a little shocked at the tone of the email Patricia forwarded to me. It was very proto-coled, as if he didn't know I was his daughter's teacher.

That's when my anxiety dissipated. I had the home-ice advantage and decided to arrive late.

First because I wanted him to be in the classroom when I came in and to wait for me. I wanted to have the upper hand. I wasn't one hundred percent sure he'd leave once he'd seen it was me.

Second, I knew I would need a few more minutes to pull it together, check myself in the mirror, and apply a little more lip-gloss.

Maybe it's superficial, but I wanted him to look at me and see what he missed out on.

Perhaps I'm not over it.

Perhaps it isn't mature, but I'm certainly not the only woman who wants to look good when running into an ex.

I need the Universe to be on my side for that meeting, along with my best hair, best outfit and best attitude.

Even if the confident, go through fire seventeen-year-old Alane he knew is long gone. I can still manage to find my way back to her on occasion, even though I had hated her as much as I hated him.

When I finally arrive in my classroom—a good ten minutes

late—he's looking at the wall with his back to me. His shoulders are broader than they used to be, and his hair is now grey.

That's what I see first.

Then I find his ass in his perfect jeans, and I can't remember ever seeing such a remarkable butt.

I thought it would be easier to have him in my classroom, but Aaron Gritt is still a piece of art, and seeing him here brings back emotions I'm not ready to face.

I had forgotten how many times he waited for me between two classes to steal a kiss.

I had forgotten how I used to wrap my arms around his waist when he had his back to me like now.

I've blocked the images of my younger self being happy with the teenager he was.

I've erased the dates, the pecks, the make-out sessions, the hand-holding, the long afternoons we spent on the ice or our discussions about the future together.

I know I was young, but to this day, it was the happiest time of my life.

Even the first years being a mother weren't as light as that time with Aaron. All was still too raw. I was hurting too much, holding my son in my arms, wondering about the what-ifs.

Even the first few years of marriage were never as happy as when I was with Aaron, racing against one another. I never found the same happiness. I never really looked for it either.

As I feel my anxiety rising, I try to calm myself down. I won't let myself have a panic attack in front of him. There would be no better sign to tell him what a fuck-up I am than to fall on the floor, crying, petrified to take any actions. As my therapist has told me to do so many times before, I concentrate on the good in the present instead of dwelling on my past issues.

Adam is okay.
I am okay.
I am enough.
I deserve to live the life I want.
Plans can change, but it could be for the best. I'm proof of it.

Facing Aaron Gritt is just something I need to do.

Clearing my throat, I summon up the courage and enter the room.

"Glad you could make it." When he turns to face me, I give him my brightest smile, even if my heart pounds in my ears, bile rushes into my throat, and my knees weaken. Because my smile is what he preferred, and right now, I'll give anything for him to look at me like he did when we were teenagers.

But around his blue eyes are wrinkles, he now has a beard whereas he couldn't grow a mustache, and his gaze toward me is indifferent.

His whole demeanor shows me that time has passed, and we're nothing to each other anymore.

"Mrs. Smith, thanks for having me," he says, reaching out his hand.

The dagger he planted into my heart starts bleeding again when I register his words.

No Al, no Alane, no Sweets, but Mrs. Smith.

It then becomes clear to me that these many years later, my first love doesn't recognize me.

7

THEN – AARON

"*S*weets, slow down," I breathe in her ear.

I'm hard and about to come in my pants. Alane and I are making out in my truck, and she's getting more and more handsy. She's always touching me when we're alone, and I have to tell her to stop, to keep it clean.

It's torturing me, but I have to.

I promised her dad nothing would ever happen, and I want to keep my promise, but tonight she's driving me crazy. She found a patch of skin dangerously close to my cock to torture, her tongue is exploring my mouth, and her eyes are burning with desire.

It's our first kiss anniversary, and we're back from a burger and a movie. That's all I could afford, but I think she liked it. I'm already putting money aside for her Christmas gift, but I'm not working enough to give her the beautiful things she deserves.

I've picked up more shifts at the diner and now work mainly in the kitchen, helping to clean and prep the food. I like it and would love to work more hours, but more hours there mean either no time for hockey or for Al.

I would drop hockey in a heartbeat if I knew it wouldn't hurt my dad. I can't do that to him. There is no way I can let Al go, but I want to do more things, to get her the best things, and these things cost money. I'm not sure what to do; I just wish I could stop playing hockey.

"I know, Aar, I'm sorry, just... I wish we could... I want you so much," she says, straddling my lap. My hand disappears under her shirt and traces along her bra.

"Me too, Sweets. I just, I promised, you know..."

"I know, and you're a man of your word," she says half-annoyed, half-content.

"That's why I love you even if..."

"You love me?"

"Didn't I ever tell you?" Alane is not the most forward with her feelings. Compared to my family, where everything should be discussed all the freaking time, the Smiths don't share feelings, or discuss issues. Do I know she loves me? Of course. I have no doubt she does. Did she ever tell me? Nope. So, I didn't tell her either, even if my heart is as much about to burst as my dick.

"Never, Sweets."

"Hmm... Well..." She's so shy it's freaking cute.

"Sweets, look at me." She does. "I love you." The blush creeps up adorably on her cheeks, such a contrast with the girl who wanted sex a few minutes ago.

"I love you, too," she whispers.

I bring my lips to hers and kiss her hard, my lips hungrier than they've ever been.

"What about dry-humping?" She breathes with a certain mischief in her eyes.

"Al." My voice is strained. My cock hardens in my shorts, and Alane moans, unquestionably feeling the warmth of me between her legs. I wish I could go to third base, but I know one thing will just lead to another, and I want to respect my promise. Alane is grinding her crotch on my length, and her actions have a contrary effect on my dick than on my self-control. One is getting thicker while the other is getting thinner.

"Aar, I want you to make me come," she whispers between kisses, her hips moving back and forth on me.

"Please, I can't. Your dad..." She shuts me up with a kiss. Her brown eyes are fiery.

"Technically, dry humping is not deflowering me," she says, kissing my neck. "I masturbate thinking of you, you know. I know what an orgasm is." I grunt.

If I visualize her touching herself thinking of me, I will come, right here and now. "Don't you masturbate thinking of me?" she asks in a honeyed voice and with a bright smile she knows I can't resist.

"Yeah," I manage to say, nervous and even more turned on.

"So, what if we masturbate each other through clothing. What's the difference?" I'm trying hard to think of why we shouldn't, but my brain is fogged by desire, and I have no reason for us to stop. As she gets faster, I lose control; and give it all to her.

"I want to kiss your breasts," I tell her.

I've touched them before but always through her T-shirts and bra. I have never seen them, I have never kissed them, and if there is a part of Alane's body that drives me wild, it's those magnificent breasts she jiggles in front of me.

I love her because she completes me, she understands me like nobody else but Luke, she is competitive and goal-oriented, but if I had to pick one piece of her body I love the most, it would be her tits.

I've stroked myself many times, wishing I could have my tongue on them or my cock thrusting between them like I saw in the magazines Chris found in his uncle's car.

"We should move into the back," she says in a husky voice, but I can't move. My dick is nicely tucked close to her folds and never wants to leave this paradise. Before I can answer, Al removes her top, and I'm faced with her sports bra and the object of my desire. She arches and brings my head to her breasts.

I inhale her scent.

She smells like peaches, but also like something new, desire perhaps, I'm not sure, but it drives me wild. I nibble on her peaks through the fabric and knead her flesh.

"Please, Aar," she pleads.

I bring my thumbs to each nipple and circle them slowly. "Kiss them. Make me come," she says, grinding harder. I bring up her bra to let her breasts free and admire them. They are big enough to fill my whole palm; I squeeze them giving all my attention to her pink nipples. They are gorgeous, pale, adorned by a few moles and a star-shaped birthmark.

It's a dream come true.

I tremble as I bring my lips to one and put it in my mouth. French kissing the bud like I do her tongue, I have no clue what I'm doing, but I must do it well because Alane is moaning above me. Her head tips back, and her blonde hair falls down like that first time I really saw her after practice. I could die a happy man right now.

"Aar, I'm about to come, please make me come. The stitching of my shorts is rubbing on my clit. I wish it were your finger." I had no idea my girl was such a dirty talker, and it turns me on. It turns me on so much that I come in my pants, without warning. It's quick and messy and mortifying.

"Shit." I mumble, "I'm sorry, Sweets." She shoved her hand into her jeans and starts playing with herself. I've never seen someone do that.

I'm captivated.

"Get your mouth on my tits and continue what you were doing. I can't stop now." She gasps.

So, I oblige, wanting to make my girl come. She's panting while I suck on her breasts, and she moans like I've never heard her do before.

"I'm so wet, you always make me so wet. I would love you to…" She doesn't continue what she's saying as her legs tighten against my thighs, and she screams my name, again and again, until she falls on my shoulder.

Seeing her come is more beautiful than anything I thought I would ever see. Her chest is red, and her whole body is shaking on my lap.

I was wrong before, now is when I can die a happy man.

I kiss her breasts a hundred times more, getting acquainted with each of her moles and her birthmark before putting her bra back in place. Her lips find mine, and she kisses me, slowly, lovingly, and sensually.

"Happy anniversary, Aar. I love you." She sighs.

"I love you, too," I say drunk on what we just did in my truck. Al gets back in her seat, slipping on her T-shirt and looks at me with so much love in her eyes that my heart explodes. There is no doubt to me that this girl is the love of my life.

"I should go," she says at the same time a loud bang comes from my hood. I turn my head to see her dad, facing us. I blush right away, guiltily, knowing that what we just did is a loophole that will lead us to Hell. He signs for me to open the window.

"What were you two doing in here for ten minutes? Now Alane is late for curfew."

Nothing comes from my mouth.

I could blurt the truth and lose my girl, or I could lie and keep her, but my brain can't choose which path to take. Losing her is not an option, but lying to a man of God, even if I'm not religious, might give me bad luck or some shit like that.

Alane's father is looking at me, ready to maybe murder me, perhaps not with his bare hands but surely with God's help. If God exists, I really hope he's going to keep his mouth shut about what he saw tonight and never tell Father Smith.

"Sorry, Daddy." Alane saves my ass. "We were just listening to a song I really like. Aaron keeps telling me to get home, but I just wanted to hear the end of it."

He looks at her suspiciously, but she smiles, the same smile she gives me when she really wants something or when she's happy to see me. The same smile she gave me ten minutes ago when she was using her sweetened voice to convince me to dry-hump in my truck, in front of her house, next to the church, in the middle of the street. The smile I love more than anything.

"Get in, Alane, you're late!" he says before turning towards the house and walking along the driveway. She leans into me and gives me a small peck on the lips, that's all her dad allows in front of him. It's quick and not enough after what we just did, especially after almost getting caught, but that's all I can get, and that's all I can give.

"I'll be thinking of what we just did when I masturbate tonight," she whispers, smiling at me.

"Fuck, you drive me insane," I readjust my hard but wet cock.

"Alane! Hurry!" her father screams.

"I can't wait for our next date, Aaron," she says, the devil on her shoulder.

She runs to her dad and gets inside while I stay dumbfounded by what we just shared. I hate myself for not being a man of my word, but I love that my girlfriend seems to want me more than she loves God.

I drive home hard and run to the shower to clean up and replay the whole scene, stroking myself, not having to imagine what her breasts taste like but knowing. I dream of my mouth going down past her breasts to her navel and lowering to her pussy, imagining what she tastes like between her legs.

I heard some guys do that.

It excites me as much as thinking of her mouth around my dick. I come again, spent by the evening and hoping we could go further. I knew that if we'd come together, I'd want more.

We opened Pandora's box, and I'm not sure how I can wait until we're married now. It seems so far away, but Alane is worth waiting for, her eighteenth birthday can't come fast enough.

8

NOW – AARON

*H*ailey's teacher is gawking at me.

    If looks could kill, I would certainly be dead by now.

Then her eyes fall on the hand I extend, and I don't know if she's going to be sick or slap me.

I'm not sure what her problem is, but I'm confident that's not standard way to treat a parent. She's hot, I give her that, but she seems as bitchy as how Hailey described.

I'm ready to walk away and go discuss the issue directly with Patricia when her cleavage catches my eye.

There is a lot you can forget about the first girl who made you come, but a star-shaped birthmark she has at the crease of her breasts is unforgettable.

"Alane?" I ask, searching for confirmation in her eyes. I can see it now. Her hair is shorter and darker, wrinkles mark the eternal teenager face I thought she still had, her hips are rounder than they used to be, and her brown eyes show she's lived through some hardship, but there, in front of me, is the girl I loved so much.

"Asshole!" she mumbles between her teeth.

"Wow, look at you. You've changed a lot!" I say, still dumbfounded not to have recognized her right away and hoping she did not realize I remembered her tits before her face.

"You did too, but I didn't need to look at your cock to know it was you though," she bites back. I cringe.

"I'm sorry... I..." Fuck. "You had the name advantage," I say defensively.

"You did, too. My name is still Smith," she retorts in a sarcastic laugh.

"Come on, you disappeared for almost thirty years, and your name is Smith. You knew Hailey was my kid, but I had no way of knowing you were her teacher."

"Whatever, we're here to speak about Hailey, right?" she says all matter of fact.

"What did you want to talk to me about, Mr. Gritt?" She sits and gets her reading glasses from her case, going through what I believe is Hailey's file. The sexy teacher look fits her well, the bitch attitude, a little less.

"I'm sorry, Al, I didn't expect you to be her teacher." I try to smooth things out, but she's still looking at me as if I'm the worst scum she ever met. "I had no idea you were a teacher, I thought you..." I trail off, wondering what happened to the girl who was leaving for hockey prep school.

Yes, I had never heard her name when the women's national hockey team was playing, but I didn't check women's hockey either. Who does? I was curious, but I never wanted to know, afraid it would hurt, afraid she would be living her dream without me, afraid I would have remorse.

"I had no idea you were a pig that needed to see tits to recognize women. I guess we're both disappointed by whom the other one has become." Ouch. I guess I deserved that.

"Can we start over?" I say, asking for a truce. She scoffs, anger in her eyes. I can honestly say that in the almost three years we dated, Alane had never once been mad or angry with me. Is she outraged that I checked out her cleavage, or is she still angry I dumped her?

Because I'm an idiot, I ask. "Is this because of what happened between us almost thirty years ago that my kids have problems in science?"

I cross my arms and stare her down like I do at the restaurant when the staff fucks up. I know I can be intimidating, and I won't let her bully my children because I dumped her almost three decades ago.

If that's her problem, she needs to get the fuck over it.

I don't know why she's back in town, but I just can't let her treat my kids this way, not with their absent mother and all the shit Hailey is going through.

Alane's breathing becomes heavier, like a bull ready to attack and she narrows her eyes at me. Gone are the eyes I met when she came in. Those eyes had no light, no drive, and no happiness in them.

That's certainly why I didn't recognize her.

The Alane I knew had the most promising eyes I had ever seen. The adult Alane has eyes that transpire fear and isolation. Now, her eyes are full of anger but also of fire and passion.

I woke up something in her, even if I just insulted her more than a moment ago, and because I'm an ass, my dick swells.

"Are you fucking kidding me, Aaron? Do I have any problem with Lawson? Did you know Hailey doesn't do her homework? Did you know she copies it from Madison? Do you realize I can tell when someone gives me a paper that is not their own handwriting but their best friend's? Has she told you how she spends her classes flirting with her boyfriend? I will fail her, and she can say goodbye to her scholarship. I don't know if she's acting up because your wife left you, or if she was always like this and everybody was too busy kissing her ass, but I don't think it will teach her anything to come here, and degrade her teacher not knowing what the fuck you're talking about. Maybe if your head was not focused on women's tits, you could pay more attention to your kid!"

"You're such a bitch, Alane, no wonder your name is still Smith!" I don't see the slap coming, but I feel it. I instantly regret what I just said. I'm angry but not with her, not really. I'm mad at Jess because she seduced me. I'm mad at myself for leaving Alane behind. I'm mad at Hailey for having lied to me. I'm mad at Patricia for not telling me Alane was back. I'm mad at Luke for not giving me any warning she was a teacher now. I'm just mad, and I lashed out at her.

"Now, if you'll excuse me, I have somewhere more interesting to be." She walks away. The appointment lasted less than fifteen minutes, and I have a feeling she hates me more than she did when I walked away at eighteen.

I'm about to climb in my car when I hear a voice coming from two cars over. Alane is holding the steering wheel, tears falling down her face, the window slightly open. Her lips are moving, but I don't think she's talking to anybody.

I hear only scraps here and there.

Something about an Adam, about being enough and deserving to live and have different plans. She seems hurt, lost, and it's my fault. I never wanted to hurt Alane Smith. I always knew she was too good for me. Even when we broke up, I didn't want to damage her.

Needing answers, I call the only other person who knows her more than I did. Luke picks up right away.

"What happened to her?" I ask my brother point-blank.

"Why does it matter now?" He always was protective of her.

"I just met with her about Hailey. You could have told me she was my kids' teacher." I enter my car and connect him to the Bluetooth system. I don't take a second glance at Alane, not because I'm a dick, but because I'm hurting for her, and I need to know I didn't break her again. Luke knows me. He knows that if I'm asking, it means it certainly didn't go well.

"What did you do?"

"I didn't recognize her, or, let's be more precise I didn't recognize her face, but I did recognize the star-shaped birthmark she has between her tits," I tell my brother.

"Ah, *the* star..." he says, reminding me how I undoubtedly shared more than I should have with him when we were kids.

"Do you have an answer for me? She's so different, I would have never recognized her."

"I recognized her, Aar. She just grew older. You did as well. You have grey hair, for fuck's sake!"

"I know... Listen, Luke, just give me something."

"I don't know what happened. All she said was that she's a teacher, she has a son, she was married, and now she's divorced. She's back in Springs Falls because her mother is sick, and she needed to work not to be crazier than she already is. There, you know everything I know. Now go apologize and grow the fuck up." He hangs up, letting me wonder why I didn't recognize her, and he did.

Luke and I never fought as kids. We never even had a disagreement. We were two peas in a pod, yin and yang, night and day, clouds and sun. The only time we fought, was when my parents told him I had broken up with Alane and even then, he didn't say a word to me.

He lost his temper, which is a hard thing to accomplish for my brother, and destroyed my room. He refused to say goodbye when I left for Seattle. He moved away two years later, once he was eighteen, and disappeared in New York City. It took me a long time to get back into his good graces, a lot of groveling, but it was never the same between us. I had Jess, and he didn't come home except once a year for Christmas, and in a way, I knew it was because of me.

He loved Alane like a sister, and he had felt he had to choose me. I don't understand why they didn't keep in touch, and I thought they had, until he told me otherwise. Trying to smooth things over once again, I send him a text.

Me: I'm sorry.

Luke: It's not me you need to apologize to. Talk to her and do not look at her cleavage under any circumstances!

I laugh. I think I learned my lesson today. Do not look at Alane Smith's tits. Maybe Luke should tattoo it on my forehead.

Once I get home, I rush into Hailey's bedroom to find her kissing face with the boyfriend I didn't know she had until an hour ago. Saying I'm pissed is an understatement.

"Out!" I growl to the punk who has his hands under my daughter's shirt.

"Dad," she starts to plead, but I don't want to hear it. I raise my hand to shut her up and sit down calmly to find her eyes. That's something I learned from my dad a long time ago. Screaming doesn't have the same effect on your kids as sitting them down, looking them in the eyes and showing them all of the disappointment you feel because of them.

"Hailey, do you think it was smart to send me in blind to meet with your teacher?"

She shakes her head, tears already falling down her cheeks. "Do you think it was a good idea to manipulate me, lie to me, and deceive me?" She shakes her head again.

"Why did you do it then?"

"Because of Mom leaving…" She sobs.

"No, Hal. I was the one who was always here. I was the one taking care of you, always taking care of you. If you lied to her for payback, I could understand, but lying to me? No. I'm sorry, but you're grounded. I'm hurt and disappointed, and worst of all, I hurt someone because of you. I want you to go to Mrs. Smith and apologize, and I want you to work hard in science class. No acting up or drama will make your mother come back. She checked out a long time ago, but if you want to jeopardize your future, continue on this path, and maybe you can work at the farm shoveling shit for the rest of your life." She nods, understanding I'm not done.

"I'll speak with Grandma and Grandpa tomorrow, but you will come home right after practice and work at the farm, shovel the shit and do anything they need. The days they don't need your help, you'll come to the restaurant and be my dish-washer. Then you'll do homework, and if I need to check it like I was doing when you were in elementary school, I will. As for the boyfriend, if I hear that you suck face or flirt in class, I will destroy him. If I hear he's dry humping you or more, I will destroy him and call your Uncle Barnabas to help me, and if I hear he gives you a bad reputation, we'll call your Uncle Luke to be in on it as well. Understood?" She nods again.

"Now give me your phone, I haven't done a random check in a long time. I thought I could trust you, but you're going to need to work to earn that trust again, baby girl." Hailey hands me her phone and comes in for a hug.

"I'm sorry, Dad."

"I hope so, Hailey. I acted like a dick because of you, and let's just say, Mrs. Smith was the last person I wanted to hurt." Hailey frowns when she looks up at me.

"Why is that?"

"Because, once upon a time, I destroyed our lives like a bulldozer. I don't regret it because I had you and Law, but Hal, I hurt her badly a long time ago and was an ass to her today. That was not fun."

"Is that the girl Uncle Luke was talking about?" she asks sweetly.

"She is."

"Shit, Dad, I'm sorry. I'll try to make it better."

"Do what you have to do. Do not meddle in my business. Just do your own homework and work hard in science."

"And I'll apologize to her. I'm really sorry," she adds, crying on my shoulder. I kiss the top of her head and make my way to the kitchen. We live in a house not far from the restaurant. I built *Gritt Your Plate* on Luke's land and our house on mine. When my parents decided to downsize, they gave us each a piece of land. Luke needed money to open the tattoo parlor, and I needed land to build the restaurant. It was an easy agreement between my brother and I.

"And you owe me by cooking my favorite meal, Hal. You had yours under false pretenses, time to pay back."

"I'll make lasagna with Grandma as a penance." As if spending time with her grandmother was ever a punishment.

9

THEN – ALANE

"Thank you so much, Mrs. Gritt. I didn't know what to do for Aaron for his seventeenth birthday. I mean, with him as a junior and me as a sophomore, hockey, and his job, we haven't had time to spend much time alone. I'm so glad you're helping us. He planned so much for our first anniversary; I just wanted to pay it back, you know?"

I'm in Mrs. Gritt's kitchen, learning how to make lasagna for the boy I love, and planning a romantic dinner for him in his parents' barn, something rustic chic.

His dad wasn't happy having to move the boys and girls practices around when his wife asked him to, but he did it, nonetheless, because the Gritts are super cool like that.

As for my parents, Mrs. Gritt called them herself and said I was invited for supper to celebrate Aaron's birthday, which is not a lie, I just invited myself and hijacked his parents' plan.

I had to promise we'd have dessert with them.

Luke wasn't happy either, bitching that we never spend time together anymore. He had planned something with Chris for the four of us to do, forgetting to invite Patricia. Unfortunately, they'll have to do something without me once they drop me off at home for curfew because I can't be late, even for my boyfriend's birthday.

If the Gritts accepted me as one of their own, my parents still look at Aaron as if he's the plague. He's never been invited in, or to lunch, nevermind supper. They only seem to remember I have a boyfriend when I'm a minute late for curfew, and when he doesn't come to church. He tries so hard to please them, but it will never be enough.

"Al!" Barnabas shouts, running into my arms.

"Hey, honey. How is my favorite boy?"

"I'm dying. I need a kiss!" he says with a massive grin on his face. Barnabas is my favorite five-year-old. We bonded a lot playing G.I Joe when Aaron babysits his siblings. If Salomé wants nothing to do with me, Barnabas is all over me. So much over me, that Aaron has to remind him that I'm his girlfriend. Barnabas keeps saying he'll marry me one day. It melts my heart every time.

"Barnabas, leave the girl alone," Mrs. Gritt says while Barn tightens his arms.

"Never!" he says, burying his face in my neck.

"You know," Salomé says, "She's never going to marry you! First, because you still pee your bed, and also because, why would she marry you if she has Aaron? He's not my favorite brother for nothing."

"Salomé! That's not very nice!" I scold her. The little bugger shrugs.

"Kids, why don't you go play upstairs and let Alane and I continue our cooking lesson," Mrs. Gritt tells her two younger children. We continue preparing Aaron's lasagna, and before I know it, everything is ready. All I need to do is shower and change into the dress I bought for the occasion.

I'm just getting out of the shower when Aaron appears in his bedroom, sweaty and smelling like melted ice, exactly how I like him.

"Sweets, what are you doing here?" He comes behind me and wraps me in his arms.

"Shit, Aar, you're early?" I turn around in my towel.

"Yeah, I drove fast here to be with you."

"Does your mother know you're here?" I whisper into his ear. He shakes his head and brings his lips to mine.

Our kisses are not so sweet anymore, they are hungry for more, like the two teenagers we are. He always tries to be respectful, but not me.

Still in my towel, a little wet, and my body against his, has me feeling warm when I should be cold. I feel pressure building between my legs, and I wish he hadn't made any stupid promises to my father. He deepens the kiss, shoving his tongue further into my mouth, and I tilt my hips toward his thigh. I can feel him getting hard just by kissing me. I want to let the towel fall, be naked in front of him and show him how wet he can make me, but Aaron backs away, groaning into my mouth.

"Get dressed!"

"Or what?" I say, bringing my hand to his bulge.

"I'm going to marry you as soon as you're eighteen and fuck you, Al, but for now, we made a promise. Please put clothes on." He nibbles on my ear.

"What if I don't want to?"

"Sweets, please. I'm really trying to be honorable here, however, if you continue pushing me, I won't be. I can't be." He kisses me softly, but I thrust my tongue in his mouth and press my body into his.

"I just want you so much," I say in between kisses.

"Fuck if I don't know it. I keep thinking of what we did in my truck. I can't drive anywhere without a hard-on."

My hand is on the knot of my towel. That could be his birthday present, seeing me naked, kissing my tits again and maybe more. I'm about to let the cloth go when a knock interrupts us, and I jump far away from him, afraid his parents are going to walk in on us.

"Aar!" Luke's voice comes through the door "I told Mom you were in my bedroom, but she was wondering if Al was ready. It seems the dish is."

"Give us a minute, and she'll come downstairs," Aaron tells his brother.

"Oh shit!" I wanted him so much, I forgot about his birthday supper.

It happens a lot lately.

My brain and my vagina are so engorged with desire; I can't think or skate properly. I need to take care of it regularly, in the dark, under my sheets, without making any noise to be sure my father doesn't disinfect my hands with holy water or worse, make his Sunday sermon about self-adulation, mind-pollution and the Devil in his home. But the fear of getting caught is half the fun.

Nevertheless, I would prefer Aaron's fingers, tongue, dick or whatever else, as long as it's him between my legs. I feel guilty most of the time, until I need a release again and masturbate some more, thinking about my boyfriend and how I would like him to take control of me. Of course, thinking about all we could do, I need a release right now. I rub my thighs together to try to ease some of the pressure, but it doesn't work. I breathe in and out, trying to calm my hormones, but Aaron is still too close.

"Are those your panties?" he says, pointing at my underwear on his bed. I nod, blushing. "Fuck! Shit! Fuck!" He rasps one hand pulling his hair while the other is shoved in his pants. "Your panties are on my bed, Al," he grunts. I pick them up quickly and slip them on under my towel.

"Are you mad?" I ask not sure what his expression means but certainly knowing it's not a joyful one.

"I'm not mad, but I need a fucking shower, a cold one!" He turns to the wall and bangs his head against it. "You drive me insane! Get dressed and go downstairs." His harsh tone hurts.

A lump forms in my throat.

I reach for my bra and dress and slip them on as fast as I can before running out of his room. I'm mortified. Replaying what just happened, I dash down the stairs, pass by a confused Mrs. Gritt and make it to the door. Once out, I have no escape. I'm sixteen, but my parents haven't bought me a car, nor have they allowed me to take the driving exam. My mom dropped me off after practice, and Aaron was supposed to drive me home. I could walk, but I'm barefoot.

"Alane? Are you alright, sweetie?" Mrs. Gritt appears on their porch, Barnabas on her hip. "Did something happen with Aaron? Did he try to touch you?"

I shake my head. If only he had, I wouldn't feel like the neighborhood slut trying once again to convince my boyfriend to put his hands on me. But that's what I am, a perverted mind, thinking about sex all the time. Not my game, not my schoolwork, but my boyfriend and all the dirty things I wish we could do.

Overwhelmed by culpability, I cry. Barnabas reaches out to me and nuzzles his perfect little nose in my neck while Mrs.

Gritt rubs my back in a soothing way my mother never has. After being around the Gritts a few times, I realized my parents were distant and cold. They never hugged me or comforted me. The first time Mrs. Gritt did, I was in shock and had no idea what to do or how to react. Now though, I know to let it all out, on Aaron's mother's shoulder, allowing my tears to soak her T-shirt while Barnabas hugs me tight.

"I don't like to see you sad," his little voice tells me. "I'll go punch Aaron for you!"

"Or I'll do it." Luke's voice comes from behind before embracing his mother, little brother and I.

"Do you want me to drive you home, Captain?" he asks.

"Luke, you don't have your license," his mother chastises.

"Is it really any different than driving a tractor, Mom?"

"I guess not, just don't get caught by the sheriff. I don't need your dad to go drinking all night long with his buddy for him to forget your stupid behavior." Letting me go, she looks at me with compassion and adds, "Are you sure you don't want to talk to him?" I shake my head, still not able to tell her what happened.

"Okay, sweetie. Come on, Barnabas, let the girl go," she says reaching for the boy in my arms. I can't let Aaron take the blame.

"It's all my fault, Mrs. Gritt. He's the noble one here," I say withdrawing from her, blushing and averting my eyes.

"I see… Why don't you come for tea this week, and we could discuss the issue that is tormenting you? I'm pretty sure your mother hasn't touched the subject of young love and sexual desire, has she?" I shake my head. What I would have given to have a mother like Mrs. Gritt.

Luke drives me home in silence, at a snail's pace. He doesn't want to pry; he wants me to tell him what happened. It's awkward, but I know I can confide in him. If someone can understand what guilt and sins are about, it's him. Breathing in, I dive into the conversation.

"Aar doesn't want to have sex with me," I say drying my cold but sweaty fingers on my dress.

"Not true," Luke says his eyes on the road.

"He keeps pushing me away."

"True. But that doesn't mean he doesn't want you. He made a promise to your father; he wants to honor it."

"But it still means he doesn't want to touch me."

"Captain, look, he's a seventeen-year-old boy with a hot girlfriend, believe me, he wants to touch you. But Aaron has a conscience. If you wanted to get fucked quick and dirty, you should have gone out with Chris. That guy will fuck anyone. Aaron loves you and respects you. That's not a bad thing." I shrug. It's not a bad thing, but it doesn't make me feel better. By the time we arrive at my house, Aaron is parked in front of the church, waiting for me.

"If you think he was going to let you go without a fight, you really don't know my brother," Luke says waving at Aaron. "Talk to him, he's just trying to do right by your father." Aaron is making his way toward me, a scowl on his face and pain in his eyes. "Go, Captain, make it better," Luke says, shoving me out of the car. He doesn't even wait for the door to close properly before driving away, leaving me with his brother.

"I'm so fucking sorry, Sweets. I should... I wish we could... You know I love you, right?"

"I know. It's just that being around you makes me lose control. My whole life is spinning with how much I want you. I need to focus on school and hockey, and I can't deal with it when I'm with you."

"What are you saying?" There is a tremor in his voice. "I

can't lose you, Al. I need you. You're the only one I can talk to, aside from Luke. You take my silence, my bad jokes, my passion. I love you and the challenge I see in your eyes. I love how you roll your eyes when I say something stupid. You can't dump me. I can't lose you. I never wanted to hurt you tonight. I was just trying to do the right thing." He sobs, breaking my heart, but holding my hands and rubbing his thumbs on my knuckles as he often does.

"I'm not breaking up with you, Aar," I say, bringing one hand to his heart "How could I? I love you too much. I just need a little space to get my head straight. Maybe we can avoid being alone for a while?" Aaron shakes his head not accepting my deal.

"That's what your father wants, you know? He wants me out of the picture. He suggests it every chance he gets. He thought you would turn me down, but once we started dating, he didn't think we would last. He also said that if I break my promise, he'd take you away; send you to your aunt in Arizona or something like that. I can't lose you, Al. Please don't make me lose you." The idea of losing Aaron burns a hole in my heart.

Could I think of going to practice without him or be at school without finding him in my classroom, a donut in his hand for me? I know I can't go back to be the girl before Aaron. I don't even know what it is to be in high school without him.

"Okay," I whisper, "but you can't make me feel guilty for what I want to do with you. I get enough of that at home."

"I'll give you anything you want, even if it means burning in Hell for you, but please don't leave me, ever." He kisses my nose, my eyelids, and my cheekbones.

"Never leave me, please," he repeats over and over drying his tears and kissing me all over.

Deep inside me, I know there is no way I could ever walk away from Aaron.

I would walk away from hockey, from my parents, from everything else before walking away from him, and it scares the shit out of me.

10

NOW – ALANE

My first anxiety attack happened while I was suspended from a ceiling, blindfolded with a tie and my wrists bound together. I knew the man kissing me, it was my husband, but I didn't know the one thrusting between my legs.

It was the first time I used my safe word.

After years of pushing the boundaries of my sexuality, I had finally reached my limit. It wasn't the first time I was suspended, blindfolded or bound, and it certainly wasn't the first time I had sex with a stranger, but for some reason I just couldn't go through with it. It was nothing violent, or at least, nothing different than our ordinary play, nothing out of my comfort zone. Adam just turned seventeen at the time, was a handsome and happy boy, looking more and more like his dad. I was happy in my marriage, Mark and I were amazing, and everything else was fine. I was living the life I wanted to and even now, after years of therapy, I don't know what triggered the anxiety.

That day marks the beginning of the end of my conjugal life.

Mark and I had met at the club, and these plays were part of our sexual relationship. Step by step, I refused any scenes that were generating anxiety and soon, I couldn't have sex anymore with anybody else but my husband, in a bed, missionary style, which wasn't what he had signed up for.

The first time Mark showed any interest in me, I was a waitress at the club trying to pay for school to become a teacher.

I had arrived in Arizona three years earlier and had needed time to get back on my feet after Aaron had shattered my heart and self-esteem.

My long-term plans had changed from one day to the next, and I had no idea what my future held. Mark was a regular, and as per my boss's rules, I wasn't supposed to get involved with him, unless he requested me. Once a member invited a waiter or waitress, it was up to us to decide if we wanted to be part of their world, but then we couldn't serve anymore, and if the regular didn't want us, we couldn't come back.

Getting involved with one of them was a significant risk.

I had seen him around. He looked magnificent in his suits, and such darkness emanated from him, that I was drawn to him right away. Needing to be discreet, I checked him out surreptitiously. I was making decent money, and even though Mark intrigued me, and the club scene turned me on, I told him no when he approached me the first time. But Mark, who was ten years older than I was, didn't give up. He said he knew the moment he saw me that we could be great partners. It took me one year to have enough money set aside so I could pay up to my last semester. Mark had proposed to pay all my expenses, but I couldn't get paid for pleasure. That's where I was drawing the line.

Once I changed jobs, I joined the club, first as Mark's guest and very soon after, as his girlfriend, and then his wife.

For fifteen years, I pushed every boundary I could.

The pastor's virgin daughter was long gone.

I never told Mark I was a virgin when we started dating, not that he would have believed me anyway, nobody ever did.

In fifteen years, I couldn't tell you how many men or women I slept with, but since our separation seven years ago, I know exactly how many people I've had sex with: zero. I haven't had sex since Mark. Sex triggers my anxiety, as well as any situation where I think Adam is in danger or I don't feel in control.

Yesterday, when I was angry with Aaron, I felt a desire I hadn't felt in a while.

Fighting and anger were part of the foreplay with Mark, so why wouldn't I be turned on by fighting with another man, and not just any other man, but the one I never experienced between my legs. Unfortunately, as soon as I left the classroom, I could feel the distress taking over.

Angst filled me, and I had just enough time to rush to my car and hide from him before the meltdown showed its face. I managed to calm myself down with my mantras, but I felt like the world was about to swallow me whole, or maybe I wished Aaron would.

Dealing with my anxiety is a daily struggle, and most of my friends and family don't understand it, not that I have many friends left. Over the years, Mark and I surrounded ourselves with people who lived the same lifestyle as us. Once I renounced it, I was alone, again. It seems my entourage is always conditional to the men I date. In a way, it's easier not to have to explain why I'm not dating and why I'm repeating the same sentences over and over.

Only my ex-husband and my son know about my condition.

Since anxiety attacks are not clinically defined conditions, the only thing doctors can do is listen to my symptoms and life events. I had anxiety, which was triggered in certain situations. That's it, that's all. The most I could do was to acknowledge when it happens, breathe, try to relax, and be mindful, which is why I am keeping a journal of probable triggers.

Thanks to what happened yesterday, Aaron Gritt has won his very own entry, which means I need to avoid fighting with the man, or maybe I should just avoid the man altogether.

"Look who the cat dragged in," a younger than me, but seriously hot guy, says with a smirk on his face that I know too well. There are boys you can't forget, even if you run into them twenty-seven years later in a coffee shop full of backpackers.

"Do I know you?" I ask while sipping my coffee to hide my smile. Joining his hands to his chest, he scoffs as if I've sent an arrow directly to his heart.

"Ask a woman to marry you, and she forgets who you are!" he says dramatically. A few steps behind him is Aaron, and I can't deny the genes they share.

"Compared to others," I point my chin in the direction of Aaron, "I recognize people easily, Barnabas," I say, wrapping him in a hug. "You grew up quite a lot since the last time I saw you."

"And you haven't changed, Alane. So, when can I marry

you?" His charming smile is unmistakably a panty-dropper all over town. He sits down facing me, obliging Aaron to come closer.

"You're almost the same age as my son. There is no way…"

"You have a son?" Aaron asks. I ignore him.

"Luke told me you haven't changed, but you are even more beautiful than I remember." Barnabas is beaming at me like he used to when he was a little kid.

"Thanks, but you were five, Barn." I blush. Aaron grunts in the back before coming closer. He's overshadowing me. I should feel claustrophobic, but I don't.

Having him so close feels natural, even after all these years.

"I came here to grab you a coffee; I owe you an apology, Al. I was an ass yesterday, and…"

"Oh shit! Is this happening? I promised Luke I would take a video of the apology. Let's FaceTime him right away." Barnabas gets his phone out.

"Shut up," Aaron sends a stern look to his brother. "Look, Al, I'm sorry. I was taken aback, and I think that's why I didn't recognize you. I've heard you were back in town, but I figured if you wanted to see me, you would have reached out. As you never did when you visited your parents, I wasn't counting on it this time either. I just never thought you were my kids' teacher, it's a little…" I raise my hand to stop him.

How did he become such a pompous ass? Why would I ever reach out to my ex-boyfriend who pulled the rug out from under my feet?

Inhaling a calming breath, I take him in.

"No need to apologize. So much time has passed by that Barn is even an adult now. I'm pretty sure you can behave like one, Aaron." For a reason I can't comprehend, he takes this for an invitation to sit next to his brother. I turn my whole body toward Barnabas trying hard not to acknowledge Aaron's beautiful face and perfect eyes. I don't want to lose myself in him again. I don't know him anymore, and I don't want to know him ever again.

"So, what do you do now, Barn? How is Salomé?" Barnabas smiles at me, understanding I'm indeed ignoring his brother. His eyes tell me that he's got me, and it's a nice change to have someone who's got my back.

"I work at the farm." He wrinkles his nose. "All my siblings followed their dreams, so it's all up to me to follow in our parents' footsteps." That doesn't sound like the parents I used to know.

"From what I remember, your parents had no problem letting their kids follow their dreams, even if it meant they were abandoning those they claimed to love behind," I say with a saccharine smile to sweeten the bitterness of my past.

"Ouch," Barnabas says. "Is that a blow for Aaron or my parents?"

I laugh nervously. "All of them?" I raise my eyebrows.

"Fair enough," Barn answers. "Sal was a big shot baker in New York until she found her fiancé balls deep in her business partner, after having learned they had bought her out. She came back home and now organizes weddings at the farm and does all the baking we sell." Having a wedding at the farm is something Aaron and I discussed a lot. I look at him, and I can see he remembers.

His smile is genuine, but I shake my head as to tell him not to go there.

"And you, Mrs. Smith? You have a son, so are you married?" Barnabas asks. I don't want to share my life with Barnabas, and even less in front of Aaron, but on the other hand, I don't want him to think I was the pathetic single girl he insulted yesterday.

"Divorced." I give in. Aaron nods as if knowing what it is about and Barnabas frowns.

"What dickhead would let you go?" The fit of laughter that follows is a nervous one at first until the ridiculousness of the situation kicks in, and I look at Aaron's contorted face.

"Shit, Barnabas, you're still the cutest!" I stand to get ready to leave when Aaron finds the ability to speak again.

"Can you let me know if there is anything more happening with Hailey? I talked to her last night, but just in case…"

"I'm sorry, Patricia said she would take care of the Gritt family for me. She even asked me if it's true, you are divorcing." I smirk, knowing it's been years that she's been trying to get one of the Gritt's to notice her. Aaron scoffs.

"I don't touch my brother's sloppy seconds." He smirks at Barnabas.

"Barn." I laugh.

"I was young and impressionable. She was sexy as fuck." He shrugs non-apologetically.

"I get that. After all, who am I to judge?"

"Now, as for the love of my life… Unlike Aaron, I see no harm in pursuing someone he has a past with," he answers before being slapped behind the head by Aaron. I chuckle while Barnabas' eyes widen.

"I really have to go. Barnabas, I hope I see you around. Say hi to your sister for me, and your parents, of course."

"Of course," he mumbles.

"Aaron." I pass by him. I'm not even at the door when I feel him behind me.

"Wait! Al!" Taking another deep breath in, I turn around to face him.

"I'm really sorry. Can we start over?" he says, handing me a coffee.

Because it's nothing new to me that I'm a masochist at heart, that I need the pain to feel alive and that I could never say no to a vanilla latte, I nod.

And when my stomach does a somersault and my panties get a little wet, I ignore it all, because Aaron Gritt is in my past, and the girl I used to be is buried under a mountain of secrets.

11

THEN- AARON

"*M*ooom! He did it again!" I scream, discovering the state of my room.

"You'd better run, Barnabas! If Aaron catches you, you're going to be in trouble!" Luke shouts while laughing from his bedroom.

"Seriously, Luke, why are you a dick to me these days?"

"Captain, oh, my Captain!" he quotes, from this stupid movie he loves so much. It's because of Alane. Luke thinks he masters everything there is to know about her.

Seeing the hours they spend together when I am away, he might be right, but I would like him not to shove it in my face on a regular basis. I feel like an outsider in my relationship, and it's not a good feeling. In fact, since my birthday, nothing has been feeling good. I lost a piece of Alane that day.

At first, she avoided me for a while, and now she never wants us to be alone. Each member of my family has had something to say about the situation. Well, with the exception of Salomé, who ignored the whole fiasco. It went from a long explanation my father gave me about women's desires, which was mortifying, to my mother reprimanding me for being a dick, and Barnabas saying he wants to kill me while destroying my room, to Luke repeating that if I fuck up, he loses her too. If Alane and I break up, it's pretty clear I'm going to be the one to lose custody of my family.

"Fuck! Can you let it go?" I ask my brother through our wall.

"Not when she's my best friend!"

"You didn't have to become best friends with her. I know you lost yours because he didn't like you being gay, but come on, she is *MY* girlfriend." I pout. Luke is about to answer when our mother appears at the top of the stairs, out of breath, followed by our dad.

"What now?" my mother says, entering my room.

"Barnabas peed in my bed again!"

My father chuckles. "Barnabas!" he calls, amused. "Come here, Boy!"

The little asshole strolls in as good as gold with no worries about getting in trouble for what he did. Being the baby of the family, he never gets in trouble with my parents, and they mainly laugh at his shenanigans. They are way more laid back than when I was a kid, which should be impossible because they were heavy stoners, which also makes me wonder if the mushrooms they grow are not the kind you should cook with.

My parents met at Woodstock.

They practiced free love for a while, until I was so confused about who my parents were that they cooled it down and reduced the partying to a few times a month. Shortly after the eighties kicked in, and the cliché of the hippies they were proud to be became obsolete. Then, they had more kids and finally got married. As I was already ten when Sal came along,

I was the built-in babysitter for a while but then my father realized that I could be more helpful around the farm. That's when Luke took over as the nanny, but as he dislikes children —because he's still one at heart— I was given back the duty to care for my little sister and brother and learned how to cook with mom.

My father continues to laugh and I roll my eyes. It's always the same. The only place my father is authoritative is on the ice or when I get into a fight. Rest of the time it doesn't matter. Nothing ever matters and should never be taken too seriously. Sometimes I feel like I'm the one really raising Sal and Barn, teaching them what's right or wrong. It's tiring but rewarding, except when the little shit pees on my bed.

"Why, Barnabas?" My mother laughs while I remove the sheets from my bed and wonder how I'll clean the mattress.

"Luke said Aaron should piss off! So I pissed off!" he says proudly.

"Be lucky I didn't tell him to shit all over your things..." Luke jokes, appearing behind my father.

"Seriously, Barnabas, you have to stop pissing on my bed!"

"He's just marking his territory over your girlfriend!" my dad explains, not caring that my bed is wet, and my room smells like pee.

"Maybe you should pee around Alane's house to mark yours?" Luke adds, raising an eyebrow.

"You know what, all of you, you're not helping. I'm not letting my five-year-old brother claim my girlfriend! This is all fucking ridiculous!"

"Language! And be a man, son! At your age, nobody gives a shit about your tantrums." My dad crosses his arms, letting me know I need to calm down.

"Of course! He pees on my bed, and I get in trouble!" I

scream before pushing my dad and Luke from the door and hurtling down the stairs. I can hear them laugh and make fun of me. I need to disappear. I don't want to be here, having them mock me and laugh at how I always take everything too seriously.

Between Alane putting distance between us, Luke pestering me to treat Alane the way she deserves, my father expecting me to be a farmer or a hockey player, and my little brother making my life more difficult than it should, I'm tired of never being enough. I need space, and if the Gritts are bad at one thing, it's to give you any. They much prefer to meddle.

"Aaron?" Salomé asks, frightened by my heavy steps on the stairs.

"What, Sal!" I bark, turning my head in her direction just enough to see tears springing from her eyes. I have never raised my voice at my little sister, and I know she's having a hard time not having me around as much as before. Since Alane, I have less time for her, which means I don't play Barbies with her as much, and we have fewer tea parties than we used to. She sniffles a little and turns her back to me before running up the stairs. Shit. The last thing I need today is Sal being mad at me.

"Sal, I'm sorry... I..." She stops in the middle of the stairs and turns around. I wish she would come for a hug, but I can see I hurt her more than I ever intended.

"I hate you, Aar. You used to be my favorite but you're not anymore. I even prefer Barnabas to you!" She turns and continues up the stairs, sobbing heavily. I rub my hands over my face and grunt in frustration before climbing the stairs, running after my little sister to do some groveling.

Two hours later, after baking chocolate muffins with her, having sat down for an epic tea party with a crown on my head and having let her paint my nails, I'm on my way to my girl-friend's. I haven't cleared my head of all the shit I need to, but at least Salomé loves me again.

I noticed shitty things come in threes. Barnabas peeing on my bed is strike one. Salomé saying she hates me is strike two. So I'm not surprised when Alane's father corners me as I pass the church on my way to see Alane. He gives me no choice but to follow him into his office to discuss an "important matter." I follow him, a knot in the pit of my stomach, stressing about what he could possibly want.

Does he know about the dry humping?

The towel encounter?

Has he guessed that I want to marry her as soon as she turns eighteen?

My ass is not even positioned on a seat when he starts a lecture, his judgmental brown eyes on my red painted fingernails.

"You know, Son, the importance in dating is to discover if the person you think you love strengthens your relationship with Christ, or if they compromise your morals and standards. You should always remember to keep God as the most impor-tant person in your life and never place anything or anyone above Him. I'm assuming you have heard of the sin of idola-try?" I nod, sitting on the uncomfortable chair in his office.

I know there is nothing I can say that would stop the lecture I'm receiving.

"As Paul says in Colossians 3:5, 'Covetousness is idolatry.' Because... you see... covetousness means desiring something so much that you lose your faith. Does this sound familiar to you?" The bleak and austere office Mr. Smith spends his days in feels like a coffin closing up on me. I quickly took it in and look around for an escape but there is none. Dizziness and nausea take over as Alane's dad hammers each word into my head. "Of course, you wouldn't understand. You're a lost soul, my child, your whole family is. What I mean is, you take up too much space in Alane's world, when she should be concentrating on God. We live in a village, boy, the whole world is a village, in fact, and there is always someone who knows someone who knows me. People can see your actions, God can see your actions, and they all tell me what my daughter does or thinks.

"Do you think I don't know when one perverted brother drives Alane home and the other kisses her? Do you think I don't know about the heavy kissing, the dangerous games you both play, and what you do in the darkness? I was once a teenage boy as well. It's time for you to renounce your demons. Do you see what you're doing to her? What you're turning her into? You made me a promise, and I intend for you to honor it. I recommend you end this relationship, and explain to her she should concentrate on God, find a person who has accepted Christ as his Savior, and play better hockey, if she wants a future. Do not disrespect God, Aaron. This story will not have a happy ending, and I would hate to have to send her to her aunt's and shatter her dreams."

I gulp heavily, hurting my throat in the process. The ultimatum is clear, break up with Alane or she'll be sent away and will never become the professional hockey player she dreams of.

"How long do I have?" I squeak, sweating in my seat.

"I have the feeling if you stay around, it will be a problem until you're gone, she might become even more rebellious and do something stupid like get pregnant."

"Sir, I would never!"

"Son, please, don't disrespect me. As I was saying, if you spend less time with her now, and decide to go far away to school, far from here and Alane, I'm certain you can date her until the end of your senior year. It's that easy. Mrs. Harbor tells me you're quite talented in the kitchen. Isn't cooking your real passion? She could talk to her husband so you could have more hours at the diner. Take this as an opportunity to hone your skill."

I'm not sure how Mrs. Harbor knows this, she barely speaks to her children or husband because she spends most of her time here, helping Father Smith or praying. I don't think I ever told Chris how much I like to cook. I know I told Alane and Luke, but I'm certain my brother wouldn't share my secrets with the Pastor or with Mrs. Harbor. In the end it doesn't matter how he knows because I would take any opportunity to stay in his good graces so she won't have her dream ripped away from her. She's too close to getting what she's always wanted.

I nod in agreement with tears of frustration in my eyes, as I realize the list of people who think I'm not good enough grows longer, with Alane's parents wanting me to break my girl's heart for her own good.

"I'm glad we had this conversation, Son. Now please, Alane is waiting for you, we wouldn't want her to wonder where her boyfriend is, right?"

I always thought going to church was supposed to make you feel at peace.

Standing up, I feel like I sold my soul to Beelzebub and made a deal I'll soon regret if I don't fulfill my end of the bargain

12

NOW- AARON

efore Alane's father died, I felt the need to forgive him for manipulating me as a teenager. Pastor Smith ignored me once I was back in Springs Falls, and I did everything possible not to speak to him.

I didn't forgive him so he could die in peace, I forgave him because I selfishly needed to absolve myself for breaking Alane's heart, for loving her so much that I chose to set her free. I never actually talked to Pastor Smith, but when I learned he was dying, I forgave him in my mind.

I guess that was my first prayer.

Talking to God became something I regularly did. It was a great way to sort through my thoughts and clear my mind. After months of praying whenever I could, the next step was to go to Church.

So, I did, not every Sunday because it depended on my schedule, but I tried to go as much as I could. I never forced my children to come with me, but I never discouraged them either. My ex-wife didn't want to, and that was okay with me too.

Over the years, I found the sermons of our new pastor enlightened my everyday life and were relatable to my daily situations and I kept coming back for more.

Today's sermon is about love and forgiveness, but the brown-eyed girl in the front row is distracting me. Not that I can see her eyes, but her short honey-colored hair that is slightly below her ears gives me a perfect view of her neck. The neck I used to caress and kiss when we were younger, even if back then, I had to swipe her mane to the side to reach it. The green dress she's wearing hugs her hips, and the curve of her back is all I can see.

My eyes keep going from the back of her neck to her ass.

Of course, my traitorous brain remembers her breasts, and I can't stop wondering if they are as magnificent as they were. I start to sweat profusely and my dick swells at the thought of Alane's body because my mind is not strong enough to keep me from getting in trouble in the house of God,

"Are you alright, Dad?" Lawson asks seeing me tugging at my collar.

"Yeah, I just need some fresh air. Are you going to be alright here alone?" He nods, and I walk out silently, but at a quick pace, feeling my chest closing up while images of my ex-girlfriend flip through my mind like porn slides of a teenage dream. Breasts, nipples, navel, neck, and pussy.

I've seen her naked, I've seen every part of her, but my undoing will always be her lustful eyes and her smile, which is why I can't understand why I didn't recognize her. I had a lot of excuses, her hair is shorter and darker, her eyes aren't filled with the same spark as they used to, her smile seemed fake, and I didn't expect her to be my kids' teacher.

The truth is, I'm the asshole who didn't recognize the girl I used to love more than anything, not until I saw the star-shaped birthmark. I'm the jerk who hasn't stop thinking of tasting her again and finally get my chance to have my dick in her.

Alane has become a very sexy woman, and because I'm such a bastard, I've let my thoughts go to every moan she ever gave me. I've also allowed myself to remember the noises she makes when she orgasms and how she used to touch me. I'm consumed by lust, and if I weren't living in a small town nestled between the mountains and a lake, I would have tried to find someone to forget, like I found Jessica in Seattle years ago.

Maybe visiting Luke in Los Angeles is what I need. I could bring the divorce papers to Jessica in Vegas, see Luke and his boyfriend, and rewire my brain not to want to fuck my kids' science teacher on her desk, in a church, in my kitchen, or wherever I can think of fucking her.

The green swirl of her wrap dress I was admiring before interrupts my thoughts, and Alane appears before me. Her eyes look erratic, her breathing is short, and she's pacing back and forth without seeing me; mumbling again about that Adam guy, about being enough and deserving to live and being able to have a different plan, about how being in church is a trigger. I don't want to spy, but I'm not sure my presence will be welcomed. However, when I hear her mumble my name, I decide it's best she knows I'm lurking in the corner.

"Alane." She turns in my direction, and her eyes widen in shame.

"Oh shit! Shit! Shit! Shit! Shit... Oh no." She begins to

hyperventilate, hiding her face in her hands while she is still pacing back and forth.

I ask, "Alane, are you alright?"

She squeaks in agreement, but it's clear to me she's not, especially since I see her fingers twist together with one another, her lips pinched, and her eyes closed.

"Sweets, what's going on?" I ask, coming closer. As if she could feel my proximity, she backs away, raising her hands defensively.

"Don't touch me. I need space. I need to calm down. I need to go over it by myself."

"What are you talking about?" She looks a little crazy, and I'm not frightened per se, I'm just worried by her behavior. The Alane I knew was always so focused, but the woman in front of me seems so out of control that I'm starting to wonder if I'm not in a parallel universe.

"Did you know I haven't entered a church since my father's funeral? Even then, I arrived late and stayed all of five minutes. Before that day, I hadn't even set foot in a church since I left home," she rambles, still pacing, totally unhinged. "I thought I could do it. I thought I could sit there and listen to a sermon, but I can't. I can't be in his church. I can't be in any church. I need to go. I need to breathe," she says walking further away from the building. It takes me a few strides and a little jog to catch up, but I do and block her path, forcing her to look at me.

"Hi," I say softly to calm her down, taking her hands in mine to stop her from twisting her fingers. She blinks at me several times as if she can't believe I'm standing in front of her, and she breathes deeply in and out. Synchronizing my breathes with hers, I hold her eyes and smile. My smile used to soothe her apprehension, my gaze used to appease her uncertainty, and my touch used to settle anything. I hope it still can.

"Hi." She sighs.

"You changed your hair," I say like the moron I am. Who wouldn't change their hair in twenty-seven years? I want to tuck the piece sticking out behind her ears like I used to, but I don't. She's not mine to touch.

"I changed a lot of things since we were kids," she answers, cocking her head to the side. "Your hair is also kind of different." She smiles.

"Kind of?"

"It's grey, but the cut is the same," she blurts out, blushing.

"Yours is darker," I say stupidly, not believing the first time we talk to each other after all this time is about hair.

"Yeah, I hide the grey." She shrugs, and before I know it, she lets my hands go. It's too soon, I still need her touch, so I trap her index finger in mine and rub it with my thumb.

"You want to tell me what that was all about?" I say, nodding my head in the direction of the church. She bites her lip and my dick twitches. She seems so unsure if she wants to share, she looks so lost. It takes all I have not to wrap her in my arms and carry her home. I need to protect her, I need to soothe her, I need to cherish her.

"I have anxiety attacks." Her eyes fall at the ground. I wait for her to elaborate. Alane always needed time to put her thoughts into words. "One day, out of the blue, I had one. I still don't know what triggered it. Now I live with it." She blinks as her eyes adjust to my scrutinizing gaze.

As a dad and a chef, I've heard more than enough excuses and drama in a lifetime. There wasn't one ounce of bullshit in her eyes, only pure pain. Alane is hurting, and I couldn't do anything about it. I hadn't known about it, and it hurts me in return.

Over the years, I've tried not to miss Alane and what we had. I've tried my best to be mentally faithful to my wife when I know she wasn't physically. I've tried to let Alane go, and I truly believed I had, until I heard she was in town. I knew then that I had lied to myself. I knew she always had been somewhere in my mind. I knew I had missed her more than a dying man misses oxygen, and the first thing I did when having the chance to breathe the same air as her again, is not recognize her.

"I'm sorry," I say tearing up. Her eyes locked on mine like a magnet.

"For what?" I'm not sure we have time for me to do penance for all I need to earn her forgiveness.

"For loving you," I whisper as the church doors open, and Lawson appears, followed by Alane's mother. I quickly let her hand go, chancing a last glance before we're surrounded by very nosy onlookers.

The residents of Springs Falls don't really get into each other's business like other small villages, unlike my family. Mrs. Smith sure doesn't like me but would surely make it her business if she sees me hugging her daughter.

Every time I've crossed paths with her before, she would scoff and mumble things under her breath that I didn't necessarily need to hear to know they weren't agreeable.

"Aaron Gritt, what a pleasant surprise," Alane's mother says sarcastically, with a pained expression on her face.

"Mrs. Smith."

"And is this your other son?" she asks presenting her hand to Law.

"Yes, this is my son Lawson. My daughter, Hailey, is away at a basketball tournament this weekend," I say with emphasis on the word daughter to correct her without insulting her. She ignores my comment while narrowing her eyes.

"Alane, don't take long. The Harbors invited us for lunch, and you know Chris is in town, and they would really like you to reconnect with him." I raise an eyebrow in Alane's direction.

"Chris?" I ask once her mother is out of range.

"They always thought he would be better suited for me than you were." I see Lawson giggle in the corner of my eye. Chris is his godfather, and he heard enough stories from my brothers and me to know Chris is certainly not better suited than I am. I love my friend, but he's an ass. Not as bad as his sister Patricia, but still an ass. What is more surprising though is that he didn't tell me he was in town.

"When did he arrive?" I ask her, trying to connect the dots.

"I don't know, my mother said he was busy last night and was only here for the weekend. I'm not sure if he really wanted to have lunch with us, but the Harbors insisted. From what Patricia told me, he has a girlfriend." My eyebrows jump to my hairline.

"Chris? A girlfriend?" I laugh at my words. "Doubtful," I add. "A piece of ass on the side, yes. A girlfriend, no..."

"Dad!" Lawson says horrified. "Can we please not speak about Uncle Chris' sex life?"

"Sorry," I say, raising my hands up in defense. Lawson comes closer, suspiciously eyeing Alane and me. I'm not sure what my son is up to, but the smirk on his face doesn't insinuate anything good.

"Mrs. Smith, did you know Dad is chaperoning the dance next Friday?" Alane turns to me.

"Are you? I didn't see your name on the list of parents," she says

"I... well..."

"He is," Lawson interrupts. "He wasn't sure if he'd be busy with the restaurant, but he will be there." My eyes widened, looking at my son. What is he talking about?

"Well, great." She smiles. "I'll see you then." She waves a hand and walks away in her mother's direction.

"You can thank me later," Lawson deadpans next to me while my eyes follow the sway of Alane's hips.

"What?"

"It's so disappointing when you realize that your father, your hero, the one you looked up to, has no game," he says dramatically.

"No game?" I feign being hurt by his words. "Hailey is going to kill you. You know that, right?"

"That's all part of the fun. Now, what are you going to wear? Do you still have your suit from prom? I can't wait to tell Uncle Luke, Grandma and Grandpa, oh my God, and Uncle Barn!"

"As long as you don't tell Aunt Sal, we'll be fine!" I mumble, knowing my sister won't be happy to hear I'm going to a dance with Al.

"Don't worry, Aunt Sal doesn't care, Dad! Haven't you heard? Uncle Chris is in town," he says, getting into the car. I follow suit, wondering what my son knows that I don't.

13

THEN - ALANE

"I can't believe your parents allowed you to be my date for the winter formal," Aaron says entering the Winterland decorated gymnasium. He looks delicious with his navy blue suit and grey tie. It's the same suit he wears for important hockey games, but I don't know why he looks better than usual tonight.

"Don't be too excited! They said yes because my mother is a chaperone, and I have to be home by ten." I remind him of the deal my parents struck with me.

"I don't care, Al. I get the chance to dance with you." Swoon. How that boy can be so adorable when I am not? Just thinking of the elaborate plan I have for tonight, I know I'm not worthy.

"Why were you late then?" I tease. He was only fifteen minutes late, but Aaron is usually Mr. Punctuality. The blush spreading on his cheeks tells me there is a good story there.

"As per usual, Barn pissed on my bed, but then Sal threw a fit when she realized she wasn't the one coming with me tonight. It seems I promised I'd bring her to a ball to meet her prince. When she heard about the dance, she thought she was coming along. She was all dressed up in one of her princess costumes, and it took me a long time to calm her down. I promised I would bake with her tomorrow. I also promised that Chris and I would take her for ice cream."

"Chris?"

"She's pretty fond of him, to her I suck now because I have this girlfriend she's not a fan of." He shrugs. "Chris made a joke about you being overrated one day when Luke couldn't stop speaking about you, and Sal looked at him like he was her new hero. So not a good feeling." I can feel the pain in his voice. Aaron has been Sal's everything for a long time. Aaron's little sister doesn't approve of him spending so much time with me, and she voices it regularly. Their relationship has been difficult, not as much as Barnabas peeing on his bed difficult, but still ignoring him and having tantrums kind of difficult.

"I'm sorry, but I'm not really sorry. You're mine, Aar. Your little sister has to understand that," I joke.

"If only my brothers could understand that too, it would be peachy." Aaron and I had a little argument the week before when he'd learned I'd watched porn with Luke. I'd come to the farm to hang out with him but had forgotten he was working.

Luke had the house all to himself, and I'd found him watching gay porn. He'd gotten a tape from Chris, which did not surprise me; Chris has a way of getting a hold of these things. I'd been intrigued by gay sex since I knew Luke liked boys, especially about the mechanics of it. So when I asked Luke if he wanted to hang, and he agreed on the condition that I watched the rest of the movie with him. I sat on his bed and started watching, trying to ignore the bulge I'd seen poking through my boyfriend's gay brother's pants.

It wasn't my first time watching porn. Patricia and I had

also found some of Chris' stash, but two men together was different. The video had given me a good idea of what I wanted tonight to be about, but it furthered my knowledge of what was acceptable and what excites me.

When I saw one man putting his dick inside another, I almost had an orgasm on Luke's bed.

The whole scene should have frightened me. It was violent, hard, rough, but it got me so wet that my nightly fantasy had involved Aaron doing a lot of the same to me.

Unfortunately, I knew tonight couldn't be about anal sex and roughness, but I was hoping I could do something else, something men always seemed to like in porn videos. Something Patricia and I had read about extensively in the magazines her brother kept hidden in his closet, not that I went in there. Patricia had brought us a few to study.

After my discussion with Mrs. Gritt, I'd felt somewhat better about my desire and sexuality. Guilt over God and what my parents thought aren't my main concern anymore, but self-reproach for trying to push Aaron to do something he isn't comfortable with is my daily self-punishment. I am, at the same time, trying to find a way around it.

If Aaron can't take my virginity, maybe we could have oral sex or even anal? I could remain a virgin, yet fulfill my wildest fantasy without getting pregnant. I just have to convince my boyfriend.

"You look beautiful, by the way, Sweets." Planning to do what I want is a constant battle in my mind. First, I needed to look presentable but desirable, so I could drive Aaron crazy. I know how to get him hard just by kissing him, but I need to have him wanting to kiss me more than usual. I need him to crave me and not be able to say no. I need him to want me so much, he can't back out. So, I bought a simple black dress that hugs my hips and caresses my breasts. The outfit had horrified my mother, the cardigan I swore to keep on all night with the perfect pearl necklace I borrowed from her, gave her the security she needed. I insisted that she would be there anyway, as well as Coach Gritt, and a lot of other parents and teachers. I also reminded them there was no way Aaron would do anything. It's funny how she always thinks Aaron is the one who's trouble. If only she knew.

"Thank you," I answer shyly like the perfect girlfriend I am, not the hussy thinking of taking him in my mouth while pleasuring myself with my fingers.

"Do you want something to drink or do you want to dance?" He's guiding me with his hand at the small of my back, and I would love for his hand to travel south to grab my ass tightly.

"Let's go dance," I say when I hear Sinéad O'Connor's hit song hit the speakers.

Being so close to him while my mother is looking over my shoulder is a mistake. I want him, and it's hard to hide. Aaron doesn't smell like his usual wet ice and sweat mix but a mixture of ocean and a fresh breeze. It doesn't matter.

What I desire is his touch, his kiss, and his smile, not the funny smell of the ice rink. His fingers on my waist are burning me up. Our hips are rubbing against each other, and my head against his chest is spinning. As my breathing becomes heavy from the desire building around me, I can feel his erection growing against my belly. I can feel his heat, and it's making me hotter. Tilting my head up, I see Aaron's nostrils flaring.

"Are you okay?" I whisper pecking him on the lips. No heavy petting is allowed at the dance. Squeezing my hips tighter, with his hands, he pushes me into him so I can feel him entirely.

"I need to kiss you," he says, dragging me by the hand toward the exit so fast I almost lose my balance. That's not the Aaron I know, but I like this Aaron a whole lot.

Unfortunately, my mother is at the door, blocking our way out.

"Give me a second," he squeezes my hand in reassurance. Aaron walks towards Chris, who winks at me over his shoulder and then strolls towards the door. Aaron is back in front of me after a few seconds while Chris is distracting my mother. We make our way to the exit when Patricia jumps in front of us.

"Finally, I've found you. I didn't know where you were," she scolds me before turning to Aaron and greets him while batting her eyelashes. He nods to acknowledge her presence.

"I need to go to the bathroom," I shout above the music.

"Let me come with you," she shouts back. I shake my head. I can feel Aaron's uncertainty and my window for sexual favors closing. I need to get the hell out of here before my mother realizes I'm up to no good.

"No, I don't feel well," I tell her, reaching for Aaron's hand. "Can you tell my mom not to worry? I just want to see if I feel better with less noise and some fresh air, and if I don't, Aaron will take home." Patricia narrows her eyes at me, but I use my poker face, the same one I use at home. She nods and lets Aaron and I pass while Chris still distracts my mother.

"Where are we going?" Aaron asks once we are in the corridor.

"You were the one dragging me somewhere, Aar. I thought you had a plan!"

"I just wanted to properly kiss you," he offers as if we haven't kissed for years. Pushing him into the girl's bathroom, I find myself pinned against the wall before I can lock the door. Aaron devours my mouth with a swipe of his tongue, nibbling my lower lip, licking my upper, trapping my body under his, but it's over before it really begins, and he lets me go.

"Saw something I want to try," I announce, diving back into the kiss.

"Okay, but you know we can't..." I kiss him deeper to shut him up. I don't want him to remind me of the stupid deal he made with my father. I don't want my father or God between us right now. I don't want anything between us.

"Don't worry, I'll still be a virgin after what I want to do," I say, placing my hand on the bulge in his pants and pushing my tongue in his mouth.

As we get lost in our kiss, I unbuckle his belt before finding its way to his length. It's my first time to have my hand on his cock. It's warm, thick, and smooth. I'm not sure what I was expecting, but it's better than anything I could ever imagine. It sends a surge of desire between my legs, and I bring my other hand to my panties. Sliding the cotton underwear down my thighs, I squeeze him before releasing his lips. I fall to my knees and stroke my clit, coating my fingers with my desire while I bring my mouth to his zipper.

"My hands are busy, pull down your pants for me."

"I don't think we should..." Releasing his cock, I tug down his pants and underwear in one move.

"Al, please... I..." I shut him up by opening my mouth and taking in his length. His whimpers satisfy my eagerness to take the next step in our relationship, and I start to work on him, following all the advice I read in the magazine and everything I saw in the videos. The tip of his dick taps the back of my throat at the same rhythm as my fingers enter me. Each moan sends vibrations in both of our bodies, and as my hand works him, I feel him swell around my tongue.

"Fuck, Al, I'm going to come," he says, putting his hand in my hair and pulling a little. As I saw in the videos, I abandon my clit so my fingers can find his balls, and I hold them tight. His hips thrust, and come fills my mouth, without any warning on his part, spurting several times before I swallow every last drop of him.

Letting my fingers travel along his dick, I rub the tip of him before I get back on my feet to meet his eyes. They are burning with lust and anger. Backing away from me, he shoves his package back in his pants and kisses me roughly, his hand cupping my pussy over my dress.

"You're not the only one watching porn, Sweets. Are you sure that's what you want?" His voice is strained, and I can see he has no more control over the situation than I do.

"Yes! Please, Aar." I groan while his hand rubs me.

"You've tasted me, now it's my turn." He pushes my dress up to uncover my core. "Do you want me to do that?" His fingers brush me tentatively. I nod fervently for his hands to caress me, for his mouth to taste me, for his fingers to enter me.

"Please."

"Fuck, you drive me crazy," he says, getting on his knees in front of me. "Stop me if there is anything you don't like, okay?" He starts by kissing my pubic bone gently, breathing in my scent.

"You're making me lose my mind, Al. We could lose everything; you do realize that?" He nibbles his way down to my throbbing pussy. When the tip of his tongue hesitantly licks me, I feel my whole body shake under his touch. I can barely hold myself up with the intensity of the sensations, so I back away. "Too much?" he whispers.

"Oh no, please more." I sigh in despair. Putting his fingers between my legs, he opens me to make room for him and licks me some more. Tracing the outline of my opening with his tongue, he pushes inside while I try to muffle my moans.

His long, slow licks move along one side and then the other, getting closer to my clit with each lap. I want to shove his head into me and have him eat me out, but I know I should let him explore some more as he let me do to him a few minutes ago. My clit is aching, and I beg him for more pressure while grinding into his face. When he continues his agonizing pace, I grab his head and move it to where I need it to be.

"You've tortured me for almost two years, and now you won't let me play?" he teases before sucking on my clit. Not being able to stay quiet while I hump his face, I bite my lip when he increases the tempo and slides a finger inside me. Synching his fingers and flat tongue, he keeps alternating between lapping and fingering me, and I slowly lose my mind, a white fog enveloping my brain.

With each of his movements, I feel every ounce of my body turning into mush. When my climax rolls inside me, I hold his head and immobilize him against my clit while my knees buckle and my eyes roll back. It's the best orgasm I've ever had, and when Aaron stands up, his face wet from me and leans in for a kiss, I don't hesitate to taste myself on him.

"You taste so fucking good, Sweets. Like butterscotch." He smiles.

"I love you," I answer, bringing him in for a hug.

"I love you too, Sweets." He kisses the top of my head. "Can I keep your panties?" He's dangling my underwear in front of me. I snatch them from him and cover back up. My dress is too short for me to walk with a bare ass.

"So when can we do this again?" he asks, caressing my back.

"Look who wants more now that he's tasted it," I joke.

"Isn't that the whole thing about Adam and Eve? I bit the apple, and now I want another bite." He shrugs. "In my opinion, it's all your fault." He's readjusting his clothes while I arrange my hair. "Joking aside, we shouldn't say anything to anybody, Sweets. I don't want you to get in trouble." He comes behind me and kisses my shoulder. It's the sweetest touch I've ever felt, like a ray of sunshine warming up my shoulder or a shower of love piercing my heart.

"Just Patricia," I mumble.

He shakes his head behind me. "Especially not Patricia. Chris said she is feeding details of our relationship to her mother."

"She's what?" I turn to face him.

"She's not a friend, Al. She's a jealous bitch and always will be. And I'm quoting her brother on that, these are not my words." He shrugs. "Luke and Chris are your friends, but Patricia. She's not. Don't forget that."

NOW - ALANE

"Thank you for picking me up," I tell my date for the night. "I wasn't sure I could walk in alone..."

The gym has been decorated as if the Queen of England was coming. Parents and students have spent hours organizing an event that will last only four hours, but nobody dares to say how ridiculous the whole shebang is. Chaperones and teachers came early to wait for the students to appear in their gowns and tuxes, or whatever it is kids wear these days.

"Because of the anxiety? I get it."

"Do you?"

He nods. "One of my exes had panic attacks. It wasn't always easy to calm her down."

"You broke her heart?"

"Not sure? It was more of a falling out of love scenario for both of us."

"I get it."

"Do you?" It's my turn to nod.

"Ex-husband, remember?"

"I do."

I smile. "We have more in common than we used to." He smirks. My laugh comes directly from my belly. Barnabas is even cuter as an adult than he was as a kid. I wasn't sure it was possible, but, man, he knows how to seduce a woman. His blue eyes are laughing as well, and the tiniest wrinkles appear around his eyes like magic.

Cuteness at its finest.

"Señorita," he butchers the word with his strong accent, leading me to the gymnasium.

"Thank you, Barn. You're a real gentleman."

"One of us has to be," he says, looking into the distance behind me. "Don't turn around. My brother just showed up with Patricia," he announces with a glimmer in his eyes.

"Patricia? Well, they would make a nice couple." I feel a pang of jealousy in my chest. Aaron and Patricia are the last people I would want to see dancing together.

"Shit, we need to take a picture of them and send it to Luke," Barnabas says jokingly. "The broody and the tramp." I laugh again at his goofiness. "He's going to be pissed at me," Barnabas adds, looking at Aaron.

"He shouldn't." I shrug, handing him a glass of non-alcoholic punch. "It's not like you're pissing on his bed like you used to."

"No, but I am your date for the night. That's almost as bad as pissing directly on you." He turns up his lips. "Oh, but look, someone else might get pissier by seeing us together." He jerks his chin in the direction of the door where Salomé and Chris appear arm in arm.

"Sal and Chris?"

"They're friends. They like to hang out together when he's

in town, it's no secret she had a huge crush on him since she was like six."

"Did she ever make a move?"

"Not that I know of. He sees her as the little sister, you know..."

"I think I know," I tease him. "Why are they here?"

"Chris is an honorary board member. He's the one who funded the school. Patricia doesn't even have a teaching degree. The only qualification she has is being Chris' sister."

"And Sal?"

"He takes her as a date when he's around. Better than taking Patricia... I guess Sal is hoping you'll distract Aaron enough so she can make a move."

"She's in for a rude awakening, Aaron and I are long over..."

"Right," he mocks me. "Long over— that's why he's shooting daggers at me right now. I just hope Patricia doesn't try to get back in my bed. I was kind of traumatized by the noises she made." I raise an eyebrow, waiting for him to elaborate. "She barks like a seal," he mumbles, and I can't stop the fit of laughter spreading through me.

"What's so funny?" Aaron's voice arises from behind me, transforming my laughter into a squeak. Turning around, I'm transported to our night at the Winter Formal. He's wearing a navy blue suit and a grey tie with a dark shirt. It matches his eyes, his hair, all of him. We are teenagers again, the only difference is that my so-called friend is hanging on his arm, and he doesn't seem to mind.

"Seals," I answer, fake-smiling with all my teeth. "Some have sex with penguins, and it seems they make a lot of noise. Have you ever seen that video Patricia?" I add before Barnabas spits his drink on Patricia's dress.

"Barnabas!" she screams, letting Aaron's arm go and running for the bathroom.

"That was cold, Al!" Barnabas smiles.

"But well deserved!" Aaron adds. I turn to him in confusion.

"You're not very nice to your date, Aaron," I chastise him. He doesn't have time to answer when Salomé and Chris join our group. Chris hugs me tightly. If I'm not mistaken, I hear someone groaning, and I'm not sure if it comes from Salomé or Aaron.

"Alane! Seeing you here with Aaron! It's like old times," he says, wiping a fake tear from his eyes. "I don't even have to distract your mother if you want to give him a blow job this time!" he adds smugly.

I don't know what's coming over me, but I can feel the growing rage inside me. When I was younger, I had the ice to take out my frustration. Later in life, I had rough play and sex with strangers. I haven't really felt rage in years. It was more anxiety and panic, but since I've been back in Springs Falls, I'm starting to feel old emotions, from desire to anger and a little jealousy stirring back up.

"Aaron is here with your sister; she might be the one blowing him tonight. If you'll excuse me, there is a colleague I want to see. Barn, I'll catch you later." I walk away without a backward glance; nervous that my anxiety will rise any minute. But it never comes. Instead, I feel delighted.

For a while, I get sucked into a boring conversation with the oldest math teacher in the country. My eyes keep darting back to the group of friends I don't belong to anymore and when I see Patricia's breasts pushing up against Aaron's arm, I excuse myself from my colleague, and stand in the corner to continue my observation. She's now touching his chest, batting her eyelashes, squeezing his biceps, over and over.

"That's some interesting nostril flaring you're doing there, Al. Why don't you go talk to him," Barnabas says, standing next to me.

"I'm sorry. I'm not a fun date," I answer, ignoring his comment.

"On the contrary. Luke is going to love this. I didn't come here to woo you. I wish I could, but I know better than to piss off Aaron, he won't hesitate to punch me. However, Luke and I thought it could be interesting to see if we could push him a little." He smiles.

"So you're using me to rile him up?" I ask, confused.

"Well no, but actually yes. But also to prove to him that he should pursue a second chance."

"I don't want one, and neither does he."

"So, that's why your nostrils are flared, your eyes are burning with hate, and you're wondering where to hide Patricia's body?" Rolling my eyes, I don't answer. "Why don't you kiss me and see what he does," he proposes.

"No, Barn… You're seven years older than my son…" I try to dissuade him. Barnabas' eyes widen, and I realize the mistake I just made.

"Or nine years," I quickly state, "what I mean is, you're a little too young for me." I don't have time to see what his reaction is because Aaron comes between us.

"Dance with me." It's not a question. Aaron was never one to tell me what to do. He knew better. Taking my hand in his, his eyes look deeply into mine to find an answer I'm not ready to give. "Please, dance with me," he pleads while I recognize the song playing, *Nothing Compares to You.*

"I'm not sure we're supposed to," I whisper, thinking how awkward it would be for the students to see a parent and a teacher dancing together. "Your kids are going to be mortified."

"Not if we stay in a dark corner," he says sheepishly. Nodding, I wrap my hands around his neck and let him bring me closer. I'm thrown back in time, it's as if no time had passed.

"I would really like to catch up with you." His lips are moving, and I can't stop looking at them. I remember how good they felt on my breasts, or how they touched my pussy.

"Alane?"

"Sorry, you were saying?"

He chuckles. "I'm wondering too what it would be like to kiss you again." He beams, his eyes now falling to my lips.

"Aaron, it's easy to forget why we didn't work, but you broke up with me for a reason, and we are both very different people than we were thirty years ago. I don't know what you're looking for, but..."

"Happiness." He cuts me off. "I'm looking for happiness. Do you remember how happy we were?"

"We were kids. It's easy to be happy when life hasn't touched you yet." We sway to the music, both lost in our thoughts. Mine are about the boy I used to love, all the firsts we experienced together and the long lasting love we never had.

"Just coffee to catch up, please, Sweets."

"What about Patricia?"

"What about her?"

"Nothing, I guess. I'm happy, if you are," Aaron laughs, and it's not butterflies I feel inside me but a charm of humming-birds. I always loved Aaron's laugh because it was as rare as an ice cube in the Sahara Desert. Like his smile, his smirk, his kisses or anything involving his mouth, it was always reserved for me.

"That's bullshit, Al! I hate your ex-husband, and I don't even know him. I hate my own brother tonight because you came with him. Don't pretend, Sweets."

The music changes to a more suitable rhythm for teenagers, and I unhook my hands from behind his neck, but he keeps me close. Inching towards me, the expression in our eyes looks as if we're both remembering the last time we danced.

I wet my lips as I look at his.

He comes even closer, and when I think he's about to kiss me, his mouth finds my cheek. All I can feel is the tingle of his beard, and it awakens more than the nerves on my face.

"Thank you," he says before backing away. "Think about coffee, okay." He smirks while I can still feel his mouth on me.

I'm on cloud nine, pondering coffee with Aaron when Lawson approaches me.

I shouldn't play favorites, but I do, especially since the kid reminds me of a certain boy who loved science as much as I did. I wonder if he knows how much he's like his Uncle Luke.

"Mrs. Smith?" He seems uncertain he should talk to me, touching his glasses nervously.

"Yes, Lawson?"

"If I tell you something, would you tell my dad?" That's something no teacher wants to hear coming from the mouth of a teenager.

"Listen, Lawson, if you or your sister are in danger, I will. Aaron, I mean, your dad seems to be an excellent father, and I'm sure you can talk to him."

"It's about Hailey though, and I promised her I won't tell

Dad, but I really think she needs help," he says, looking at his shoes.

"Your uncle, godfather and aunt are here, why me?"

"If I tell one, they'll all know, and every one of them will have something to say. We'll have to discuss it at the family dinner, and have my Uncle Luke weigh in through FaceTime... I don't think what happened tonight is worth a Gritt council."

The only council I attended was when Luke came out. It was chill but still intense. With everybody as adults now, I can't imagine the mess it might become.

"Where is she?"

"In the bathroom. Can you let me know if she's okay afterwards?" I know too well how easy it can be to get the adults distracted when you want to be alone at a dance, so I walk-run in the direction of the bathroom to find Hailey crying in one of the stalls. She's inconsolable at first and doesn't seem to mind that it's me she's crying on. I would much prefer Sal to be here, but I know how it's easier to speak to an almost stranger. I did the same with Mrs. Gritt many times. If only I could be for her half of what her grandmother was for me, I would be happy to do so.

"Talk to me, Hailey. What's the problem?" Pinching her lips, she shakes her head, refusing to tell me. "Okay, so don't tell me. Just let me know if you are hurt." She shakes her head again. "Do you need medical help." It's another silent no. "Did someone hurt you?" She nods. "Physically?" No. "Why can't you tell your Dad?" I ask an open question, so she will answer. It's a trick I learned as a teacher. Teenagers like to respond by yes or no. You need to open the question to get a more elaborate, but a short answer. Still no answer, so I continue, "I was never an overly dramatic teenage girl, but Patricia was. I consoled her more than once about a boy, a bad date, her crush being gay, or whatever other things that brought her to tears and made her feel like her life was over. So you can confide in me." It seems to do the trick.

She sighs before saying timidly, "I wasn't supposed to date."

"Your father told you not to date?" I say surprised. She nods, and I can't help but roll my eyes. "That's grand." I scoff. "Look, when I was your age, I lost who I thought would be the love of my life. I survived. We always do. I also lost my best friend and left town, moving far from my parents. Talk to your father, or any other adult in your family. I know for a fact your Uncle Luke is a great listener, and your dad and grandfather might look scary, but they are huge teddy bears. Your father might get a little mad that you disobeyed him, but he'll listen and help. He always did."

I shouldn't use myself as an example, but I want her to know it's going to be fine even if I'm not the greatest role model for teenagers. In fact, if most of the parents here knew my past, I certainly wouldn't be teaching their kids. "Now, hand me your phone, so I can tell your aunt to come and get you. I'm sure she won't tell."

"She always tells Dad everything. She's not cool at all." I smile remembering the little girl who babbled about everything to her older brother. She used to tattletale on what Luke and I were doing when Aaron was at work.

"What about Mrs. Gritt then?"

"My mom?" My heart shatters. Of course, there is another Mrs. Gritt, and it's not Aaron's mom.

He has a Mrs. Gritt in his life.

Why am I here taking care of his daughter and considering coffee with him when he didn't choose me and ended up married to someone else? Can I forget the hurt and despair he put me through? Am I strong enough to risk my already broken wings breaking once again?

"My mom is far away and never really cared," Hailey says, having taken my silence as an invitation to speak about her mother.

I'm dying from the inside.

Almost thirty years of suppressed pain come crashing into me, and I feel myself slipping into a world I'm all too familiar with. Misery, sadness, and hopelessness. Three encounters were enough to give me faith again when I should have been concentrating on my mother getting better.

Aaron is just someone I used to know, like an old song you can sing knowing the lyrics by heart but don't remember who sang it or what year it came out. Despite that, I won't leave one of my students crying in the bathroom because a boy broke her heart.

"Okay, Hailey, this is what we're going to do." As I lay out my plan of action: from cleaning up the mascara that transformed her face into a panda, to walking with her head held high, and to finding the cutest boy out there and asking him to dance with her; my thoughts somehow keep going back to Aaron and how my traitorous heart was ready to give him time to catch up with the possibility of a future together.

He's my past, and it's time I move forward and learned from it.

15

THEN - AARON

*S*ince Alane and I crossed the line into oral sex, we've been busy sneaking out.

We've put our confidence into Luke and Chris to be sure we have people covering for us, and for all I know, Al hasn't said anything to Patricia. She has even put some distance between them, spending most of her time with my brother when I'm not around.

I'm more envious than jealous of the bond they are building and also annoyed that Luke spends more and more time with us, but as he had lost a lot of friends when his former best friend blabbed to the whole team that Luke was gay, I can't bring myself to ask him to leave us alone.

The three of us are hanging out in the back of my truck. Alane has her head on my chest, lying down next to me while I caress her hair, and Luke is at our feet lying down as well, and throwing a football in the air. We're just talking about the future, our hopes, and the latest gossip. Time stands still, and I would like to stay like this forever.

"What is Chris going to do after graduation?" Alane asks. I see Luke's ears perk up. I'm not dumb. I see the way he looks at my best friend. Chris was one of the only ones standing up for Luke. When Alane and I hang out, they do as well. I know Chris got his hands on some gay porn for Luke, and I suspect they even watched some together. I'm discreet, and I don't interfere. I hate when my family gets in my business, so I won't get in my brother's.

"I'm not sure," I respond, "It depends on what his father wants him to do," I scoff, dragging my fingers along her arm.

"He wants to become a sport's agent, but his dad wants him to be a doctor," Luke answers, throwing the ball in the air.

"What does Patricia want to do?" I ask, not interested but curious to know what someone as shallow as Patricia has planned for her future.

"Except marrying Luke?" Alane jokes. "I guess teach? But I think her dad wants her to be a nurse."

"Dads always end up getting what they want." I'm defeated in the choice of career looming in my future. I still haven't told them what I want to do. I told Alane, Chris, and Luke, but every time I try to broach the subject with my dad, he comes back to the farm and hockey. I'm so afraid to disappoint him; so I shut up and pretend we have the same dreams.

"You need to talk to Dad. If I could tell them I like boys, you can say you want to go to culinary school. First, they'll say they need to plan for the money, but then they'll be happy for you that you've found your calling. Even more, once you are a famous chef if you promise to come back here one day and use the farm products in your restaurant."

I sigh at the amount of faith my brother has in me.

If only I could take everything as easily as he does. He likes boys, no problem; let's tell Mom and Dad. He wants to go to art school, let's show them how he can draw and jump on the artistic bandwagon.

Everything for me seems harder to talk about, and knowing I'll be crushing my dad's hopes is the worst feeling.

"Where is the best school?" Alane asks, her eyes closed as if she's afraid to hear the answer.

"Seattle, but that's not where I would like to go. I want to stay close by."

"I could do some research and see what hockey prep schools there are in Washington State," she says without a doubt.

"No, Al. I'll never get in anyway, even if I speak to my parents about it. Your scholarship is already secure for next year; you're not changing plans for me. I'll talk to them, and I need to apply soon. The deadline is coming up."

"Okay," she whispers, unsure. "And you, Luke, where are you going to go?"

"I'll stay around next year, and then I'll see. I'll miss you both, that's for sure."

"I'm not gone yet," I tell my brother. Luke sits up abruptly and looks at me with an intensity I've never seen in his eyes before.

"Remember, I'm doing it for you, Aar." He smirks. "Dad! Aaron has something to tell you!"

"What is it, Son?" My father comes closer and pops his head in the bed of the truck. He's always so nonchalant if it's not about the farm or hockey.

"I… well…" I stammer my words, not sure I can say what Luke wants me to.

"Come on, Aaron," he insists, "he's not going to kill you." Alane has sat up as well and is looking at me with encouragement.

"Well, son. At least we know you're not gay." My father chuckles. "Should I call your mom?" I nod, still fighting with my words. I was never good at saying what I want.

"Bella!" he screams. "Aaron is finally ready to speak."

"I'm not sure I am," I mumble, trying to find the nerve to do so. Alane has her hand on my thigh, supporting me. Luke is amused, but I know it's his way of helping; he always pushes me to pursue what I want. He did it with Alane, with my job —he's the one who begged Chris and Patricia's father to give me a chance— and now with my future.

"Finally," my mother says, standing close to my dad, "I was wondering when the boy would tell us."

"What are you talking about?" I ask them confused.

"That's not how it works, Aaron Jax! You're the one who has to tell us, not us putting words into your mouth." Luke chuckles, and if I didn't know he was doing this for me, I would kill him.

"Well, I'm not ready, but…"

"He is!" Luke interrupts, "Right, Captain?" Alane nods.

"Go on, Aar, it's going to be fine."

"I want to be a chef!" I say quickly. I don't know how Luke had the courage to come out to my parents. I feel a knot in the pit of my stomach, a fear of disappointing, a hope that they'll still love me and a dread waiting for an answer.

"Darn, Son! You couldn't say baker? I just lost twenty bucks to your mother!" my father complains while getting his wallet from his back pocket and pulling out a twenty. My mother is beaming, with her hand out, pride in her eyes.

"You knew, and you're not mad? I mean... the farm, the hockey?" My mother rolls her eyes at me and slips the twenty in her pocket.

"Those were only fallbacks until you fessed up and told us what you want to do, Son. When I walked away from the life my parents laid out for me, I chose not to impose our wants on our kids." I'm shell-shocked by the ease of this conversation.

"I really wish you were my parents." Alane yearns with amazement in her eyes.

"Oh, sweetie. Whatever happens with this one, you'll always be a part of this family. Now, can I go back to work? We'll discuss more over dinner. Alane, are you staying?"

"I can't tonight. My parents are expecting me for supper with the Harbors," she apologizes for having to choose. I still haven't been invited to share a meal with the Smiths, but I prefer to avoid the pastor anyway.

"Let me drive you home," I slide off the bed of my truck and shove Luke on the shoulder.

"You're welcome," he chimes

"You knew, didn't you?"

"I heard them talking about it last week. I could have told you, but I didn't want to take the fun out of the whole experience for me." He laughs.

"Revenge is a dish best served cold, Luke. But thank you." I hug him.

"Drive the girl home. I'll call her parents in thirty minutes saying you just asked me to call to tell them you are on your way." He winks at Alane, who doesn't blush a bit. She initiates what we do more than me, and I end up being the one blushing from head to toe.

"That's sexy," she whispers, and I end up nodding at Luke, telling him silently to call her parents for me in a little while.

As I come back home, I know I'm late for dinner, and my hair is sticking up. Alane held on to it so tight when I went down on her, I look like someone shoved a stick of dynamite up my ass. Everybody is sitting around the table, and there is no way I can avoid them and run to shower, so I sit down, hoping nobody comments on the state of my hair, but that's not how my family works.

"I hope you're being careful," my mom chimes, passing me the potatoes.

"We're not doing it," I answer, trying not to speak about sex in front of my younger siblings.

"Well, you're doing something," my dad adds, shoveling some stew in his mouth.

"Yes, but not that. Her dad gave me enough warnings."

"You're young and about to leave for Seattle. You shouldn't promise Al anything."

"Seattle?"

"Yes, Mr. Harbor said that's where the best school is. I think you should go."

"Of course, he did. That's Pastor Smith's plan. Sending me away."

"I don't want Aaron to go away," my little sister complains, and it feels good in a way that she's not giving me the cold shoulder. My mother shushes her, explaining this is a conversation between grown-ups.

"Aaron," my dad shakes his head dismissively, "if his plan is giving you a good education, I don't see a problem."

"What happened to Alane being part of the family?"

"What happened to you wanting to become a chef?" My mother pushes food into Barnabas' mouth indicating he should finish his plate. "So what's your plan? Going to a local school for one year and then follow her around, depending on where she's going?"

"Pretty much. And marrying her." My parents' eyebrows jump to their hairline. Salomé groans.

"Aaron, you're still young, Alane is your first real girlfriend. I'm all about love, but maybe you should go to Seattle, work a little and then marry her." My mother sounds more upset than concerned. I thought she would be supportive of Alane and I getting married. Telling me I'm too young when she married my dad, certainly while high on mushrooms and practicing free love for years, is the most ridiculous thing I've ever heard. If 'experienced' means sleeping around, that's not for me. Alane is it. I'll follow her where I need to. She can stay focused on her game, and I'll be happy to provide for her. As much as going against her dad scares me, I've thought a lot about it, and I can't let her go or walk away, I need to fight for us.

"Do her parents know about your plans?" My mother winces.

"Of course not. Pastor Smith asked him to break up with her as soon as school is done and leave so she can follow her dream," Luke pipes into the conversation, knowing I would never share this information with my parents. I send him a pointed look, but he shrugs it off.

"Aaron, listen to me. If you and Alane are meant to be, you can leave for Seattle and come back later. Don't jeopardize your future and hers; it's not worth it. I'll talk with Father Smith."

"If going to culinary school means leaving for Seattle, I'm

fine just working at the farm," I say, playing with my mashed potatoes.

"But if staying means you threaten your whole life and you never do what you love, it's going to be a very long fucking boring life," my father says.

"But what's a life without Alane, Dad? It seems I can't win."

"You can, by creating a future she can be a part of one day."

"Like in ten years? I want her to be my future tomorrow, not once I'm fucking thirty years old!"

"We're not saying you should wait for her career to be over; we're just asking you to think about your life as well. Don't decide anything around her plans, she might not even make it as a hockey player."

I sigh, pushing my plate, and stand up, needing to be alone.

"And you wonder why I never share anything," I say, climbing up the stairs.

"Aaron!" I hear my father call while I shut my door and lie on my bed.

"Don't give up, Aar," I hear Luke telling me from the corridor. "If she's the one, and you and I both know she is, don't give up."

"I'll try, Luke," I say, turning my back to him and closing my eyes. All I can do is try.

16

NOW - AARON

*a*lane is ignoring me.

I've begged Barnabas to give me her phone number, sent numerous texts and emails asking for a coffee date, and she's ignoring me.

All I want is to understand how the girl I knew became prone to anxiety attacks.

Who is Alane Smith now?

I'm not asking her to marry me. I mean, I'm not even asking her to give me a shot, not yet, maybe never. I need to sit down with her first to discuss and clear the air, to see where we are at. I'm not even sure I want a second chance, or maybe I do, or just a chance to fuck her.

Shit, I'm so confused, I just cut my finger.

Fuck.

My sous-chef looks at me with concern, as he has for the last few months since Jessica left and Alane came back.

"Take over," I mumble, making my way to the first aid kit to bandage my index finger. My phone chimes, and I look, hoping it's her, but knowing it's not. It's Luke.

. . .

Luke: I heard you cut yourself. Who were you thinking about?

I look around to see which traitor would have announced this to my brother, but there is nobody who knows him in my kitchen. It only means one thing. He's here and asked to talk to the chef, saying he was my brother. Then the waiter inquired about me and reported to Luke. I have no private freaking life, even in my own kitchen for something as stupid as a cut.

Making my way to the dining room, I see the icy blue eyes of his boyfriend staring back at me. Dex stands up and walks toward me, greeting me before I can slap the back of my brother's head.

"He's going to be an idiot, and I'm going to be an asshole. Fair warning, we're not here to blow smoke up your ass," Dex smiles and shakes my hand.

"Fair warning, I'm not in the mood for you two," I answer, hugging my brother.

Dex and Luke got back together a few weeks ago when I was in Los Angeles. They're madly in love, but my brother is too laid-back, and Dex is too much of a prick to show his love. I don't know how their relationship works, but it does, and we all adopted Dex quickly. Not that we had the choice anyway. I like the guy more than my two brothers. The only thing I dislike is how he needs to fix shit, and hearing his little speech when he greeted me, he's here in fix-it mode. I start to sit in the only empty chair around the table when Luke stops me.

"That's the Captain's seat. She's meeting us for supper."

"She accepted to come here?" I snarl, which doesn't fall on deaf ears.

"Is that why you cut yourself? Is she ignoring you?"

"Do you have to know every fucking thing, Luke?" Dex puts his hand on my brother's arm to tell him to let it go. Rolling my eyes, I make my way back to the kitchen. Why did they have to come here? What am I supposed to do now?

She has been pretty clear she doesn't want to have anything to do with me. That said, we're both adults. She could send a text or email just telling me so, but it seems even that is too difficult. Yet, coming on my home turf to dine with my brother isn't though. The icing on the cake would be if she brings Barnabas as a fucking date like at the school dance.

I didn't bring a date. I ran into Patricia in the corridor.

She constricted me like a boa before killing his prey. I couldn't breathe or get rid of her. It felt like she was crushing the life out of me.

The only moment I could breathe was when I danced with Alane. I could feel our old chemistry still lingering, and I was hoping she would give me a couple minutes of her time.

She reconnected with Luke, Barn, Chris, and whoever else but me. Next thing I know, she'll have tea with my mother while still ignoring me. I know I hurt her, but twenty-seven years should be enough to get over whatever grudge she has against me.

I spend the rest of night slamming things and snapping at the staff, getting more pissed off by Alane's behavior.

Every time the door to the kitchen opens, I can hear Luke having a good time, and I feel like punching him in the throat to get him to stop laughing.

When it finally calms down in the kitchen, I retreat to my office with a brandy and wait there for the night to end, knowing Luke and Dex won't leave without saying goodbye.

So when my second-in-command, Jacob, enters my office to tell me the staff are all gone, and there is only one person left in the dining room, and is waiting for me, I'm surprised to find Alane sitting alone, sipping a glass of amaretto.

"You requested to talk to the chef?" I make my way in her direction but stop a few steps away from the table, scrutinizing her.

Even if I don't want to show her any of my emotions, I'm buzzing.

She's sitting in my dining room and I'm barely holding on. She sips her drink, her eyes slowly roaming over my body. I feel naked under her gaze. When her eyes stop on mine, I see a glimmer I know too well.

Alane Smith wants me.

My dick stirs just thinking about it, and she must recognize the signs of me desiring her because she chuckles while biting her lower lip.

"Talking is not really why I asked you here." She finishes her drink in one gulp and sits the glass on the table before standing up and coming my way.

Her walk is a little unbalanced, and I'm pretty sure she drank more than the usual tonight.

"How much did you drink?" I keep my hands in my pocket while she stands before me, her eyes never leaving mine.

"Enough that if you want it rough, I shouldn't get an anxiety attack. Not enough that I don't know what I'm doing." Fuck that's sexy.

"So, you don't want to talk?" She smirks at me.

"What do you want to say, Aar? I got married then I divorced. You got married, then you divorced. I never made it to professional hockey. You became a chef. I have a son; you have a son and a daughter. There, all caught up."

"That's it? There is nothing more to know about you, Al?" She narrows her eyes at me as if she can't grasp why I'm not jumping at the opportunity to fuck her. I don't understand it either.

My conscience is telling me something is not adding up.

I can't reconcile the woman I saw at the church with the woman standing before me. Something doesn't make sense, and I don't know why.

She leans back on the table, her legs opened just slightly, and her back arched. She's pure sexiness, and I feel my restraint failing every damn minute.

"You want to know more?" She opens her silky shirt button by button. "I have thirty years of regrets to never have fucked you and seven of those were pent-up frustration because of anxiety. I'm offering this to you because even if you betrayed me and destroyed me, when I'm close to you I feel kind of safe for a reason I can't comprehend. My brain rejects you every chance it gets, but my body craves you. I haven't wanted sex so much in a decade, Aaron. Tonight might end up with me crying and begging you to stop, or it might end up a great night. I can't predict what will happen, but since I don't care much about giving you a second chance, I'm proposing a better deal. One night, no inhibitions, no holding back. We do what either of us has ever wanted, and then we walk away."

Her hands have disappeared behind her back during her monologue and unzipped her skirt. She's now in a white lace bra and panties, with a white blouse open, and heels that are begging to be around my neck. She steps out of the skirt and it puddles on the floor while she leans back against the table, her head tipping to the side, offering me her neck to bite on.

I'm hypnotized by the woman in front of me, her body is like a siren to my desire. As my brain tries to fathom all she just told me, my body has a life of its own. My fingers close around the bridge of her bra between her two breasts, and I drag her to me in one rough movement. Her hands fall to my chest, and I don't need more of an invitation to claim her lips in a hunger I didn't know I had.

Every swirl of her tongue reminds me she didn't wait for me. She used to be a great kisser, but I can feel she's now an expert. Anger spreads inside me, and I pin her vehemently on the table.

"How many men, Sweets?" Her vicious smile gives me the answer I don't want to know but need to.

"Too many to count." She wraps her legs around me and brings her body to mine, my bulge nesting between her legs. I thrust against her, and it feels like I'm sixteen again.

"I didn't wait three decades to dry hump you, Aar."

"And I didn't wait all this time to fuck you on a table, but here we are..." My hand snatches her panties and when my fingers enter her, she's so wet I can't restrain a groan. "You're so perfect." I kiss her again.

"Fuck me, please" Begging Alane was always my favorite Alane, not that I told her so when we were kids. But now I can, so I do, and she begs again, giving me control over her body.

I can't help myself and bite her nipples. She cries, but I feel her contract around my fingers, so I do it again. I'm leaving marks all over her, and I like how it looks. I'm still dressed, in my chef uniform and seeing her opened for me, almost naked on the table has me as hard as a rock.

My fingers push into her, and she whimpers a little more, so I bite harder as an answer. Her body is mine. I replace my fingers with my tongue and push my creamed fingers in her mouth so she can lick them clean. The tip of her tongue mirrors the strokes of mine. I bite her clit, sending a jolt of pain through her body. She bites my finger for me to stop and our eyes find each other. She's so fucking perfect, it hurts.

"Fuck me, Aar," she begs.

I stand up brusquely, freeing my cock and slam into her in a sharp thrust that sends her eyes rolling back into her head. I'm literally fucking her brains out, hard, fast, dirty, and she loves it. We are two animals grunting and moaning until I feel her clenching around me, and she orgasms, screaming my name like she did so many times before. As my eyes see the marks I left on her, I need to stain her even more. When I feel my balls tightening, I pull out and stroke myself to come on her stomach and make her as mine, like I did before.

I rest my forehead on her shoulder, still shivering because of the intensity of our orgasms. I'm not sure what the protocol is for fucking your ex on a table, so I wait for Alane to do something.

Peeking through my eyelashes, I see the moment when the reality of what we've done comes crashing down on her. She starts to mumble the few sentences she always repeats, and tears sprang to her eyes.

Because I don't know what to do, I kiss her.

I kiss her deeply like we used to, holding the back of her neck and helping her find peace.

I kiss her until she stops crying. I kiss her until she can stand strong and take control again.

I kiss her until she shoves me back, grabs the tablecloth

under her ass, wipes my cum from her body, gets dressed and leaves.

I kissed her until she decided we were done, and only then, I put my dick away and close up the restaurant, emotionally exhausted by the best sex I've ever had.

17

THEN - ALANE

*a*aron has been more distant than usual.

I know he has his job, his schooling, his hockey, and our future on his mind, but I have the feeling I'm spending my time with a giant plastic doll. He has retreated into his broody self. He doesn't smile anymore, he's always in his thoughts, and he never shares them. He also disappears on me a lot, saying he needs to be alone.

Today, we were supposed to babysit Sal and Barn for his mother, but he's not here.

Nobody knows where he is. I think Luke has an idea, but he's walking the fine line between his loyalty to his brother and his friendship with me, so I don't ask him. Mrs. Gritt felt guilty that Aaron ditched me, so she asked Luke to stay and help out.

I was relieved because if Barnabas does everything I ask; Salomé tends to lash out at me when Aaron is not around. I can stand on my own, but I'm not comfortable scolding a sister who isn't mine, even if she's mean to me like she is now.

"You're the worst, Alane. I hate you! Now he's going to leave because of you. I wish he had never fallen in love with you!" She sticks her tongue out and stomps her feet.

"You know he's not leaving with me, Sal. He'll come back every second weekend or so. Don't worry." I try to appease her, but I wish Luke was taking care of her instead of washing the peanut butter Barnabas spread all over his face.

"I know how to read a map. Seattle is far far away to come back on weekends!"

"Seattle?" The wind is knocked out of me. I sit on the floor, my head spinning and my pulse racing as Salomé stands fierce, her arms crossed, despising me.

"Yeah! They all say he should go far away from you! I wish you could be the one leaving so he could stay!" She runs upstairs, leaving me behind confused. Luke comes to sit next to me and squeezes my hand.

"Is that why he has been so distant?"

"It's not like that, Captain. He's trying to find a solution between how to stay here and not disappoint my parents. Saying he wanted to be a chef opened a can of worms he wasn't ready to deal with. He thought he would stay nearby, but they want him to get the best opportunity. They are breathing down his neck, but in the end, you know he's going to choose you, you have to have faith, Alane."

"Where is he?"

"Where do you think?"

"The ice?" Luke nods.

"I wish I could be with him." Luke and I are stuck with Salomé and Barnabas, and we don't have a car. All I can do is wait here for Aaron to return or for Mrs. Gritt to drive me home. But what if I could join him? I've already said so before, but there is undoubtedly a prep school for hockey at Washington State, and if not, there are some in Canada, or I could do my last year in a public high school with a hockey team and stay closer to him. After feeling crushed, I'm giddy, excited, and hopeful. Kissing Luke on the cheek, I get up laughing.

"What's going on Captain?"

"I'm going with him, Luke! I'll go to Seattle. I'm sure I can play hockey there. I need a plan to convince my parents, but I'm sure that's what I want to do!"

"Alane, are you sure? I mean, you have a spot reserved, a scholarship, your future is pretty well pathed already. Aaron is working on something to stay here, why don't you let him do it?"

"Because it's not worth living without him. You'll get it one day."

"Don't do any dumb Romeo and Juliet shit, girl."

"I won't, I just want to be with the love of my life. Is it so hard to understand?"

Luke sighs. "Hopelessly romantic but not hard to understand. Tell me if you need help."

Lightheaded by my newly made decision, I go to Aaron's bedroom and wait for him, lying on the bed. I love being surrounded by his smell, and I wish we could spend the night together one of these days.

Waiting is unbearable.

I feel like we're trapped in our little town, never able to ever do what we want. If he stays here and I go to the school my parents want me to, that's thirty minutes away, it will be the same. We'll never be free. But if we both moved to Washington State, we could be unrestrained by the adults around us. We'll meet on weekends and sleep all night together. We'll be able to live the life we want, and not have to sneak around because I'm the Pastor's daughter. I'll be Alane, nobody else. I'm dying to be myself.

When Aaron finally arrives, only thirty minutes have passed, but it was enough time for me to organize the whole plan in my head.

"You forgot about me," I start because he truly did. Him thinking he can disappear on me is disturbing after being together for so long.

"Sorry, Sweets, I needed to think." I can see the distress on his face. I've seen it several times in the past few weeks.

"No, you forgot to include me in your thinking. We're in this together. I know your parents want you to go to Seattle, I know they think we should go our separate ways; I know my father is certainly not helping with all the rules he has, but we are in this together. You want Seattle? Well, that's what we're going to do. I'll follow you." Aar sits on the bed and puts his hand on my knee.

His eyes are sad, and it hurts me to see him in pain. I already know what he's going to say before he opens his mouth. I can read him better than Luke, I think, but he doesn't see that. He doesn't see me anymore.

"I can't let you do that. I'll find a solution to stay, even if it means working at the Harbor's diner." His body language tells me it's the last thing on earth he wants to do.

"I'm not changing my dreams for you; I'm changing my trajectory. You, staying here and working in that diner is changing your dream. No way. You can't do that for me, like I won't give up hockey for you. But I can change where I'm going, and we're going to Seattle together."

"How are we going to do that, Sweets? Your parents are never going to let you go."

"I don't know, but I love you, and if I need to put a plan in place as complicated as escaping Alcatraz, I will. We're going. I might be able to transfer, I might be able to convince my parents, I might be able to have it all. So please, let me share the burden of figuring out our future together. Now, kiss me."

I want to wash his worry and sadness away, and the best way to do it is to make out.

He starts with small pecks.

I open my mouth to let him take over, but he doesn't. I want him to lose control again, so I kiss him harder, my tongue swirling and our teeth almost knocking by the intensity of our embrace.

Our lips break apart only to remove our T-shirts, our hands busily undressing each other until we're both in underwear, on his bed. We've never been so naked together. Even if we had oral sex and jerked each other off, we always had clothes on, Aaron never wanting to pass the point of no return. We're so close to having sex; I feel my excitement wetting my panties. I climb on top of him and rub myself on his hard length.

I would give my first born for him to be inside me.

"Slow down, Al."

But I can't, I continue kissing him, my hands roaming his body and our underwear getting wet. When I feel him at my entrance, I whimper, ready to push our underwear aside to have him in me. My hands find my panties, and I'm eager to remove them, but he clasps his fingers around my wrists and stops me. In one movement, he's on top of me, his head in my breasts. Bringing down my bra, he cups my tits and brings a nipple into his mouth. My hands free, I remove my underwear and rub against him, my clit loving the texture of his cotton briefs.

"Please, Aaron, fuck me," I beg.

He shakes his head, still in control.

So, I continue to hump him without penetration, his tip playing at my core, his underwear the only barrier between us. I take his hand in mine and bring it to my pussy. I need something inside me. Aaron seems to understand what I want and pushes one finger in me while licking my breasts one after another. His fingers are trapped between our bodies, and I beg him again to give me what I crave, but he still refuses. He adds a second finger and bends them a little to reach the sweet spot he discovered during previous explorations. My back arches, and I feel myself starting to fly.

When I come, I forget where I am and begin to scream his name. Fortunately, one of us is still thinking, and he muzzles my cries with his hand. A surge of pleasure bursts inside me by the restraint he's imposing. I come hard, like I've never before, my whole body shaking.

I open my eyes to find Aaron sitting on his heels, naked, and spreading my juice on his length. His other hand is still on my mouth, and I love the feeling. I'm aroused by the sight of him. His blue eyes are darkened by pleasure. His chest is bulky, and his long fingers are wrapped around his dick. If I weren't hypnotized by what he's doing, I would take him in my mouth.

"Please, Aaron, come on me." I want him to mark me the way I saw a man doing it in a video. I want to be his, even if he refuses to be inside me.

My words seem to excite him more than I intended, and he strokes faster while putting more pressure on my mouth. His grunts are erotic, and I can't help playing with myself while our gazes are on each other.

A few strokes have me panting at the same pace as he groans.

When he's about to come, he positions himself, so it splashes on my stomach, but his aim is trumped by his orgasm.

His cum shoots on my pussy, and I continue pleasuring myself, my fingers dripping of him pushing inside me, hard and fast. I come again; my orgasm provoked by the naughtiest thing we've ever done together.

Falling on me, his dick rests between my legs, and I kiss him, with no care in the world, because he's my world and always will be.

♥

"Can you drop me off at Pat's?" I ask Aaron when we make our way home. "I haven't seen her, and I need to catch up." He grunts. It's a different grunt than the one he uttered before, but it still sends a message to my senses. Nevertheless, he changes direction and drives me to the Harbor's house.

"Remember what I said, don't tell her what we do. I don't trust her." Aaron kisses me languorously before letting me go.

Patricia's house is not far from mine, and before Aaron was my boyfriend, we used to walk back and forth from hers to mine, discussing the world and gossiping a little. I've missed our long chats. These days, all she wants to talk about is whom she'll marry.

Of course, she wants to marry a Gritt, but the only one available is Barnabas, so that's not in her near future. She joins me outside, and we start our walk to my house. I share my new plan with her. I want her to know that I might be leaving, she's been my best friend since elementary school, and I can't blindside her. Also, I would need her help to announce it to my parents and do research.

"You're changing your life for someone you haven't even had sex with?" she scoffs.

Because that's the other thing she speaks about all the time.

Sex.

She's sex crazed. Not that I'm not, but I have a boyfriend. I get upset by her thinking my relationship with Aaron is based on it. Yes, I want it, but it's so much more.

"Not everything is about sex, Pat. Aaron and I are about love. Maybe you should try..." I know I'm not being fair. She tries hard to find a boyfriend, maybe too hard. She shrugs at my words as if to tell me I haven't hurt her, but I know better. "I'm sorry," I whisper.

"It's okay, I know you're in love, but how can you plan your life with him if you don't know if you're compatible?" I don't know if she's saying this to antagonize me even more, but it's working. I clench my jaw and try to ignore her.

"Or maybe, he's like his brother, and you'll end up just as a friend with both of the Gritt boys," she snarls.

Since she walked in on Luke and her brother, she has been vindictive towards Luke, but Chris threatened to tell her parents about the blowjobs she gives behind the bleachers if she says anything to anybody.

I only know she saw Luke blowing Chris because Luke told me.

That's how I hear the little comments she puts out there, they are quite passive aggressive otherwise, and you would need to know that she knows Luke is gay to understand what she's saying. She's clever in her meanness. I want to shut her up so badly, I walk into her trap and tell her the one thing I told my boyfriend I wouldn't share with anybody.

"Of course, I know we're compatible!" I grumble. "We've done other things, you know, like oral sex and masturbation."

"And you didn't tell me?" Patricia stops, and when I turn to look at her, I can see she's offended that I didn't share with her, yet there's so much she hides from me. "Good luck convincing your parents you want to follow your boyfriend." She grimaces.

It's clear to me she won't help me with my plan. Without saying a word, I walk away, having had enough of her drama for a lifetime.

18

NOW – ALANE

I learned a few things last night.
First, Aaron Jax Gritt is a dirty lover.

Fucking me on a table, only his cock out, biting me and marking me, dominating during intercourse is not for every man. Aaron grasped what I wanted and what I needed. It was as if he had read my mind and knew the fantasy, I acted out so many times with other men in scenes I created at the club. The only thing missing was his hand on my mouth to silence me. The restaurant scene, with customers sitting around watching me was my favorite play.

I've been fucked this way many times by my ex-husband, strangers or regulars, but it has never been as good as last night. Aaron knew what I needed, even if it was our first time. He remembered my body and understood I craved pain to come. I thought I would get into my head and not enjoy it, like how it happened in Phoenix, but the anxiety showed up only afterwards, once I realized I hadn't panicked while doing it. When I realized I could still have sex the way I liked it as long as it was with the right person.

That brings me to the second thing I learned.

Aaron can appease my anxiety.

After the church incident, I thought it was a one-time deal. But last night when I started to lose control and the anxiety took over, Aaron's kiss melted away my angst. Nobody has ever been able to calm me down, even my son, but in one touch, or in one kiss, Aaron could. It's unsettling, and my teenage heart is hopeful when my adult heart knows better than to trust my ex.

With that in mind, there is indeed room for more than only one night together. There is still something going on between us. Not because of the sex, I am the first one to know you can have fantastic sex with people you don't feel anything toward, but because of how I feel when he's close by.

The last thing I learned was that Aaron doesn't like to be ignored.

Nobody does, but I didn't think he cared until Luke and Dex laid it out for me to see. When they left after a lovely evening, and I asked to talk to the chef, that's what I wanted to do, talk. The plan changed, as every one of my plans had always done where Aaron is concerned. Seeing him angry with me, his face in a scowl and his fiery eyes got my panties burning, and I just decided to go for it, consequences be damned. I was sixteen again, wanting to fuck my boyfriend, and I could finally have him if he wanted to. Oh, boy, did he want to.

As I recall every little bit of last night, Patricia strolls into my classroom with the determination of a woman on a mission.

"You seem different, is everything alright?" She pries not so subtly.

"Mm- hmm" I pretend to be correcting a paper on my desk as to not engage with her.

"I wanted to make sure you were okay with me seeing Aaron."

Here is the thing about Aar, he's not a cheater, so I do know that after what happened last night, he's not seeing Patricia, he's not even thinking of her. She is obviously fishing and wanting to be with him.

"I was with Barnabas that night. I hope it's okay with you, he told me you two have a history." I give her my most beautiful syrupy smile and try hard not to imitate the bark of a seal.

"Kids these days, he has to blab it to everyone. Do you think Aaron knows?"

"Oh, he does. Barnabas is not shy about oversharing, never was." I want her to realize that Aaron will never go for Barnabas' sloppy seconds.

"Shit, I thought I had a chance this time around." I can't hold my laugh at the thought of her believing she has a shot with Aar.

"Well, sorry to disappoint," I simply say. Patricia narrows her eyes on me deciding whether she wants to push the issue. It seems to me she's jealous, but when was she not?

"Don't get your hopes up, Al. Why would it be different from the first time around? Aaron didn't change that much." I don't have time to respond when she turns around and leaves angry. I don't even know what happened, and I don't care. Maybe what we did is written on my face?

"Do you never learn from past mistakes?" Luke appears at my door. Is today an open house in my class and I wasn't notified? Sure seems like it. For all I know, Mrs. Gritt will be next, coffee in hand, telling me she waited long enough for me to come say hi.

"What do you mean, Luke?"

"You shouldn't trust her." He sits in the exact same seat he would have sat in class. Fourth row, next to the door. His tall frame and tattooed arms barely fit in the chair, and I can scarcely see the scrawny teenager I used to know.

"Seeing how your face is as blank as the mind of Salomé's ex-boyfriend, you haven't talked to Aaron." His voice is amused, and he clearly knows what happened between us already. I don't think Aaron told him, but I do believe Luke always knew where we were at and what we were up to. He has a sixth sense when it comes to his brother and me.

"You two always did everything backwards, Captain. One piece of advice, ask him what happened, why he dumped you. I didn't talk to him for two years until I learned the truth. All I can say is, it wasn't his choice." Yeah right. Poor Aaron was forced to break up with me.

"He found someone extremely fast for a guy who was heartbroken." I snarl, reminding Luke that not even two months after dumping me, Aaron was with someone else and happy to be. How do I know? I saw him with my own eyes, and then my parents confirmed it over the phone. It was the last time we spoke about the Gritts. I asked them never to share anything about him ever again.

"True, but he was just trying to push away the loneliness. Plus Jess had a magic pussy, but their relationship was doomed from the beginning."

"Why?"

"Because she wasn't you," he merely says, his eyes full of mischief. If someone knows how to push me to his brother, it's Luke. Without saying a word, I reach for my phone and compose a text to Aaron. I know Luke finds it amusing and is proud of his accomplishment. I would slap the bastard if he weren't out of reach.

Me: Hey. Can we talk?

He could say no. Luke has piqued my curiosity now, and I need an explanation, but maybe Aaron doesn't want to give me one. He said he wanted to know what I had been up to, not relive the past.

"He's going to say yes, Captain" Luke is standing up, walking next to me. "Also, my dear boyfriend had a message for you. It's cryptic like Dex is, but it seems you should give him a call. He said you should know secrets don't keep. Whatever he means." I freeze.

What does Dex know about my past? Did he look me up? Will he say something to Aaron before I do? Luke kisses my forehead and walks away, leaving me with my doubts and fears. My phone chimes, and I feel somewhat relieved seeing Aaron's name on my screen, even if I know we need to dig up some skeletons for us to go forward.

Aaron: Ok... Working tonight but I'm free now. If you're done at the school, I can pick you up.
Me: I'll wait out front.

As I wait for him in front of the school, I get edgy. The last time I was nervous about meeting Aaron was when I was fifteen. I feel ridiculous in my skinny blue jeans and a shapeless white sweater. If I had known I was going to see him today, I would have made an effort. My leather messenger bag is thrown over my shoulder, and my enormous scarf covers my neck, my three-inch low-cut boots being the only fashionable accessory of my outfit.

A nice SUV pulls up to the curb, and the passenger window rolls down.

Aaron appears before me, nodding and shooting a short wave like he did in high school. He has his aviator glasses on, but I know the livid-blue sweater he's wearing matches the color of his eyes, and I imagine how it will make them pop.

Just seeing him, my heart starts galloping, and I tighten my grip on my bag to be able to walk.

But when I come closer, Aaron tilts his head while pushing his sunglasses down his nose, greeting me with a wink and a subtle, "Hey, Sweets."

My knees buckle, and my body heats up like never before. Shit, he's sexy. Sliding into the passenger seat, I'm fifteen again.

The car smells like the man he has become. The smell of melting ice and sweat is gone, but the musk of his aftershave sustains.

He kisses me on the cheek and puts the car in drive. I try not to get distracted by the arm porn in front of me. His sleeve is rolled three quarters up his arm, and it takes all my willpower not to slide my hand in his on the armrest between us like I used to. It's depressing how I can revert back to how it was, so easily with him.

"Want to go skating?" His smile is genuine and if only he knew his words just ripped my heart out, I know he would never have asked.

"Well, um no." He looks at me briefly, confused, before turning his eyes back on the road.

"Alane Smith doesn't want to go skating?"

"Nope," I shiver by the cold feeling invading me. That's the first sign it's happening.

"Come on, Sweets, for old time's sake?" he insists. That's all I need to go spiraling into anxiety. My chest tightens, my heart palpitates under the stress, my limbs tingle, and my brain starts to get foggy. I try to breathe, to calm down by reciting my mantras, but I'm too far gone. The car stops and I jump out, dying for fresh air. Aaron is embracing me in seconds, and his touch feels magical, but I'm still shaking.

"I'm going to kiss you now, because I know it calms you down. It's simply therapeutic." His eyes are filled with humor, but I can't laugh. His hand traces my jaw, and he crashes his lips onto mine, giving me small pecks at first until he feels me relaxing a little and requests entrance to my mouth. His hand massages my neck, while his tongue erases all my worries. I feel the anxiety leaving me, and while I have no idea why he has so much power over me, I'm glad he found a way to calm me down, even if it means kissing him more than I intended to. He breaks the kiss, and his eyes look deep into my soul.

"What the fuck happened to you, Al?" I sigh. If I have to tell him what happened, it's certainly not going to be on the side of the road, leaning against his SUV. I climb back in his car and wait for him to drive again.

"Where to?"

"Do you just want to drive around and talk?" He nods at my proposition.

"Can I ask why you didn't want to skate?" He takes my hand in his to calm me before my anxiety even starts, and it works.

"I haven't skated in forever. In fact, since we were together." He brakes abruptly and looks at me.

"What happened to hockey prep school and your career?"

"I never went. I went to Arizona to live with my aunt." From all the emotions I've imagined Aaron would be feeling the day I'd tell him I never followed my dream; sadness wasn't what I was expecting. Tears fill his eyes, and he mumbles to himself something about how he sacrificed us for nothing in the end.

"What do you mean you sacrificed us?" I have a bad feeling about this. Between what Luke told me about knowing the truth and Aaron's comment, I'm sure now I don't have all the pieces of how our story ended.

"This is not the place to discuss what happened. I'm not doing this in my car. Why don't you come to my place? I'll cook for you tonight and explain it all."

"Didn't you have to work tonight?" He shrugs.

"I think clearing up our past is more important. I'll give instructions to my sous-chef." His voice is stern and resigned as if our lives had brought us to this moment of truth.

"Okay," I whisper, afraid of what I'm going to learn, how I will react, and wondering if I should also open up about my past.

"Drop me off at the school, I'll follow you in my car," I tell him, so I have time to organize my thoughts and make a decision on what I will share with him tonight.

As Dex said, secrets don't keep, but that's not a reason for you to have to blurt them out before you're ready to do so.

19

THEN - AARON

*P*astor Smith is not the small, ugly, bald man I wish he were.

He looks charming and can convince everybody in his congregation that what he says is evangelical. So, of course, he convinced my parents I didn't understand what he meant when he wanted me to stay away from Alane, and he was, in fact, happy his daughter had found such a respectful boyfriend. I'm so respectful that he wants to have a talk with me. That's why I'm sitting once more in his office, waiting for him to deliver another lecture.

"Aaron, I hope you can understand my disappointment when I heard you were having sex with Alane. I thought I had been clear." Fidgeting on my chair won't help my cause so even if I feel like fire is burning my ass, I stay still and stoic.

"Father Smith, we did not have sex." But he doesn't hear me.

"You compromised my daughter, Boy, and now you're lying. I'm not stupid, and believe me when I say, I know. I. Know. Patricia came directly to me and told me what Alane had confided in her. You really don't leave me any choice. Do you?" Of course, Patricia betrayed Alane. She certainly thinks that by removing her from the equation she can get in my pants. She's tried for the last three months, propositioning me every damn day.

"Father Smith, I promise Alane and I did not have sex. Patricia is jealous of your daughter and is spreading rumors to get her in trouble" I'm on the defensive. After all, I tried hard to resist Alane, and if the results are the same as if I had fucked her, then maybe I should have done it.

"Boy, boy, boy," he says shaking his head as if I had disappointed him. "We had a deal and it's time to call it quits. You can't jeopardize her future. It's easy now, either you go to Seattle, or she leaves for Arizona. You have no other choice."

"But we have a future together!" He scoffs at my words.

"What future? Hers is to pursue her dream because I won't pay a penny if she doesn't do what I want. Do you really believe I'll let her go to Washington State with you? Do you think I will let my daughter out of my sight so she can fornicate with her boyfriend and live without adult supervision? Are you that naive or totally stupid, Aaron?"

I can see all the disgust he feels towards me perspiring from his skin.

He's spitting his words.

"Your whole family is perverted. I'm not surprised you follow in their footsteps. Now, you break up today, or she leaves tomorrow. I want you to go see her, and I want her heartbroken by tonight. I checked with the principal, and as you were a good student, you have already graduated; I believe you can leave for Seattle tomorrow or the day after." He doesn't even look at me when he shoos me away with his hand as if I was a bug on his shoulder. I don't see any solution to my problem.

If I want Alane to have a future, I need to break up with her. I knew that day would come, and I was a fool to believe I could get out of the deal I shook on last year.

As I step out of his office, Alane is waiting for me. She is beautiful. Her long blonde hair is braided on the side, her eyes are filled with love, her cheeks are red, and I feel like the worst asshole knowing that by the end of our conversation, everything we believed we could achieve together will be destroyed. Skipping my way, she twirls in front of me and smiles until her eyes stop on me and what I'm sure is a somber attitude.

"What did my father want?" she asks her smile waning. It sucks the last hope out of me. I need to be strong, for her, her future. What else am I supposed to do?

"He heard about our plans for Seattle," I say walking away toward her front porch. I sit on the stairs. If I have to break her heart, it's better doing it where she can run home, let her have home-ice advantage so I can leave. It's a cowardly move, but it's all I have in me.

"How?"

"How do you think? I told you to keep it under wraps, Al."

"I only told Patricia." She doesn't see that's the problem. She doesn't know her best friend like I do. She's so trustful. I say nothing, not wanting to alienate her from her friend. She'll need her once I'm gone. "So you told him we're leaving?" Resting my arms on my knees, I put my head down and shake my head slightly. My throat is tightening, my stomach is flipping. I want to hurl the words I need to, but emotion is taking over. Her face hardens, and her eyes darken.

"Aaron..." She tears up, putting her hand on my arm. I don't need to tell her what's next; she can read me better than anyone. I know she deserves hearing the truth, but I can't tell her. She only has her parents, I can't destroy their relationship, that wouldn't be loving her, it would be obliterating her from the only people she has. I sigh heavily. "Aar... Aaron." I know I broke her even before uttering what I have to tell her. "Please don't..." she whispers.

"I'm sorry, Sweets. It's just... I have to," I say, kissing the hand resting on my forearm. "I'm going to Seattle, but you're not. You can't come with me. I wish it were different; I tried to find a way, but there is none. You have to stay."

"I... I can run away." She sniffles. "I can come with you. We'll get married in one year; we'll live together and create a future, you and I, with nobody telling us otherwise."

"And then what, Sweets? How do we live day by day? How do I care for you? How do you follow your dream?" I wipe the tears from my cheeks and lay my hand on hers. I know I have to rip away the hope she has that we have a future together, because we don't. She'll become a hockey player, somewhere here or in Canada, and I'll work in restaurants. We were always on borrowed time.

"I don't want you to come with me," I add, squeezing her hand, hoping I'm telling her how much I don't mean those words, how much I really do love her, how much I'm hurting, and will regret my actions forever. Telling her I'm sacrificing us because I love her will only confuse her more. How can you profess your love by walking away?

"Will you come back for me?"

I stand up, not able to look at her. "Don't wait for me, Sweets." I snivel. I hear her cries and imagine her beautiful face hidden in her hands. In a way, I wish she'd stand, throw herself at me, beg me to change my mind, fight for us the way I should.

I wish she'd show me love and mercy, but I'm relieved she's doesn't. It would be harder for me to walk away.

I don't deserve her anyway.

I gave up on our future a long time ago.

I thought I could fight our destiny, believe in our fate, but there is no such thing as long-lasting love in our story.

She calls my name, pleads for me to come back, to give her a last kiss, but I continue walking away until I'm standing in front of the Harbor's house. I don't know how I found my way here, everything is a blur. Thankfully, Chris is the one opening the door, not Patricia. I fall apart in his arms, in total silence, bawling my pain out.

Pretending I'm fine would be stupid.

I'm not.

I'll never love someone the way I love her.

Chris drags me to his bedroom and finds us some beers from his father's stash. I drink, in my mind replaying my story with Alane, from the moment we met until our time ran out. Chris' voice breaks the noise in my head as he says what a best friend should say, that it's just young love, that I should experiment anyway before getting married, that if it's meant to be, we'll end up together again. It sounds like bullshit, but he's trying to have my back. The beers keep coming, and I drink them all. I can't drive home, I don't want to go home, I want to leave, tonight or tomorrow and never come back, ever again. I mumble it to Chris, who puts his hand on my shoulder to ease my pain without succeeding one bit.

"I'll take care of everything, bud, don't worry." I crash on his bed, sadness crushing my heart. My world is spinning. I need to leave for an alternate universe where it's possible to survive without Alane.

Finally closing my eyes, I feel like death.

Guilt takes over imagining how she feels. I should have told Luke to check on her. She's alone when I have my best friend. I fall asleep on his bed, still thinking about her, and wondering if I will ever stop.

When I wake up the next morning, my parents are standing over me. My head is pounding from the alcohol I drank last night and the heartache I inflicted on myself.

"I'm sorry." My father smiles apologetically. "Seattle is the best school for you." His voice is sweet, and his eyes are conflicted. "It's no fun seeing you hurt, Son, and we know it seems insurmountable now, but it will get better. Trust me, I broke my own heart before finding your mother." I shrug, lacking the energy to do anything else. I reek of beer and remorse. Tears fill my eyes again, but I wipe them away quickly, not wanting to cry in front of my father.

"Let it go, sweet boy." My mother sits on the bed and takes me in her arms. "I'll miss you," she adds in a strangled voice. That's when I see my suitcase next to Chris' bed.

I look at it, trying to understand. I know I said I wanted to go, but it seems the last fifteen hours are a little blurry. I never thought yesterday morning that I would be leaving so fast, not graduating with my class and spending my summer almost three thousand miles away from home.

"Mr. Harbor and Pastor Smith organized everything. You can stay at a family friend of the Harbors before school starts, discover the city, and spend the summer on the west coast. With the money you've earned, and what we've put aside for you, you'll be comfortable. They even found you a job. Don't worry, it will all work out," my father says ruffling my hair. I feel betrayed and abandoned, but it's my own fault for not sharing with them what happened over the last two years. I hid it all. They can't help me if I don't give them all the pieces they need, and I can't tell them. I don't want them to fight my battles for me; it would only compromise Alane's future. I need to leave town, it's the only option I have for Alane to get what she deserves.

"Luke?" I ask, knowing well enough my brother will never forgive me for what I've done. He'd already warned me that he would choose her over me.

My mother shakes her head sighing. "He destroyed your room. He'll calm down. You know how he gets when he's hurt."

"Sal?" I ask, hoping my little sister will say goodbye to me.

"She's too mad that you're leaving. Give them time. You didn't only break Alane's heart. You also broke the heart of your siblings."

"Even Barn?" I half-laugh, half-cry because I'll miss everybody, even the bed-pisser.

"He wants to punch you for hurting her. I'm not surprised. I think Alane was his first crush." My mother brings her hand to my face and caresses my cheek to reassure me.

"Aaron, it's going to be okay. Believe me. It will all be for the best. Now, you have to go. You have a flight to catch, sweet boy. I'll see you at Thanksgiving or Christmas, okay?" She kisses me, crying. "It's hard for a mother, preparing the chicks to fly from the nest, but that day has come. You can finally fly alone. I'm hoping you won't crash without me. You're an amazing person, Aaron. Be young, have fun, enjoy your life away. I love you, my boy."

My father has to separate us, reminding her I need to dress and get ready if we want to make the flight. He explains how the family I'm going to live with in Seattle has a son who's one year older than me and promised he would show me the Emerald City and the life of the Evergreen State.

I sigh.

Becoming a Seattleite is the last thing on my mind but the only escape I have. So, I get up, get dressed and leave for my new life, knowing I left my heart behind in Springs Falls, NY.

NOW – AARON

When I was a teenager, and I thought of my adult life, Alane sitting at a kitchen bar while I prepare supper is what I envisioned.

Except that instead of having teenagers sent to their grandparents for the night so I could relive a hurtful past with my ex-girlfriend, we would have been sharing plans for our next vacation with the kids happy to be around us. It was a dream, a fantasy that I never shared with Alane and even less with Jess.

Jess was never home and wouldn't be the kind to plan any vacation. In the summer, she would ask us to follow her wherever her assignment sent her. She never took time off, and when she did, it was because I needed her home during the busy season. Summer should have slowed her down, with most of the sports being on a break, but she always found a conference to attend, a seminar to go to, and a class to enroll in. We joined her when the kids were little. I traveled alone with them when they grew up.

I wonder if my life with Alane would have been any different. If she had been a hockey player, would we have followed her wherever, or would I have resented her like I did Jess? Would our marriage have been doomed anyway? I'll never know. What I do know is that fucking her on a table woke up feelings, kissing her stirred up desire, and seeing her sitting at my kitchen bar awakened a nostalgia I wish I could suppress.

We never had a fair chance, and I always said if I could, I would beg her to be with me again.

But should I?

Her father is dead, and we live in the same city. Father Smith broke his promise and sent her to Arizona anyway, but Alane became a very different woman than what I thought she would.

On the other hand, she doesn't seem to resent me for having become what I wanted even if she didn't, and her body reacts to me as it always did. Her mother and Patricia are still around, but they are irrelevant to the man I've become. I just have to tell her what happened and hope she'll understand that I thought I had no choice. She takes a sip of her wine, zooming in on my working hand.

"So?"

"So, your father thought we had sex." I continue cutting my vegetable in julienne style, avoiding her gaze as best I can.

"Yeah, I know that."

"You do?" She nods. "Is that why he sent you to Arizona?"

"No, I asked to go." Her revelation chills me.

"I went to Seattle for you not to go to Arizona," I admit. She waves me off rapidly.

"No, you went to Seattle for school. You cut off all communication with me, dumped me because you wanted to live your life, be single and have fun with girls." I put the knife down as a precaution.

"No, I went to Seattle because your father said if I didn't, you would never go to the school you wanted, and he wouldn't pay for anything else. I was a young, stupid kid, and I didn't think I had any other choice," I explain, my hands gripping the counter.

"That's not what they told me!" Her voice is pained and lost.

"Who are they?" She shakes her head vigorously not willing to answer my question.

"Start from the beginning!" she demands, breathing rapidly. I throw my julienne vegetables in the frying pan to start cooking.

"So, the first time I spoke with your father I was, I don't remember well, but I was maybe sixteen or just after my seventeenth birthday."

I wince, trying to remember the chronology of our story. You would think I'd remember the exact moment I fucked myself over, but I don't. I blocked it out for so long, I can't remember the details.

"Your father told me that he would allow us to date until I graduated, but after that, I shouldn't be an obstacle for your future. I knew that our time was limited, but we were in love, we were young, we thought we were forever. I didn't really forget about it, but I believed I would find a solution, or he wouldn't remember. I truly thought he was saying it more to scare me about having sex with you than anything else." I pause to look at her while I continue stirring my dish. Her eyes are closed, and she gestures for me to go on.

"Then we tried to find a solution, my parents pushed for Seattle, and I told them your father didn't want us together. They spoke to him, he convinced them that I misunderstood him and said he had contacts for me to get into the culinary school in Seattle. Anyhow, my parents were on board and were pressuring me to go, saying we could pick up where we left off once I came back. Then you said you'd come with me, and I had hope, Al, but reality came crashing down on me."

Her eyes are still, and a single tear runs down her cheek. "Continue," she murmurs.

"So, the day we... I..." She opens her eyes and narrows them on me. I swallow trying to gather my courage.

"The day you broke my heart?" she scowls.

"The day I broke both of our hearts." I gulp, reducing my pan to a simmer and closing my eyes. "That day, your father said he knew we were having sex, and I had a choice to make. I had two days to leave for Seattle, or you would be sent away. Patricia told him the plans that we were hatching, she told him that we were having sex, and all we had done together and more. I couldn't see any other solution. I didn't want you to throw it all away for me, so I walked away, went to Chris'. I slept there, and the next morning, my father drove me to the airport. Your father and Chris' dad had everything laid out for me: my early graduation, where I would stay, where I would work, who I would hang out with."

"You didn't fight for us?" It's a punch to my gut. She purses her lips and lowers her brows. I'm hurting her all over again.

"I told him it wasn't true. I told him Patricia was spreading rumors, but what else could I have done? Having you follow me, and then what, Al? I did what I thought was right to let you have the future you wanted." I defend myself; my stomach hardening by who the man I am now, now knows as cowardice, when the teenager I was then thought was bravery. "I loved you, and I just wanted you to have what you deserved."

I walk around to her side of the bar and reach out for her.

She jerks back, flinching at my touch. "I really thought you went to school and were playing hockey somewhere. I never really looked you up, I couldn't. I never left because I wanted to be with someone else. I met Jess, but I truly believed we were over." My hand is on her knee, and I push her legs open to walk in between them. I engulf her in my arms and hug her like I should have when I destroyed us. "I'm sorry, Al," I whisper in her ear.

Not that I can erase what I did or forget our lives without each other.

We both have kids from different partners, and I'm confident she wouldn't rewrite her story and not have her son like I wouldn't rewrite mine and not have Hal and Law in my life. But I believe we need to heal, and the first step is apologizing and taking responsibility for what I did to us.

We stay like this for what seems like a long time, just breathing each other in.

"I'm so mad," she finally says.

"I know. I hope you can forgive me." I step back, tucking a piece of hair behind her ear. Our gazes lock, and I get lost in all the emotions I see in her eyes.

"Forgiving you is not an issue. I got over it a long time ago. I'm mad at myself for not seeing whom my father was, but we were kids after all. I'm mad at Patricia. She made me believe you told Chris you were happy to be without me. She said you were happy to be single, living the perfect life in Seattle. I barely talked to her for years. I'm just…"

"It is what it is, Al. I can't regret meeting Jess, and you can't regret meeting your husband. We have kids. We are here together again, and as much as I hurt you, we are adults now. I would like to date you, but if I need to do some more groveling, I will." I see her hesitate, biting her lip and looking anywhere but towards me.

"I'm not the same Alane you used to know, Aar..." she starts.

"I'm not the same Aaron."

She laughs. "You so are! The only difference is that your shyness transformed into assholeness with age. You're still very intense, broody, serious, and driven. I'm just a fuck up with a lot of trust issues and anxiety attacks." She shrugs, and it hurts me to hear her speak that way about herself.

"What happened to you?" I ask her softly as she sighs heavily. It feels like eternity passes us by before she finally decides she can share her story.

"When I met Mark, I was waitressing in a sex club." I keep my face blank. I always knew Alane was adventuress, and even if her declaration stirs my dick and heats me up, I refuse to show her anything else but relevance. If she's opening up, it's not for me to judge. She closes her eyes and breathes in slowly. "Over the years, we went pretty far. I was rebelling against my father's values, I guess. I was finally free of his hold on me, so I was living all my fantasies. I did most of the things you can only imagine..." I rub my hand on her knee to encourage her to continue. "Anyway, one day while we were doing a scene," she adds, and I want to know details, but I won't pry. I can't get aroused while she's telling me who she has become. "I panicked. Over time, I couldn't participate in what Mark and I used to like. I wanted more 'conservative sexual encounters', as my therapist would say. Mark and I divorced. I had become too vanilla for him, and I understand that."

"Sex on a table in my restaurant is all but vanilla," I say, remembering last night, and getting a little bit harder at the thought of what we did.

"I guess it depends on the experience one had before. I was also slightly drunk, or maybe it was because it was with you." She hesitates.

"What triggers the anxiety? Sex?"

"It does. You calmed me down yesterday, and I can tell you it's the first time someone has actually appeased me. Mark and Adam were never able to. I have a list of triggers and the mantras to calm me down, but you just block everything else."

"What was happening in your life when it happened?" My hand is now soothingly caressing her thigh.

"Adam had just turned seventeen, we were happy, I was teaching. Everything was fine. It's as if from one day to another, I was done with the clubs, the BDSM and all of our lifestyle." I'm so aroused by her that I could fuck her on the stool, but I won't. I step back to attend to my vegetables and turn off the stove, trying to regain some control.

"What about your son?" I ask, trying to change the subject from her sex life.

"What about him?" she answers nervously.

"Did he know what kind of life you were living? Did he say something that day that could have triggered something?"

"Of course not. We are very close, and I tell Adam everything, but I never spoke about that with him. I'm not as cool as your parents." She smiles, but it fades fast. "I also can't speak about his father with him. Aaron, he's—"

"I understand." I cut her off because I don't want to hear about her ex. "It's hard for me to speak about their mother to the kids, to explain how I think she was cheating on me for years and I never caught her. But in a way, I was cheating on her, too. I never stopped thinking about you, wondering about all the what-ifs and all the what-nows. I was a cheater long before she cheated on me." She sips the last drop of her wine, and I come closer again to top it off.

"The what-ifs…" she murmurs, looking at my lips.

"And the what-nows," I whisper, wetting mine. I lean closer, not able to control the pull she has on me, her magnetic eyes tugging on my soul and her whole body screaming for my touch.

"Sweets, let me kiss you." I sigh while brushing her lips with mine.

"And then what, Aar?" Her hands are on my back, and I feel my skin burning under her fingers, even through my T-shirt.

"Then let me remind you how we were happy together." Her tongue darts out and licks my lips. I groan.

"Let me show you we can be even happier." I push my tongue in her mouth, while she stands on the footrest and wraps her legs around my waist.

"Fuck me like it was the nineties, Aaron Gritt," she says in my mouth. I laugh because I don't want to fuck her like the virgin I was. I bring her to my bedroom and shove her to the middle of the bed. I'm not intimidated by her past because I know it wasn't just sex with me. She might have slept with a lot of men, and I slept *only* with Jess, but I know that Alane and I are something else. We always had more chemistry than we could bargain for.

"Strip," I tell her, and there is a glimmer of amusement in her eyes.

"You first." She bites her lip. "I haven't seen you naked in almost thirty years." She opens my pants. I shove her hands out of the way, and I strip fast, standing at the end of the bed, waiting for her to do the same.

"Holy fuck, Gritt. You grew up nicely." She chuckles. I

narrow my eyes at her and stroke my hard cock a couple of times.

"Strip. Last time you were on my bed, I had many reasons to fuck you but only one not to, and I let my head convince my dick. I have no reason not to fuck you tonight. Get naked, Sweets."

I see the moment she hesitates, certainly afraid to let go and losing her battle against her anxiety. I crawl onto the bed and straddle her, my dick resting in the fold of her jean-covered thighs. Bringing my hands to her face, I caress her cheeks with my thumbs and bring her in for a soft kiss.

"Sweets," I groan. "If you feel the anxiety coming, I want you to kiss me. If you need to stop, if it's too much, if you need a break, I want you to tell me. If you don't want sex with me, you can stop it all, no questions asked. I want you to take your time, okay?" She smiles at me, and I smile back, knowing exactly what she needs to hear.

"Hey," I say like when I was sixteen.

"Hey." She kisses me.

The rest of the night is a collection of kisses, touches, scratches, bites, groans, and orgasms.

I lick her and find the same butterscotch taste on my tongue that I did years ago. I play with her clit until she asks me to bite her to come, and I do, remembering the pain she needs.

I never break eye contact while my head is between her legs.

Later, I ask her to look at me when she blows me while I'm sitting on the bed and she's on her knees on the floor. She swirls, takes me deeply, bobs her head, but her eyes are still staring profoundly into mine.

When I sit her on my shaft, wrapping my arms around her,

our eyes are still connected. I wait for her panic to surge, but it doesn't come.

I tilt her backward, letting her head lean between my legs while her hands hold my ankles. Still watching her, I bend forward, playing with her erect nipples with the tip of my tongue. She glides up and down, and the more I bend, the more she glides, taking control of our pleasure. Her clit rubs against me, and I reach deep inside her with my dick. I hold my gaze on her when her pussy clenches around me, and she screams my name, her eyes hooded but still on mine. I'm ready to blow, so I move her around not to come inside her.

"Stay inside," she says, gliding fast.

"I don't have a condom," I tell her between clenched teeth.

"I always used a condom at the club or with Mark. I'm clean," she says in a breath. So, I let go inside her, coming harder than I ever have, recognizing the familiarity of our bodies intertwined but at the same time noticing all the differences. Crawling into bed, we fall into each other's arms, not bothering to get dressed or pull the blanket over us.

"Did you turn off the stove?" she utters, her eyes closing. I smile, not because I could burn my house down, but because of the casualness we fall back into right away, as if nine thousand, eight hundred and fifty-five days never separated us.

21

THEN - ALANE

I haven't eaten since Aaron left. Every time I try to put food in my mouth, it doesn't go down, or it comes back up. I feel miserable inside and out, and I have no strength to get out of bed. My lack of energy is such that I can barely walk without being exhausted.

Taking a shower is a challenge, but my mother forces me to.

Every day, she knocks quietly, helps me walk to the bathroom, bathes me, and dresses me, as if I was five again. She tried to shove me under the shower the first day, but I crumpled to the floor and cried for hours.

She decided to give me a bath with little water then, adding that I wasn't to be trusted not to drown myself as she reminded me suicide was a sin. I was only allowed to be sad for one day for my heart being ripped out of my chest, and then I was asked to move on.

That's when my flu symptoms started, and my mother came to the conclusion I was sick. She convinced my father that I should stay home until I was feeling better.

I know it's the heartbreak, but I didn't tell her, otherwise she'd force me to go to school, and I'm sure I can't bear walking the hallways where we would hold hands or skating on the rink where we kissed. I can't even imagine looking at Luke.

Patricia passed by to check up on me, and she told me Aaron had reached out to Chris. He's happy to be single, delighted to be in Seattle, glad to be without me. That's the report she gave me. I cried a little more when she left. Luke tried to pass by, but my mother didn't let him in. I even think I heard Coach Gritt's voice, but I didn't move from my bed. Aaron's parents are the last people I want to see. I believed they liked me. I thought I would always be welcome and that they were on our side.

There's being naïve, and then there's being stupid. I guess I am naively stupid.

"Can I come in?" The soft voice of Mrs. Gritt tears me apart from my self-deprecation. I don't move, I feel the bed sag a little where she sits down. Her hand comes to my ankle, but I shift away.

"He's miserable too, you know."

"Isn't it what you wanted?"

"Oh honey, no. I thought you'd make it work long distance. That's what Ridge and I did when we met, so I believed you had a chance. I didn't think he would break up with you."

"I don't want to talk about it."

"I understand. Remember, you can talk to me about anything, right?" I stay silent. I know that, but I don't want to.

"These symptoms you're having, your mother says it's the flu. Should I worry it's something else?"

"What do you mean?"

"I mean," she breathes heavily, "could you be pregnant?"

"No," I whisper, "we never had sex." I peek through my eyelashes to see if she believes me, but it's too dark to see any of her reactions.

"It's a bad heartache then. You're going to need to get out of bed eventually and face the world, Alane."

"Why? So I can be reminded he's not around anymore?" I sob, again. "Can you leave please?"

"Of course, remember, I'm always here for you." When she leaves, I feel uncomfortable in my own skin.

Something she said is bothering me. I think for hours about our conversation, but I can't pinpoint what has me conflicted.

And then it clicks.

I didn't get my period last week.

Shit!

I get out of bed faster than a cheetah and run to the bathroom to throw up.

How could I be pregnant when we didn't have sex? We didn't... I'm panicking. My heart beats faster; I'm cold and hot at the same time, shivering with sweat dripping from my body. It can't be. That's the worst that could happen to me.

Fucking pregnant.

If I tell my parents, they'll want me to marry Aaron, and he was clear it's not what he wants. He wants Seattle; he wants to become a chef. I can't rip that out of his hands. Following him for love is different than trapping him with a baby. I won't be that girl.

If I tell my parents, they'll think I'm not a virgin anymore, and I'll bring shame to our house. My father can't be the Pastor of the town and have a pregnant teenage daughter. Everybody will know, it will get back to Aaron, and he will abandon school, come back here for me, and work at the diner all his life to support the baby and me.

The other solution is to abort, but... it's something Aaron and I created, and I can't go there without guilt. Even if I lost Aaron, I could still have something from him.

I'll have to say goodbye to hockey and find a place to live. I need someone in my corner, someone who could understand, and someone to support me, but first I need a pregnancy test. I need to be sure before I make my arrangements to go where I know nobody will judge me for what happened. My aunt always said whenever I'm in trouble she would come in the next twenty-four hours, if I needed her to come.

The house is quiet. I'm alone. Picking up the phone, I call my Aunt Clarisse. She's my mother's sister, but she didn't marry a man of God. She's as open as the Gritts. She lives the life she wants, and I know she'll help me.

"Hello?"

"It's Alane," I whisper into the phone "I don't know what to do, I need help, Auntie" I speak fast because it's expensive to call her. I know my father will see the long-distance call in the middle of the day and blame my mother. I won't let her take the blame though.

"What's the problem?" She cuts to the chase, knowing that if I call it's because it's serious. We never speak on the phone, and I barely see her anymore. My parents don't approve of her writing. They say it's pornography, when it's just sex help books for couples in trouble. Nothing to be ashamed of. Not like being a teenage mother out of wedlock.

"I..." I exhale. Saying it out loud makes it more real. "I think I'm pregnant." I don't need to say more. She knows my parents more than anybody else. She knows about the shaming, she knows I'm stuck here, she knows I need her.

"I'll be there tomorrow, Alane. I was flying to New York anyway to see my publisher. I'll rent a car and come. I'll bring a pregnancy test, sit with you and your parents, and we'll find a solution. Is the boy still in the picture?"

"No, he left for Seattle two weeks ago. Dad helped him get into one of the best schools in the country... But we never had sex, he was never in me..."

"Just because he didn't put it in, doesn't mean that you didn't have sex, girl. Clearly, something happened. We'll talk tomorrow. Wait for me before you say anything to your parents. Your dad might send you overseas to deal with you, and I won't let that happen to my only niece. Hang in there, kiddo. I'll be there soon."

The next hours are excruciating. I think I might be pregnant, but I don't know if I am. I can't go to the pharmacy or the doctor because it will get back to my parents faster than me going home and peeing on a stick. I can't drive to another city because I don't have my driver's license, and I can't ask anybody for help. All I can do is wait, and cry, and worry, and of course, throw up.

I fall asleep wondering what my life is going to be like if I'm pregnant. I would need to finish high school, find a job, and raise my child. I would need a place to stay. I would need to leave Springs Falls and everybody else I know and love.

People fighting downstairs wake me up. It's a clear indication Aunt Clarisse has arrived, and I might have slept more than I thought.

"Let me see her, Thomas, or for the love of God, I promise you there won't be enough of you praying to Jesus to save your life!" my Aunt Clarisse screams.

"Why do you want to see her?" my mother says.

"Why do you think, Penelope? Because she called me!"

"She called you? Is it because of that stupid boy again?"

"You mean the boy you sent away, Thomas?"

"I gave him an opportunity. She needs to go to Bishop's for hockey!"

"Well, dear brother-in-law, your plan might have failed," Aunt Clarisse raises her voice. I come to the top of the stairs to see my father and my aunt staring at each other.

"Aunt Clarisse?" I'm worried that this was all a big mistake.

"There you are!" She scoffs at my dad while climbing the stairs. I brought what you need, let's go to the bathroom." She guides me away. "You need to know like yesterday."

"Why do you think she needs something in the bathroom?" I hear my dad say while my mother gasps. "Alane, are you?" I don't answer and run to the bathroom. I hear my parents fighting in the back, and I start crying again. Aunt Clarisse takes care of everything for me. I think if she could pee on the stick instead of me, she would do it.

"Why don't we go out there, break up the fight and speak about the options you have," she says calmly, as if my life wasn't about to implode

We find my parents downstairs, still blaming each other, and it solidifies my decision to leave this house.

I sit at the dinner table and wait for them to join me. They are not much calmer than they were one minute ago, but I have to come clean. I open my mouth to tell them my story, but of course, my father doesn't let me speak.

"I'm going to call his parents, he's going to come back, and you will marry him. He can work to support you, and we'll find you something to do."

"No." My father sends me a disapproving look. "You

worked hard for him to have such an opportunity. I don't want you to ruin it because of me. I don't want him to choose me by obligation. I don't want him in my life if he doesn't love me."

"Love... you're such a child, Alane," he answers coldly. "I guess that's how you got pregnant! Being a child but playing at being an adult. That boy looked me in the eyes and told me he didn't have sex with you."

"We didn't, Dad. We did other things, I won't deny it, but we never had sex!"

"Then what? Are you saying this is an intervention from God?" I can't look at the disappointment he's throwing my way. I'm a failure. I know it. My lips start to quiver, but I choked back my tears. I need to be strong.

"I understand that if I'm pregnant, you'll be ashamed if I stay here, but you'll be more ashamed if I don't keep the baby. I want to keep it, but I don't want the Gritts to know. So, I was thinking, if it's okay with Aunt Clarisse, I could go live with her. Finish high school by being homeschooled, have the baby and find a job. I would need help until the baby is born and a little afterwards, but I thought about it, and I think it's the best solution."

"If you leave for Arizona, it's to go live with MY family, not with your liberated aunt!"

"And what would your family say, Thomas, if you send them a pregnant daughter? Think about it."

My mother is quiet, letting my aunt and father fight about me. Her eyes find mine, and I can see the embarrassment and pain I'm inflicting on her. I wince and mouth a pathetic "I'm sorry," but she ignores me.

She stands up abruptly and leaves the room.

My father and aunt fall silent for a moment until falling back into their argument about my future.

When my mother reappears, she's holding the pregnancy test in her shaking hand, tears in her eyes. She looks at me without really seeing me, and behind her tears I see all the shame, dishonor, and disdain a mother should never feel towards her spawn. She's not crying because she's sad her only daughter might be leaving, she's crying because she's ashamed of whom her daughter has become.

She clears her throat, and with a shaky voice, she decides on my future.

"You're pregnant, Alane. I'll pack your bags."

22

NOW – ALANE

"Hi, Mom." Adam and I haven't talked in a few days, and I'm glad to hear his voice. We never spend more than a couple of days without talking, but with the time difference and me not keeping up with his schedule, I lost track of his whereabouts. I also have been busy spending time with Aaron, rediscovering one another and remembering how much we loved about each other. I can still see the sweet, patient, determined boy behind the loving, sexy and authoritative man. It's familiar and new. It's a home away from home.

"Hi, sweetie, how are you?"

"You seem cheerful. That's… not what I was expecting."

"Well, I kind of reconnected with someone. Maybe when you're closer to my part of the country, we can talk, I need to tell you something, but it's not something I want to say over the phone."

"Okay… I'll be in New York next week. Maybe I could head your way, see where you grew up?"

"Oh no, sweetie, there is nothing to see here, and I don't want you to change your schedule. I haven't been to New York in years, why don't I meet you there?" I don't want him to set foot in Springs Falls before I tell him about Aaron or before I tell Aaron about him. Them meeting before I come clean would be a disaster.

"Mom. Come on, I can take a few days off to come see you."

"Let me think about it, and I'll let you know. How are things otherwise?" Adam tells me about his life on the road, signing the sci-fi graphic novels he wrote. He's become a sensation with fans everywhere. Teenagers love what he writes, but he's still new in that world. We hung up promising to talk soon and to think about meeting here instead of New York.

Later, I meet with Aaron at the rink. He decided it's time I get back on skates, and I would be lying if I say I wasn't nervous.

I'm petrified to put skates on, but I believe that the only person who can help me overcome my fear is Aaron. It's been a long time. Aaron assured me that it's like riding a bicycle, and I shouldn't have forgotten it, but I'm still shaking as I lace the skates he bought me.

"Remember, Sweets, I'll kiss you as soon as you feel your anxiety rising." He winks, jumping onto the rink. I'm thrown back to years ago when we would practice together. His style hasn't changed much. As his hips sway while gliding, I find the courage to come closer, hesitating to set my blades on the ice.

"Come on, or do you need me to hold your hand?" he teases, daring me at the same time. In a game of truth or dare, I always took the dare. Challenge me to do something, and I would have done it. It was like that until I started to second-guess most of my moves. That's why I never thought twice before pushing my boundaries, in sports, in life, in sex. That's who the old Alane was. Being here with Aaron, that Alane wants to come back, and I'm not afraid of letting her. She's like Aaron, familiar and appeasing, I liked her much better than who I became over the last nine years. I know skating won't erase my anxiety; I know Aaron is not a magical remedy, but if I can at least enjoy some of whom I was before, I'll take it. So I step onto the ice, one foot after the other. Aaron is watching me; I'm pretty sure he's ready to slide to my rescue if needed. I'm still in control. I breathe in, breathe out, and I let go. As I skate faster, the wind kisses my face, and I feel my fears, my hang ups, and all the weight I've carried on my shoulders since I left town, chipping away. It's liberating. Laughing, I charge towards Aaron and side stop quickly next to him.

"You look so beautiful, so free." He leans in to kiss me, but as his lips come closer, I back away.

"Race you to the other side, Gritt." And I leave, giving it all I have until I feel his hands on my waist because he's caught up to me. He pulls me to him, and nips at my neck. It tickles more than it used to, sending me in a fit of giggles. We continue skating, holding hands like the two punks in love that we used to be.

"Let me ask you something," he says in all seriousness. "Who taught your son to skate if you didn't get on the ice for so long?"

"Nobody. He doesn't skate." Aaron stops in his tracks.

"Your son, doesn't skate?" He raises an eyebrow. Speaking about Adam with him is uncomfortable. Him speaking about Adam, me having to tell him the truth, him realizing he could have been the one teaching him how to skate, is agony. I need to tell him, now.

I open my mouth, but nothing comes out. The words are shouting in my brain, "Adam is your son" but I can't voice it.

That's when my anxiety strikes.

Everything flashes back in my mind. How I was alone raising Adam because Aunt Clarisse traveled a lot, how the neighbor babysat him while I was studying or working, how I met Mark when Adam was almost four. How those two accepted each other from the first time they met. How Adam looked more and more like Aaron over the years. I break out in a sweat, my breath becomes short and wheezy. I feel like choking and vomiting. I'm losing control, and fast.

"Stay with me, Al." Aaron holds my hands, looking into my eyes. "Breathe. Slowly in, slowly out." But his proximity is not working. My body trembles under my sobs, and he wraps his arms around me, holding me tight, and tighter, and tighter until I can't breathe anymore, and I feel like he's crushing every one of my bones. It hurts, but I need to feel the pain to erase the misery. That's when he kisses me, soft little pecks like he used to that turns into full on making out. His hand is pulling my hair slightly but hard enough for me to ache. I ache for him to have me. He bites my lower lip, and I moan into him, forgetting why he was holding me in the first place. "I've got you, Sweets."

"Thank you," my words are whispers that I wish held the truth I need to tell him.

"Looking good, Captain!" Luke's voice beams around us. I rest my forehead on Aaron's shoulder, frowning while he flips the bird to his brother. I missed an opportunity to tell him again. I can't open up with Luke around us. It would be even more insensitive than not telling him at all.

"Let's skate with this asshole and his lovely boyfriend. Then I want you to come back to my house, so I can fuck you until tomorrow, Al." He skates away towards his brother and body-checks him.

Being silly, Dex separates them, rolling his eyes but smirking at the same time.

Aaron and Dex seem to get along just fine.

They are communicating through quiet conversations and both smirk trying to get Luke to lose his cool. Not happening, he's the most laid-back guy I know, except when he looks at Dex. He looks at his boyfriend like he's his world, but I see concern lingering in Luke's eyes with every move Dex makes.

"Why are you worried about him?" I ask him when he comes closer.

"Because he hates being taken care of," he answers. "Like, Aar." He adds, pointing at his brother with his chin.

"So untrue. Aar always let me take care of him."

"But nobody took care of him for a long time, Alane." My eyes are on Aaron who's shoving Dex, laughing at something the other one says.

"They get along well?"

"He would prefer to have Dex as a brother over me."

"Untrue again. What happened to you, Gritt? Do you live in a parallel universe? Did LA change you that much? Are you so famous now that you can't see what's in front of you?"

Luke laughs. "And you, can you see what is in front of you?"

"I think so. Do you think we are fooling ourselves?"

Luke smiles. "I think you both fooled yourselves enough over the years thinking someone else could be by your side."

I close my eyes. "You might be right, Luke."

"I'm always right, Captain!" He shoves me hard.

"Asshole," I mumble while shoving him back. He skates away, and I follow, delighted to be on the ice once again with these two.

"Aaron, control your woman, she's being mean to me again." *Aaron's woman.* Oh, how I like to hear that.

"And you should control your man! He wants to take Al for coffee. It can only be a bad idea," Aaron shoots back before skating behind me, pushing me towards the bench.

"The lockers are great if you bend forward enough," Luke shouts when we make our way to said lockers.

"Alane, I'll wait for you outside for coffee," Dex adds, not giving me any choice in the matter.

"There is one thing that not many people know about me, Alane," Dex sits across from me.

We're at the only place that serves decent coffee, to his standard. He continues to study me as he did all afternoon. From the message Luke passed on to me, I'm positive he knows something about my past, but I'm not sure what. I tried to grill Luke, but he said he had no idea. I'm a little scared of Dex. He's as intense as Aaron can be, but colder and much more lawyerish. "Are you listening?" I nod.

"So, I was saying, there is something not many people know, not even Luke, and I'm telling you because your secret is a little bigger than mine." He waits for me to flinch, but I don't. "I'm a closet graphic novel reader," he announces triumphantly, as if this will raise his case. It does, but I won't give him the pleasure to acknowledge it until he gives me all the details of what he knows. He waits for me to crack, but I don't. Not even a little. Even if Luke and Aaron seem to love the guy, I don't know him from Adam or Eve. Seeing that I won't give in, he continues. "I like the novels by Jax S." He smiles.

There it is... He knows Adam is a graphic novel artist

publishing under the name Jax, the same middle name as his father, and S. for Smith. Dex has surely seen pictures. "Why Jax, Alane?" He smiles, ready to eat me alive.

"You know why, Dex. I don't think I have to tell you. I'm pretty sure you did your research." I seem calmer than I am inside. Someone other than my parents and aunt knowing my son is also Aaron's should send me into a tailspin, but I feel strangely in control.

"Should I give you a dollar and hire you as my lawyer?"

"He can't sue you for not telling him. And he won't sue you because he's not that big of an asshole." We look at each other, having nothing else to add until Dex pulls up a picture of Adam on his phone.

"The resemblance is uncanny." I nod while he continues, "I suppose nobody knows?" I shake my head. "You have to tell him, and tell Luke, as well as the whole family, before it blows up in your face and they get hurt. Because it will blow up, and it will hurt."

I sigh. "You think it's that easy telling the father of your only child he has a twenty-six-year-old son?"

"Why did you wait so long?"

"Because he had moved on. Because I did, too. Because we weren't supposed to ever find each other again. I don't know, Dex. Adam has Mark; it's not that he grew up without a father. He has a great relationship with him, always did. I tried to tell Aaron, but every time I speak about Adam's father and I try to tell him who he is, he changes the subject and talks about Jess, or I panic. Adam is on a book tour right now, I'll tell Aaron soon. I just need a little more time."

"So that's why you left town? So, nobody would know?"

"Well, the Pastor's daughter couldn't be pregnant, right? So, I left, in the middle of the night, two weeks after Aaron had broken my heart, and I never came back except briefly ten years ago for my father's funeral, without Adam or Mark." Dex says nothing, but there is a spark in his eyes.

"What is it, Dex?" The spark has spread on his mischievous lips.

"I see a great anger fuck in my future once Luke knows. I'm sorry, but Thor Luke is very sexy, and it makes me kind of horny." He laughs, and I join him, nervously. He stands up, throwing a couple of bills on the table and leans toward me.

"Don't fuck it up, Captain!" he says, knocking on the wooden table twice before walking away. "Don't fuck it up."

I come out to find Aaron leaning against his car, waiting for me.

"That was fast." He removes his sunglasses and his eyes looking into mine.

"Yep. But intense…"

"What isn't with Dex?" He snorts, pulling me to him to kiss me. I stop him, looking around to see if anyone sees us.

"Not here, Aar." I don't want other parents to know the science teacher is fucking one of her student's parents and thereby thinking his kids are getting special treatment.

"Oh no, Alane Smith, we're too old to hide. I don't care who sees us and what they have to say." His eyes are the color of a rainy sky, and I know I've hurt him, even if not intentionally.

"But I can't lose my job, Aar."

"You won't. Chris got you the job, you're safe." He takes my hands in his and starts rubbing my knuckles with his thumbs.

"I thought Patricia got me the job."

"Right… Believe that, Sweets. I had a nice little chat with Chris about him not telling me you were a teacher at the school he's a board member at. The asshole thought it would make a nice reunion. He knew what he was doing; he just wanted to push me out of my comfort zone. As soon as I told him Jess and I were over, he plotted to get you back here."

"Don't tell me he poisoned my mother so I would come back?"

"That just sped up the process. He was about to hire a PI to find you though."

"He's still as ridiculous as he used to be, I see."

"He's just Chris." He shrugs "How is your mother, Sweets?"

"She has early dementia. Some days she's fine, and some others she's not. I'm here to help, for the moment. I was hoping she would come with me to Phoenix, but she refuses to leave Springs Falls, so here I am. I'm not sure what the next step is. We'll see what the doctor says. Your parents?"

"Same old. They want to see you, you know." I avoid answering. Seeing his parents will be hard. As if he understands my silence, he changes the subject.

"You should have seen my mother when Dex came home the first time with Ian Porter and Ryan Marley." I tilt my head to look at him to see if he's joking. He's not.

"The actors? How? What?" Ryan Marley and Ian Porter are two of the best actors of our generation. They are handsome, talented, fun, or they seem to be. Ryan Marley knows so much about hockey; I had a celebrity crush on him like forever. I know he's about to marry Ian Porter's sister, but he's still dreamy.

"Fuck! You too?"

"What were they doing at the farm?" I ask eagerly, wanting an answer to why two of the sexiest men on earth were in Springs Falls. "Did you just say Dex knows them?" He nods.

"Dex is best friends with Ian and Ryan is Luke's partner at

the tattoo shop. There are a lot of links between them and their wives, and it's a complicated group, but they are very close friends with Luke and Dex."

"Darn, I know I had the wrong brother all along," I tease him, pushing him against the car. He raises an eyebrow as if I just challenged him.

"Want me to remind you why you don't have the wrong brother?" He pushes his hips toward mine, his erection poking at my thigh.

"Lead the way, Gritt. Didn't you say you wanted to fuck me until tomorrow, or was that you just babbling?" I tease him, hoping he'll bite.

"Get in the truck, Sweets. We're done playing nice." I do, because who can say no to that.

23

THEN - AARON

Since I arrived in Seattle, I've received a few letters from my mother and Chris, but nothing from Alane or Luke.

Their silence is killing me.

I know I don't deserve to hear from them. I know I shouldn't expect Alane to write me any letters, but I still have hope. It's stupid of me, mainly because the letter I sent was returned to me, unopened.

My mother called me once or twice, and when I asked to speak with Luke, he refused to talk to me. So I wrote him a letter as well, which was returned to me, also unopened.

Because of Patricia, I lost my girl and my brother. This girl is growing like cancer on me. She sends me two letters a week, when she's the only one I don't want to hear from. I opened the first one, thinking it was an apology for what she did to Alane and I.

It wasn't.

It was a love declaration.

She was proclaiming how she had always been in love with

me and how I deserved more than the Pastor's daughter. She described in great detail how she would suck my dick and fuck me until I forget everything about Alane. Her plan failed.

All I could think about while reading her words, was Alane's mouth on me, Alane's smile while I enter her, Alane's eyes burning with desire while I suck on her clit.

I was more turned on by the images of Alane and I than what Patricia's words drew in my mind. I was a little disgusted with myself after I jerked off thinking about my ex-girlfriend while cleaning my hands on the letter her friend sent me, but even more disgusted by what Patricia was pulling off.

I wish I could tell Alane or Luke.

I could tell Chris, but would he believe his sister's behavior? Would I lose my last friend in Springs Falls? He's my only link to home, and I asked him not to talk to me about Alane. I want to hear from her not about her. I don't want to hear about whom Alane is dating, or the fun Luke, Chris and Alane are having without me.

I'm alone in Seattle when they are together at home.

I never minded being alone before Alane.

I had Luke anyway.

Now I'm with no one, and I feel isolated. I've become a hermit. I go to work, go home, watch TV, and sleep. Michael, the son of the family helping me out here tried hard to get me to go out at the beginning, but he has given up now. He brings me beers, and we drink, in silence most of the time.

Tonight though, he's insisting that I come out with him. I don't want to, but he's trying hard to convince me, and I want to be persuaded. I want to let go, but I don't deserve to, I don't want to enjoy life without Alane, or Luke, or Chris. I want to be miserable. I want to hurt. I want to be unhappy.

"Come on, Aaron. You're not going to punish yourself forever. Let's go out tonight. Some of my friends are hitting up a bar, and you should come with." Michael is a nice guy. We get along just fine. He's easygoing and unperturbed. I was afraid we would have nothing in common, but his parents are much closer in style to my parents than the Smiths, maybe not as hippie as mine, but free, open, friendly and understanding. That's a pretty good start.

"I don't know, I mean, I don't want to impose."

"Bullshit, you're not imposing. Come."

"I'm... I." I don't have any excuse to say no; being alone all the time makes for a long summer.

"What's the worst that can happen? You could have fun? Come on, Aaron. You arrived six weeks ago, summer is almost over, and then you'll be starting school and working. We'll never see each other much anymore. I like you man, but you need to light up. You're not the first guy on earth to dump a girl. You need distractions, you need fun, you need to go out with me." It's not the worst idea. I could go out with him for once, walk away from my self-imposed misery. I could taste the water with one beer or two and come home if I hate it.

"Where are you going?" I ask shyly, feigning a small interest.

"To a bar. You won't even need a fake ID. Come on..."

I'm debating. There is nothing and nobody holding me back. I wish Luke and Alane would give me a good reason to stay home. I hope my parents would tell me to stay home. I wish it wasn't up to me to decide.

"Okay." I shrug. "Let's go out." Michael is way more excited than I am. He's bouncing off the walls.

"Shit! You're going to love my friends! Don't forget an ID. You're eighteen, right?" I nod. " We're going to have the night of your life! Get ready, we're leaving in thirty minutes."

The fucking idiot that I am didn't ask questions when we passed the border, and I'm now sitting in a bar in Canada, drinking away my pain, joyfully. Michael's friends are fucking awesome, or maybe it's the alcohol talking. I feel good. I danced with a lot of girls, laughed with a lot of people, chugged many beers, and now I'm enjoying a beautiful black girl hanging on my arm.

My heart is still in Springs Falls, but my dick is waking up.

She's telling me about her family, her Vietnamese father, and Nigerian mother, and I get lost in her beautiful brown eyes with some green sparkles shining with lust. Her straight long black hair brushes the crook of my elbow, and she keeps touching me, batting her eyelashes and laughing with her mouth wide open.

I would love to push my dick in her mouth.

My head is swirling with hot desire, my cock is hoping more and more for a happy ending, and I close up my heart that's begging me to go back to Alane.

Whatever the consequences, I will fuck this girl tonight.

If I can't lose my virginity to the one I love, I want to lose it to Jess—I think that's her name. I'll certainly never see her again. If being in love wasn't enough to end up with the girl I adore, fucking the first one I meet after that shouldn't come with any complications. I lean towards her and whisper how beautiful she is to her ear.

She's a different kind of beauty than what I'm used to, but she's still stunning. She beams at me and drags her fingers along my thighs. I feel my body getting warm, and my dick hardening. I shouldn't pursue anything with this girl. She's not the one I love. She's only the one I want. She bats her eyelashes again, and I lean in slowly, more because I'm losing balance than anything. She takes it for an invitation and bites her lip. I'm still lost in her eyes. She murmurs something, but I can't hear it, so I come closer.

"You're going to be trouble," she whispers before wetting her lips.

I can smell her shampoo, and my heart squeezes with heaviness. She doesn't smell like Alane. She's nothing like her. The only thing they have in common is that they are both athletic girls, but what's her name? I don't know where my head is at, and she continues coming closer to me, so close I have to shut my eyes not to see her in double. She takes it as an invitation, and her lips touch mine. It's a soft caress. I stay still at first, but then, I realize I have nothing left to lose, nothing holding me back, nobody waiting for me. I kiss her back, opening for her so her tongue can play with mine, and when it does, I can feel a tear falling from the corner of my eye.

I'm moving on, even if I don't want to.

I kiss her with more passion, throwing all my sadness into it, and I let her stroke my dick through my jeans. I let her touch my chest and straddle me, too.

I let her lead, she takes my hand, and we walk away from everybody. That's how I end up in a hotel room after stopping at a pharmacy for condoms. Our mouths are still on each other. My brain is too lost to the alcohol to stop the train wreck of my first time.

She undresses me fast and pushes me onto the shaky bed.

I'm not sure who's paying for the room. I know I can't afford it. I think she used her credit card, or her parent's, but I don't know for sure. I should have asked, but I didn't. Lust is clouding my thoughts.

She's hot, and I'm hard.

She strips slowly for me, swaying her hips, humming a song I don't know, and I stroke myself, looking at her, remembering how many times I said no to Alane, all to end up without her anyway.

This girl is gorgeous.

Once her panties are the only thing left, she crawls onto the bed, like a tiger hunting her prey. It's intimidating and hot as hell at the same time. She replaces my hand with hers, and I focus on not coming in her hand.

I love seeing her hand on my length.

I breathe laboriously, trying to gain more control, and she smirks at me. She reaches for a condom and sheaths me. I let her do it, impassive and not caring, drunk on beer and pain because she's not the one I wanted to lose my virginity to, but she's the one giving me an opportunity I cannot pass.

Removing her panties, she climbs on top of me, and when she positions me at her entrance, I whimper, half afraid of what's to come, the other half too excited by what she's doing to me. It's driving me crazy, and I bite her lower lip with my teeth. She pulls away, shaking her head and directs my head to her breasts. I take one in my mouth and roll it between my teeth. She moans, and it shoots a jolt of pleasure through my whole body. She chuckles, and it's the sexiest chuckle I've ever heard.

"I'll make you forget anybody you want, Aaron. Just let me fuck you, and you'll forget, I promise." She lowers herself, and all I can do is grunt. Once I'm deep inside her, I'm not sure what takes over me, but I need to put all the pain I feel into her. I need to fuck her hard. Flipping her around, I hover over her, holding her tight until she can't move. I'm not sure she can even breathe when I thrust into her, hard and deep trying to hurt her; for me walking away, for Patricia, for Pastor Smith, for Alane and for Luke ignoring me.

I thrust wishing she wasn't who she is.

I fuck her until I come undone, not caring if she came.

But seeing her lazy smile and hooded eyes, she certainly did.

She asks for more, so I give her more, and we fuck all night, her screaming my name with each orgasm, and me punishing her for not being Alane. When we're about to fall asleep, sated and weary of each other, the alcohol is long gone, and guilt fills me. I wait for her to fall asleep before letting tears wet my cheeks and sadness take over. By sleeping with this girl, I closed the door to a future with Alane. I broke the promise of her being the only woman in my bed. I broke the promise of marrying the girl with whom I'll have sex with for the first time. I destroyed my last connection to what Alane and I had. I barely recognized who I was tonight, but I like this new guy. For the first time since I left home, I like who I am with who I think is named Jess and who I am without Alane.

As much as it hurts, I know I need to shrink Alane to the size of an ant in my thoughts and forget everything about her.

I need to do it to really move on.

I need her to be a blur in my life, to forget who she was to me, or who she could have become.

The girl wakes up, grinning at me, and with just a smile, I get hard. Her nails travel to my navel, leaving an excruciating trail of desire, hardening me even more. I don't understand why I react to every one of her moves, but it feels like my body has known hers forever. I don't like it, but I accept the effect she has on me. How couldn't I when it feels so good? She wraps her hand around my dick again, pulling hard and squeezing tight, spitting on the head, her mouth torturing me, brushing my tip. I feel like I'm inside her again, warm and tight, and I beg her to blow me.

When she takes my dick in her mouth, I realize there are worse ways to forget the girl you love. It should be easier from now on, especially if her tongue swirls around my length and her hands continue tugging at my balls in such an expert way.

I fuck her mouth as if it was my last fuck on Earth.

I'm done being nice. I'm done being the guy fighting desire.

I give her all of me and tap the back of her throat, again and again. I give her all the power to please me, even when her fingers push inside me in a way I wasn't ready to explore.

I don't care.

She can do whatever she wants with me as long as she continues sucking me off for the rest of my life.

24

NOW - AARON

*F*amily dinners at my parents are loud and exhausting.

My siblings spend most of their time trying to rile me up, and tonight should be no exception. It started with my mother harassing Dex and Luke about their famous friends.

I ignored my daughter's giggles when Dex spoke about the two actors he considers as family or when Luke described the new tattoos he designed for Dan Darling, lead singer of the Darling Devils. I met the guys, and they are nice, kind of, if you like good-looking celebrities who love their wives. Seems like it's a thing that girls like.

Now, my mother is trying to talk weddings to the happy couple, but my brother stops her, reminding her the promise she made about not ever bringing up the subject, which served as her payment for a favor Dex made to her.

"I didn't speak about babies just a wedding. The deal was about you two having kids." My dad, a handsome old hippie with white hair falling to the base of his neck and a subtle beard, raises a brow in my direction and chuckles.

We look a lot alike. I'm a mini Ridge, and I know how to read him. I spent a lot of time with him on and off the ice when I was younger, and he always understood my silence, more than my mother did. I recognized his as well, still do. Right now, his face tells me he's about to fuck with my mother, and he's laughing about it even before doing so.

"Since when are you such a conservative, Bella? I thought weddings weren't for you."

My mother didn't want to marry my dad for a long time. As a joke, she always said she'd marry him only after giving birth to their fourth kid, never thinking they would have four.

I was twelve when Barnabas was born, and thirteen when my parents got married. I stood there with Luke, looking at the frown on my mother's face when she had to say I do, surrounded by a few people during the strangest wedding I've ever attended.

She refused to take my father's name and still tries not to use it, but our friends and teachers, as well as the whole town, still calls her Mrs. Gritt. She hates it with a passion.

Arabella Russo is a free bird you can't clip the wings off, but she has no problem with her kids getting married. When I married Jess, she was over the moon, trying to organize the biggest wedding of the year. We had to elope to escape her. She got mad, but then Jess got pregnant, and it all went better.

Being a grandmother is the best thing that could have happened to my mom. She took care of Hailey more than we asked for, she still does. Unfortunately for her, Luke doesn't want children, and Salomé and Barnabas are not ready to deliver any either. So, she has only two grandkids to spoil, not that my kids are complaining.

"Shut your mouth, Ridge. I didn't want to marry the alpha

hippie you were. There is nothing wrong with making Dex our official son."

"Of course." Luke laughs. "I should have known it wasn't about me spending my life with someone I love, Mom. It was about you having another son."

"Not my fault if he's my favorite," she chimes, knowing too well what she just said.

"I thought I was your favorite!" Barnabas plays along.

"No, no, no, I am," Luke teases. "You told me last week."

They look in my direction for me to play along, but I don't.

"I'm Dad's favorite." I shrug, winking at my dad, who rolls his eyes at my joke.

"Sal?" Luke says, still trying to get the ball rolling.

"I'm their favorite daughter." She smiles, knowing she's bugging Barnabas. She used to tell him she was the favorite daughter and he was not, because he wasn't a girl and he was the last one. Nobody ever liked the last child. Looking at Barn, I know he's going to bite back, and it's going to hurt. I prepare myself for what is to come, but I'm not ready for the low blow he delivers.

"Not long though, now that Alane is in the picture again." Salomé's face falls, hurt and anger replacing the easygoing teasing she was showing just before. All eyes turn to me, and all I can do is sigh. I haven't talked to my kids about Alane and I yet. I haven't touched the subject with my parents, and not at all with my sister, who still dislikes Alane after all those years, blaming her for losing her big brother. Alane's name has never been said out loud around this table since we broke up, except for a few months ago when my mother said she was back in town.

"Asshole," I mumble for only Barnabas to hear.

"Dad?" Hailey's shaky voice forces me to find her eyes.

"What does Uncle B mean?" Clearing my throat, I start to open my mouth to explain, but Luke cuts me off.

"Your dad rekindled with his first love." Hell. He always has been better than me with words, but right now is not the moment to steal the words from me. My kids need to hear it from me, in private if possible.

"You remember when we said my first girlfriend was back in town?" Hal and Law both nod, hanging on my every word. "Well, I ran into her several times, and one thing lead to another. We kind of are seeing each other." Luke chuckles, certainly knowing we are more than just kind of seeing each other. I ignore him and look at Dex for help. He nudges his boyfriend in the ribs for him to stop.

"It's new and complicated, so I wasn't going to share this with you or anybody here, until I knew where it was going. I don't want to get anybody's hopes up. We're catching up on lost years and spending time together."

I look at each of them around the table. My mother has tears in her eyes, my father looks confused, Barn has a smug look on his face, my kids seem kind of shocked, and Salomé is hurt. She gets up and walks away without saying a word. I want to follow her and talk to her, but right now my priority is my kids, not the feelings of my adult sister, who should have dealt with her shit concerning my ex-girlfriend a long time ago.

"Is it who I think it is?" Lawson asks. I nod before bringing my eyes back to Hailey, knowing what I'm about to say could be taken very badly. I'm not sure if she likes Alane or not these days, but I know she won't like me dating one of her teachers. She was very clear on the subject after seeing me with Patricia at the dance. I was not to hang out with any adults she knows, not anybody from the school, not any of her mother's friends, no one in her circle.

"Alane's last name is Smith. She teaches science at your school." I took extra-care not saying it was *their* science teacher. She was mine before being anything to them. As dramatically as her aunt, Hailey leaves the table and strolls in the same direction as Sal. I look at Law for any positive reaction, and as usual, he doesn't disappoint. His smile reaches his eyes behind his glasses; I've never seen the kid so happy.

"That explains why she looks at me that way. I was a little worried she was a creeper. She also mumbled a few times how I reminded her of someone she knew when she was young. It makes sense now."

"I think you remind her of Luke, they used to be best friends," I say, looking at my bro across the table.

"Makes sense," my father adds. The intensity of his gaze tells me we need to talk. Late night talks with Dad on the porch with a glass of whatever we feel like is something we have been doing for years. I don't speak much. I prefer to stay quiet and let my siblings be the center of attention, but my Dad got worried after I came back from Seattle engaged to another woman than the one I said I would marry, so he asked me to talk with him on the porch. Twenty-five years later, we still do, at least once a month.

"This is wonderful, Aaron," my mother says, breaking the eye contact I had with my dad. "Don't break her heart this time." She doesn't have to add more, I know what she means. We all know what she means. "And when you're ready, bring her to dinner. I would love to see her again. I've tried hard to give her space since she came back in town, but I would love to meet the woman she has become. I heard she has a son."

"Adam," I tell her.

"That's a name she always liked, as well as Hailey and Lawson," my mother says as if she is announcing the weather.

But what she just said is like a punch to my stomach. I remember the conversations we had when we were just kids, speaking of our hypothetical children, our two boys, and one girl: I never knew the names, but.... She used to tell me I was like Adam because she felt like she was the forbidden fruit to me, and I always resisted until the day I bit into her. I remember hearing her discuss the names Hailey and Lawson with my mother once, when I was doing... I don't know what in the kitchen. She could spend hours discussing names with Mom.

My mother goes nuts for different names and even has a little book she writes every name she likes in, so she can give ideas when one of us is expecting a child. That's what she did with Jess and I. She proposed the names Hailey and Lawson. I think now, she was doing much more than just suggesting names. She was meddling, not giving me a fair chance to make my marriage work, planting an Alane seed in my brain, over and over.

"You proposed those names!" My voice is full of reproach, and I stand up abruptly.

"Son!" my father warns me to be respectful with whatever is on my mind right now.

"I never knew if you actually didn't remember, or if you wanted those names for your children, to remember Alane. I never said anything to Jess," my mother says apologetically.

Truth is: I had forgotten about the names, like a lot of other details time erased. First, I put Alane in a small box to be able to love Jess. Then years apart did the rest. What I had with Jess was never what I had with Al, but I still loved my wife. I pretended my high school sweetheart didn't exist; my first love wasn't somewhere happy without me, and I forgot almost everything else, except the star-shaped birthmark. I could never forget that mark. Eaten up with guilt, and the need to be alone seeps into my veins. I should check on Hailey and Sal, but I can't. I don't know where they are, and I have no energy to look for them.

"Aaron, wait!" Barnabas says behind me, never wanting to leave me alone especially when I need just that. Always wanting to know what I think, the same way I'm with Luke. It might be the only thing Barn and I have in common. I know Luke, Dex and Dad will stop him. They know I need time to process what happened tonight before finding me and getting me to speak.

I find Hailey at home, crying on our sofa, wrapped in a blanket, a cold tea in her hands. I want to ignore her, but I can't. Sitting next to her, I wrap my arms around her and hum the song I used to when she was a baby.

"I'm sorry. I didn't know Alane was your teacher until that meeting. I didn't even recognize her at first, and she didn't want to talk to me. Then we spoke, and one thing led to another..." Hailey raises her hand to stop me.

"It's too fast, Dad." She wipes the last tear off her cheek.

"It's thirty years in the making, Hal. I sacrificed Alane, and I thought I was doing the right thing, and then I met your mom. I'll never regret it because I have you and Law, and you are the most important people in my life, but Alane and I had so much unfinished business. It was time."

"I like her as a teacher, but I'm not ready to have a stepmother. I know Mom already has someone, but I don't want to have someone here, in our house. I don't have to see mom's boyfriend, so it's not the same. I don't want to have to share the house with someone I don't know."

"We're not there, yet. We are just two adults enjoying each other. I don't know what she's going to do in the future; it depends on her mother's health. But, Hal, if we want to make our life together, you'll have to accept it. I love you, you're my daughter, you'll always be my girl, but it's not your place to tell me who I can date and who I can make my life with. Do you understand?" She nods, hugging me tightly.

"She helped me a little while back with some boy drama, and she said she lost the love of her life when she was my age. Was that you?"

"I guess."

"Don't fuck it up, Dad. She said she survived it once, but I'm not sure she would a second time. I know I wouldn't."

"Who do I need to kill, baby girl?" I say, ruffling her curly black hair.

"Nobody. He chose Madison over me. I wish he loved me, but he chose her because I didn't want to..." She looks at me guiltily, and the desire to kill that fucking kid makes me see spots. I close my eyes to calm down.

"He chose her because she did something you didn't want to do?" She nods, tears falling again on her face.

"So, you crying is not about me dating, it's about your heart being broken by an asshole?" She nods again. "Wait 'til I tell your grandpa and uncles; this kid is dead!"

"Mrs. Smith said you would listen. She didn't say anything about you killing anyone!"

"Alane forgot I can be very overprotective, and she doesn't know me as a dad, Hal. I'll have a talk with her too, she should have told me what was happening."

"She doesn't know! Please, Dad, drop it," she pleads.

"I'll drop it if you promise me you won't date until you're done with college." I'm joking, kind of.

She rolls her eyes at me before scoffing. "Even Rapunzel found a guy locked up in her tower, Dad. You had a girlfriend in high school, why can't I date?

"Because I was a respectable kid and still broke someone's heart along with mine. Imagine if you find someone like Chris, it can only end up in tears."

"I'm already crying, I don't see what it would change." She stands up and walks away, leaving me alone on the couch, thinking of all the pain Alane and I went through, to finally end up back in each other's arms, to our paths crossing again. I don't want to lose her. I want to share the next forty years with her, die in her arms, surrounded by her love. But to do so, there is a conversation we need to have, about us, what we are, and what we want.

As Lawson comes in, followed by Luke, Dex, and my Dad, I know nothing will happen tonight. Taking the bottle of scotch Dex got me as a thank you for helping him move when I was in LA, I grab four glasses and settle on the porch with them.

The night is going to be long and full of unwanted advice.

I'll speak with Alane tomorrow.

25

THEN – ALANE

"All I'm saying, Alane, is that Aaron has a right to know." My Aunt Clarisse comes closer to me, holding my newborn son in her arms.

"I don't know. Last time I saw him, he was heavily kissing another girl in a hotel in Vancouver. Seems to me he's moved on."

I had been a little shocked when the elevator opened, and I saw Aaron shoving his tongue in a beautiful girl's mouth, who was apparently waiting for a room. I had come with my aunt to Vancouver for her last book tour. She wanted me to go with her for a change of scenery. It took some convincing, but I caved in, thinking I could see something other than the four walls of my aunt's house.

As for a change of scenery, it really was a change, but it almost destroyed me. After I walked by them, Aunt Clarisse had to pick me up off the floor like a dropped spoon and then I fell into her arms crying. I waited to be back in our bedroom before literally falling to the floor, and then stayed there until the next morning. Empty, hurt and disheartened, I still don't want Aaron to choose me by obligation. I wanted him to pick me because he loved me. Seeing him with someone else crushed any last hope.

The pregnancy has been hard on me.

Not physically, but mentally.

I wouldn't say I was depressed, but I was on the verge of it. As soon as I held my son, it almost all faded away.

Nothing matters anymore but him.

He's so beautiful with all his wrinkles and his few blond hairs. He looks a little like Yoda but less greenish. He's a bundle of love. My bundle of love. Even if I still don't understand how we made him, he's what's left of Aaron and I. He's mine, only mine, for me to take care of.

"You don't know if Aaron was with this girl only for one night, and you don't know exactly what happened either. So, you saw him kissing someone else. You can't draw conclusions on one fact. He has a son, he should know."

She places my boy in my arms for me to breastfeed him. I set him up and start feeding him. I needed a C-section, and I can't really move right now. It hurts like a bitch every time I cough, move, sit or make any type of movement. They gave me some ibuprofen, as if it will make a difference.

I'm glad Aunt Clarisse is here to pass me the baby back and forth. I wouldn't like to disturb the nurse every time I want to pick up my son.

My parents didn't show up, even after Aunt Clarisse told them I had given birth. I barely talked to them during my pregnancy. I'm disappointed they're not here for me, but happy they decided not to come if it was just to lecture me and see the disappointment in my mother's eyes.

I'm an embarrassment to her.

She's the one who sent me away. Like Aaron, she forgot I existed, or at least she does everything she can to forget. My father was a little easier to talk to at the beginning, but after a few discussions about adoption, I understood he would never accept my son. I gave up on reaching out, and he didn't want to talk to me either.

"On another note, have you thought of a name? We can't continue calling him 'boy'."

Did I think of a name? It's all I thought about since I felt him move for the first time. I didn't want to know if it was a boy or a girl, but I thought of names, nonetheless. I went through books and thousands of lists, but only one keeps coming back to me. I'm not sure if I should use it though. It's a name Aaron and I liked. It's a name to honor my baby's father, even if he'll certainly never meet him. It's a reminder that Aaron is not mine anymore.

"I have a name, I'm just not sure I can get used to it."

"Okaayyy, as long as it's not Phelony or Banjo, I think we're fine." She tries to make me smile, but I can't. There is too much on my shoulders. The responsibility of choosing a name for a child, something that will define him, something that is for life...

"Adam Jax," I whisper softly, looking at him. Sitting next to me, Aunt Clarisse strokes my hair softly.

"Want to tell me what it means to you?" I sigh, avoiding her eyes.

"Adam was a name we chose together for our hypothetical son. I used to tell him he was like Adam, he would one day bite into my fruit, and we'll be kicked out of the Eden that Springs Falls was. It was a joke. A stupid joke. But it's what happened, and my son is the only man in my world now. The only man on Earth I can care about."

"It's a good strong name. And Jax?" I can't hold the tears anymore. Thinking of Aaron still hurts. Calling my son Adam Jax might hurt even more, but no other name fits.

"Jax is Aaron's middle name," I weep, fully crying now.

"Sweetie, you still love him. Call him. And if that's what you want to name your son, do it. After some time, it would be his name, not anything of his father's. If Aaron is ever in his life, he'll absolutely love the fact that you named your son after him. But first, you have to tell him." The tears on my cheeks are falling on Adam. I nod, desperately wanting to change the topic.

"I'll get you his number. All you'll have to do is call him, and if he wants to come to Phoenix, I'll pay for the plane ticket." It's a pity Aunt Clarisse didn't have children. She is more suited to be a mother compared to my own. She's compassionate, loving and understanding, everything my mother isn't.

Aunt Clarisse steps away with Adam long enough for me to truly rest. They tell me to nap when the baby is sleeping, but it's not always easy. I'm afraid he'll stop breathing while I'm asleep, so I usually keep an eye on him. After the first day without any sleep, the nurse promised to check on him regularly while I was getting some rest, but I don't trust her. What if she kidnaps him while I'm snoozing?

I know I'm a little neurotic, but I'm all he has. Aunt Clarisse is a big help, but I soon know Adam will be my full responsibility. I refuse to be depending on her for money or anything regarding my son.

Raising him alone is my penance for my foolish behavior, or maybe he's my reward. I'm not sure anymore. What I'm certain of is that as soon as I can, I'll find a job and go back to school.

The last six months, Aunt Clarisse and I discussed my future.

Now that hockey is off the table, I'm still not sure what I want to be. My aunt keeps saying I don't have to choose until later, but I need a plan. I need to know because I feel like my life has imploded. I need my head to be in the game, even if the game has changed.

"Honey, I've got you his number," Aunt Clarisse says entering the room. I open my eyes to see her pained expression about my situation.

It's not pity, per se.

It's just an acknowledgment that what I have to do isn't easy. I want to ask her whom she asked, but I won't.

I try not to ask for anything from anybody. I wish I could still talk to Luke, but he's a casualty when I lost with my boyfriend. I can't lie to him. I lied to Patricia, saying I had left for a hockey camp abroad. I don't want anybody telling Aaron or any of the Gritts.

My secret is very safe.

Only my parents and Aunt Clarisse knew I was pregnant.

Letting Aaron know is allowing the whole Gritt family into my son's life. I won't ask them for anything, I just want Aaron to know he has a son. I don't want him to quit school and move to Arizona. I don't want him to send me money or be in our son's life if he doesn't want to be.

One hour ago, I didn't want to tell him, but Aunt Clarisse is correct, he has a right to know after all. His whole family has a right to know. She hands me the phone handset and the piece of paper she wrote his number on. I take both, my hands shaking.

Sighing, I muster up the courage to talk to him before entering the few digits on the phone separating me from my first love.

"Hello?" a female voice answers. I'm not ready to have a woman talking to me. Words get stuck in my throat and tears fill my eyes instantly. "Hellooo?" the voice insists.

Aunt Clarisse put her hand on my shoulder and shakes me a little to get me out of the solid state I just fell into. I'm totally frozen. My aunt shakes me a little more, her eyes wide, trying to tell me to say something.

"Um... Hello... Is this Aaron's number?" I stupidly mutter, hoping I made a mistake dialing.

"It is. Who's speaking?"

"Hi, I'm a friend from back home, I was wondering if I could talk to him." I stumble on each and every word I pronounce.

"Oh! Are you the ex-girlfriend Michael told me about?"

"Michael?" I'm lost. I want to know who she is. I want to know who Michael is. Aaron clearly has built a life without me while I was creating life in me. Our time apart couldn't have been more different.

"Yes, the friend who introduced us. Anyway, I'm Jess, Aaron's fiancée. He's not here right now, but he'll be home soon. Is there anything you wanted me to tell him? I can tell him you called."

Fiancée.

Home.

He moved on.

He's in love with someone else.

He's engaged to another.

I can't do that to him. I can't tie him down to me if he wants to be with another girl.

"It's fine. I just wanted to know how he was. No worries. Don't even bother telling him I called. And... Congratulations on the engagement. He's a great guy. I'm sure you'll be very happy."

She says something back, but I don't hear it, I hang up, crying at the loss of Aaron, hating that I'm back at square one, missing him and wondering why I wasn't enough for him. Why I'm not the one engaged? Why didn't he choose me? I don't want to live a life without him. But I have to. I have Adam to think about now. Closing my eyes, I pray my son will look more like a Smith than a Gritt because seeing him looking like his dad would be an agonizing life sentence.

Aunt Clarisse gives me back my son, understanding I need him close by so as not to crumble.

"Please look like a Smith," I tell him softly.

But when I look deeply into his eyes, I already know those are like his father's. This shade of blue is undeniable, the same color as Mr. Gritt's and Aaron's eyes.

As my son starts to cry, surely needing to be changed, I cry with him, promising myself that they're the last tears I would shed over Aaron Gritt and vowing I would always be in control of my life, my desire, and my son; that I would never be helpless again.

Head in the game, Alane. Head in the game.

NOW - ALANE

*B*lindfolded, legs spread, sitting naked on the edge of a chair in my old room, Aaron is hot. His chest hair covers his toned body and sends a trail to his hard length that my tongue is happy to follow.

Taking him in my mouth, kneeling between his legs in my room is a fantasy I'd played in my mind since I was sixteen.

We never did anything in here. Aaron was never allowed inside my house. Now that we're adults, and my mother is out, I'm not letting the opportunity escape us, even if it feels kind of creepy being with Aaron in a room that seems frozen in time. It looks the same as when I left years ago. My parents never took the time to change anything in it, and as I never came back, never went through what I left behind. There is even an old Polaroid of Aaron and I still pinned on the corkboard.

"Alane, not that I'm not enjoying what you're doing with your tongue, but I really wanted to talk to you." Planting my hands on his thighs, I rise and lean forward, my mouth brushing his ear and my breasts against his chest.

"Do I need to gag you, Aar? Because I will. I'm not sure that's something you're into, but if you don't let me do what I want now, I will shut you up." I kiss him while my hand finds his dick and strokes him hard.

"Please, Sweets, proceed," he moans once I back away and kneel again. I know from past experience that some men hate not seeing the blowjob actions, but I also know that not having his sight will give him a great orgasm. I thought a lot of his ex-wife and about his first time not being mine, and I decided I could still be some of his firsts if the Alane I were before made an appearance for him to enjoy. After asking him what Jess mostly did, I decided to push boundaries and give him the best, so I could erase her mouth from his dick. Young Alane's blowjobs had nothing on me now. He's ready for a great ride. Straddling him, I push him inside me so my juices can cover him.

"I'm going to ask you questions, and you can only answer yes or no. Do you understand? If you break the rules, I'll stop." I feel in total control. Nothing can stop me.

"Have you ever had a threesome?" I go up and down on him.

"No," he whispers, and I kiss him as a reward.

"Have you ever tied someone up?"

"Yes." I circle my hips and he grunts. Knowing his dick is wet enough from me, I stand up and back away. "I answered, why are you stopping?"

"I'm just starting, don't worry." Bringing my mouth to his hard dick, I lick it clean from balls to tip. I love tasting myself on him.

"Have you ever spanked someone?"

"Yes." I lick the tip like an ice cream.

"Been spanked?"

"No." I lick his whole length again.

"Was I in any of your fantasies?" I don't know what he's thinking about, but his dick springs. I engulf it in my mouth and plunge my finger inside myself. He grunts while I moan around his shaft. "Tell me about it."

"I've thought of fucking you every time I fucked Jess from behind." His honesty sends a jolt of pleasure to my pussy and sadness into my heart. I bring my fingers to his mouth and paint his lips with them before pushing them in his mouth. He sucks on them while I lap at his dick. Putting my hand at the base to cover it all, I turn my wrist for my hand to twirl in the opposite direction my tongue does.

"Alane, I'm..." I stop. Popping it out of my mouth, I make Aaron stand.

"I said shhh." Taking back my position on my knees between his legs, I open my jaw wide and dip one testicle in my mouth while my hand strokes him slowly.

"Shit, Alane. Teabagging? Seriously, I need to see this" Closing my mouth around him, I slide down his ball, pulling on his most sensitive skin.

"Remove the blindfold, you can help me and dip deeper into my mouth if you want." He does and without saying more, I let him take control. Loving the domination he has over me while he plunges, I allow him to replace my hand on himself. He jerks off while I gently swallow him.

"Fuck, I should have never let you go," he says while stroking himself harder. Releasing him, I beg him to fuck me. He pushes me on the bed and flips me on my stomach, his mouth finding my ass right away, biting hard.

"Higher, Sweets," His hands find my hips and positions me, so my pussy is wide opened for him. He continues biting my ass, not putting his mouth near any part of my openings, torturing me while I beg him.

"Did you do any of the things you asked me before?" He nibbles hard.

"Yes," I moan in the pillow.

"Did you ever think of me while doing it?"

"Always." I can't lie. "I never stopped thinking of you." I'm rewarded by two fingers entering me while his tongue circles my ass.

"I've never fucked an ass, Al, and I really want to fuck yours. Would you let me?" His fingers are finding their way inside me, scissoring me rapidly while he repositions himself above me. His whole body is now restraining me, and his dick is rubbing against my ass cheeks. I'm on the verge of climaxing when he stops everything. Waiting for my answer.

"Do as it pleases you, Aaron." He starts to move his fingers again, slowly bringing me back to where I was.

"Do you have a vibrator?" I nod, trying to reach the night table to bring it out. Aaron moves to get it, and I miss him right away. Hearing the drawer open and close, I look back to find him turning on my toy.

"Fuck, you're sexy. There is so much I want to do to you. Are you okay with having this on your clit while I take your ass?" I had no idea Aaron could be so dirty, eager to please, I feel my pussy getting drenched by the possibilities we could explore.

"I could even take it inside me if you want." I bite my lip, wriggling my ass as an offering to his desire.

"Whatever you prefer, Sweets. I've waited a long time to take you all the ways I dreamed of. I just want you to come as much as I know will." His pushes his tip inside me, and I enjoy stretching wide for him. The pain I feel makes me come alive. I cry his name when he pulls out, pleading for him to take me once and for all. When his hand brings my vibrator to my clit, I sob with pleasure, loving that he can give me what I thought I'd lost, what I thought I was done wanting. "Push it inside you, so I can take care of your tits." My head is plastered in fog, and when I push the tip of the toy inside me at the same moment he pinches my nipple and thrusts in me, I come like I never did before. My vagina is soaring, warmth spreading inside me as fast as an army of ants, and I scream Aaron's name until he pulls out and comes on my ass.

I, who wanted to bring him to places he didn't know, am the one who went back to where I belong.

I stay lying on my stomach, sated while Aaron runs to the bathroom to get a towel to clean me up. It's soft and loving, and when he pulls me into his arms and kisses the top of my head, a single tear falls from the corner of my eye.

"If you hadn't let me go, I wouldn't have been able to discover what I liked. Maybe we wouldn't have been together long," I say, nuzzling myself in the base of his neck.

"Or we would have discovered all this together." His hand is caressing my arm while he takes a big breath. "My family knows we're seeing each other again." I freeze. Is that what we are doing? Aaron's arm brings me a security I thought I'd lost. I feel like me again after so many years having tried to find the missing piece. He completes me. But what happens tomorrow? What happens once he knows? What happens once his family knows?

"The whole family?"

"Yes. Did you tell yours?"

"Well… my mother thinks you're the antichrist, and as for Adam… It's complicated."

"Complicated?"

"It's a long story. Can I put some clothes on before going into it?"

"Of course, I mean, you don't have to tell me if you don't want to..." I get out of bed and start getting dressed, dreading losing the bliss I felt moments ago. He does the same, his eyes analyzing me like he used to do when we played hockey against one another, trying to decide what my next move would be, and trying to read me like he could.

"Sweets, what is it?" As I finish buttoning my blouse, I take a deep breath, knowing the moment I feared the most is here. I was never meant to see him again. I avoided our hometown for years, and even then, I thought he would be married, and I would be able to ignore him when I came back a few months ago.

"Adam is twenty-six years old," I announce, hoping this will be enough for him to understand.

"Yeah, about that. I realized that Jess and I named our children by the names you liked when we were kids. I had forgotten about it until my mother, who had never forgotten, told me last night." Our children. The freaking irony of his words is not lost on me. My phone rings somewhere in the bedroom, and I let it go to voicemail. Paralyzed by what I have to do. It rings again. The heavy silence between us growing like a fungus. When it rings a third time, I decided to pick up the conversation after answering. It could be Adam needing to reach me. I feel the anxiety rising when I see an unknown number on display.

"Hello?"

"Alane Smith?" A voice I don't know asks. Aaron steps closer to me.

"Yes," my shaky voice answers.

"It's Doctor Parks. Your mother has been brought to the

Health Center after she lost consciousness at the grocery store. I'm currently running some exams, so I don't have to send her to the hospital, but I would like you to come down, if possible."

"Of... of course, Doctor Parks. I'll be right there. Tell my mother I'm on my way."

"I'll drive you." Aaron takes my hand.

"We need to finish our conversation, Aar. It's important."

Kissing me on the cheeks, he smiles at me the way he used to.

"Later. First, your mom, then we'll talk."

When we arrive at the Health Center, Mrs. Gritt is here with Luke and Barnabas. I don't take the time to ask them why they're here before running to a nurse to get more details.

My mother is having a full exam done, and for the moment, there is nothing to tell me except that she lost consciousness at the store, and the Gritts found her in the chocolate aisle. They tried to reach Aaron, who had left his phone in his car, and Luke had tried to call me, but it seemed we were so busy I didn't even hear my phone.

"She was supposed to be at the Harbors, not shopping at the grocery store. I don't get it," I say to myself. Mrs. Gritt comes closer to me and wraps me in her arms.

"That's the problem with early dementia, Alane. They forget what they are supposed to do. They get confused."

"How do you know?"

"The whole town knows. Mrs. Harbor can't keep her lips sealed. Don't worry, honey. Her losing consciousness is a little concerning, unless it's because she didn't eat."

Oh, how I've missed this woman. She was more of a mother to me than my own. She taught me so much.

When Aunt Clarisse died after years of battling cancer, I thought a lot about Mrs. Gritt, wondering how she was doing, and feeling guilty for keeping her grandson away from her. That's when I learned Aaron just had a second kid. That's when I decided once again that I couldn't ruin his perfect life. That's the last time I thought of Aaron's mom.

"I'm sorry I never reached out."

"It's okay, you had other fish to fry." She smiles, lovingly.

"It's good to see you."

"You too, Mrs. Gritt. You haven't aged a day."

"You're lying, Alane, but it's okay. You should see Ridge though, he hasn't changed. Those Gritt genes are strong." I feel uncomfortable speaking about the Gritt's genes, knowing the secret I bear. I need to finish the conversation I started with Aaron.

"Mom?" I freeze, hearing Adam's voice coming from the corridor.

"I'm sorry," is all I can mumble to Mrs. Gritt before my world collapses. Adam strides in, more handsome than ever; looking like his dad certainly did eighteen years ago.

"Adam, what are you doing here?"

"I came to surprise you, and when I arrived in town, I heard at the gas station that a Mrs. Smith had collapsed at the grocery store. I was afraid it was you, so I asked where they brought her, and I came as fast as I could." He hugs me tight. I'm well aware of the silence that's fallen behind me. Once Adam steps back, I hear someone swearing, while another person is sobbing.

· · ·

"Fuck, Aaron, that kid is your doppelganger," Barnabas says, realizing a little too late what he just alleged. "Oh shit! Alane, what the fuck?" He gasps. I turn to find Aaron teetering between anger and confusion.

"He's twenty-six?" His voice is matter of fact, certainly computing all the crumbs I gave about Adam since we found each other again. I nod.

"Almost twenty-seven," I mumble between my teeth.

"I guess this conversation can't wait any longer, Alane, right?" I shake my head; mortified he learned the truth this way. I owed him more than this small hospital encounter. I owed him more than this fait accompli.

"Adam, I'm sorry." I step closer to my puzzled son, reach my hand to his shoulder to soothe him.

"What's going on?" Adam asks, looking for confirmation of what I'm certain he already knows. His livid-blue eyes shows his understanding of the situation. I can't look at Luke or Mrs. Gritt. I know I owe them an explanation too, but at the moment, I have to focus on my son and Aaron.

"Adam," I say, stepping away so that the two men can face each other without me in between them.

"This is Aaron. Your biological father."

NOW – AARON

 acophony.
Discord.
A mess.

That's what I'm surrounded with while Luke, Barnabas, Adam and my mother are screaming at each other.

Oh, the kid is a Gritt alright.

He has passion and protects his own fiercely.

I can see he's angry at his mother – it's not hard to see the mirror image of my own feelings,, but right now, he won't let my family— his family— blame her.

He's protecting her.

His body is in front of her, while she's disappearing behind him. It's not that she's hiding, but guilt and fear are eating her alive. Shaking, she's looking for an exit, for an escape, and as much as I'm infuriated with Alane, I can't let her disappear or run away. I need to save her. I need to hear her words and understand what the fuck she was thinking, keeping this secret from me, from my family, from everybody.

Because we all knew she had a son, but nobody knew he was mine. When I see Adam ready to punch Barn, I step in.

"Enough!" My voice rises above all. "Alane and I are going to discuss this as fucking adults. Luke, go fuck your boyfriend if you need to release some anger. Barn, do what the hell you need to do. Mom, call Dad and tell him to come and discuss this all with him. As for you, Adam, stay here and wait for news on your grandmother." I turn to Alane, who is sitting on the floor, hiding her head in her hands. "Al, let's go outside." I take her by the elbow and pull her to her feet. She can barely walk.

"Mom? Are you okay?" Adam comes closer.

I send him a pointed look for him to stay where he is, but he passes by me and takes his mother in his arms.

"Do you need me to come with you, Mom?" I let Alane go and walk away a few steps to give them some privacy.

It's evident I'm not part of whatever they have together.

It hurts but I won't let my emotions run the show until I have all the facts.

I'm angry, frustrated, disappointed and wounded, but I need her to tell me what happened before letting it all out. I need to process, and for that, I need all the details.

"I'm fine, sweetie. Let me speak to Aaron, and then I'll explain it all to you. I'm sorry, Adam, that's not the way I wanted you to find out who your father is." He shrugs. The fucking kid shrugs as if knowing me wasn't important.

"It's okay, Mom. I kind of always wondered why we never came to see your parents and realized later in life something must have happened here." He kisses the top of her head and walks back next to my mother, who has tears in her eyes.

She pats his leg when he sits back down next to her.

Sighing, Alane turns to me. "I'm sorry, Aar. I..." I turn my head towards the exit not wanting to hear her apology. Not here, not yet.

"Let's go out and talk." I walk towards the entrance and stop, waiting for her at the door. She follows; her legs wobbling, and all the bravado gained in the last weeks gone from her body.

The Alane before me is the shell of the Alane I reconnected with, the one who was blossoming around me, the one I care so much about. "Sweets, come on." I hurry her, trying to sweeten it with the only nickname I always called her.

Once outside, we find a bench to sit on. There is a nervous tension between us. Alane removes the ties from her tiny ponytail and fidgets with the elastics on her wrists. I wait. I sure as hell won't be the one to start this conversation. First of all, because what I would say would destroy her, and secondly, because she had twenty-six years to prepare her speech. I'm pretty sure she came to a conclusion as to what to tell me the day she would.

"So…" She closes her eyes, "We have a son…" She lets her words hang between us.

"Look at me." She shakes her head. "Look. At. Me." When she finally does, her brown eyes are filled with tears of regret. Under any other circumstances, I would reach over to take her in my arms, comfort her, kiss her, but not today, not now, maybe never again.

"How? We never…"

"Yeah, well… It clearly happened nonetheless." Bringing my fingers to the bridge of my nose, I breathe in deeply, trying to calm myself.

"I'm going to need more than elusive answers, Alane,

because I'm trying to keep cool, I'm trying to give you the opportunity to explain yourself, but knowing you sat on such a huge secret for so long is hard to swallow. Very fucking hard to swallow. Why didn't you ever tell me?"

"Seriously, Aaron?" she grumbles "Remember us at seventeen and eighteen. Would you have believed me, knowing we never had sex? My parents clearly didn't believe me; even my aunt had trouble believing me. I had to tell her all we did, all we experienced to pinpoint the moment Adam was conceived. You want to know when? When you came on my pussy instead of my belly while I was fingering myself. Is that enough details? I realized I was pregnant after you were gone. I had no way to contact you. And after you broke my heart and told me I wasn't enough, I wasn't the one you wanted to spend your life with. What was I supposed to do? Chain you to me by obligation? Make you come back? You had the life you wanted. You followed your dream. I got pregnant. Became a teacher. End of story." She shrugs.

"End of story? That's all you have to say? So, you did that for me? You didn't even give me a choice?"

Is she delusional?

Should I feel guilty that I didn't know we had a son.

I still don't understand how it happened, for fuck's sake. She left soon after me and never came back. I thought, well, we all thought, she went to that hockey prep school. That's what her parents said. My mother asked about her over the years, and the Smiths never said anything except she was married and had a son. I just assumed she had forgotten about me; how could I have known she was hiding a son who was mine.

"Did you give me a choice when you left for Seattle, leaving me behind? Did you allow me to decide on our future? Were you the one heartbroken when you were kissing Jess in Vancouver?" I gulp, jerking my head back.

"How do you know?"

"Funny story, I was maybe two or three months pregnant when my aunt had a book signing in Vancouver. I went with her, and I was wondering if I should drive to Seattle, try to find you to tell you, when I saw you kissing another girl while I was still pining over you. So then what? Should I have interrupted your make-out session in the hotel lobby and announce that you were going to be a dad?"

"Twenty-six years, Alane! What about when he was born?"

She scoffs, "You mean when I called wherever you were living, and Jess answered telling me you were engaged? Great timing, too. Don't tell me I should have told you. I know that, Aaron. I fucking know it. I tried so many times, but something always happened, and after a while, I thought I would never see you again, and I did everything not to see you again. Adam had Mark anyway. He had a father. It didn't matter. We were nothing more than a sad memory. You didn't matter anymore."

Bile comes up my throat, but I refuse to give in. Adam had Mark. He had a father. He still does. For the thirty seconds I saw the kid, he seems like a good one. I don't know who this Mark is for shit, but it seems he did a good job raising my son.

"And since you were back in town?"

Tears begin to fill her eyes again. The anger of a few minutes ago being replaced by guilt.

"The first time I spoke about Adam's father, you stopped me to speak about your ex-wife, then I had an anxiety attack at the rink, and today my phone rang. I tried Aaron. I fucking tried." She sobs, but I can't ease her. She can put it any way she wants, blame me for leaving, for meeting someone else, for getting engaged, I had the right to know. She deprived me of my own son. I stand to put distance between us, and without saying a word, I leave her crying on the bench, wanting her to hurt as much as I'm hurting.

Walking back inside the Health Center, I want to be sure my father's here for my mother. I find her with my dad, having a civil discussion with Adam. As soon as they see me though, they stop talking. Both my parents look at me with a smile on their face, Adam seems suspicious of my intentions.

"I'm going to check on Alane." My mother stands up.

"I'll come with you." My dad follows her. I stand alone, wondering if I should approach Adam or just leave. Not wanting to lose an opportunity to talk to him, despite my anger with his mother, I sit next to this son I don't know, my legs spread, my elbows resting on my knees, and my hands joined by the tips of each finger. It's a pose I find myself in a lot when I think things over.

Glancing over, I realize he sits in the exact same position. For a reason I can't really understand, it makes me smile, my heart filled with pride. He looks like me, he reacts like me, and he has some of my expressions. The only thing different is his hair. It's darker than mine ever was.

"Is my mom okay?" He sits up straight like a good student would.

"As much as she can be. You're going to have to take care of her because I'm not sure I can right now."

"I get it." His shoulder slumps.

"So... um... What do you do?"

He lights up a little. "I write sci-fi graphic-novels, you?" Of course, he's an artist. Luke is going to love that.

"I'm a chef."

"Cool."

"Yeah... my son, I mean... my other son, loves sci-fi and graphic novels." He perks up.

"I have siblings?"

"Yeah... A sister who's seventeen, and a brother who's fifteen. You also have two uncles and an aunt. You've met Luke, the tatted guy with the beard, and Barn, the younger one who was here, he's about seven years older than you. Salomé is thirty-five, so, nine years older than you."

"Wow, until a few hours ago, I had Mom, Dad and Aunt Clarisse. Neither of my... parents had siblings, so that's new." He laughs uncomfortably.

My eyes stay on him, trying to reconcile the fact that I'm not the one he calls Dad. He might look like me but is far from being mine. Once his laugh dies, he turns towards me and looking his resolute eyes into mine.

"She's not a bad person, you know. My mom? She's the best, in fact. She gave me everything. Even when she divorced Mark, she let me have a relationship with him. I always knew he wasn't my biological father. I always knew it was someone from here, but I never looked for you either. I never asked, so I guess she thought she was protecting me. All I know is that I saw her parents only twice in my life, but she didn't hesitate when her mother's friend called and said she needed help. She knew what she was risking, and she came back. She's not a bad person."

As I feel my chest tightening from his honesty, I see my mother approaching, holding Alane by the shoulders.

Bella Gritt is the incarnation of forgiveness.

She's undoubtedly hurt that she missed out on her grandson, but she won't hold a grudge. What's done is done for her, and it wouldn't make anything different to hold on to the past.

I know her speech by heart. Adam stands up and runs to his mom, taking her in his arms.

My mother approaches me slowly, her eyes on Adam.

"I told her we'll sit together in the coming days, and she can tell me the whole story. I don't want to hear it from you. I know it hurts, Aaron, but you'll get over it. You have a chance to build a relationship with that man, and if you reject his mother, he will never contact you. Be smart." She pats my cheek. "Now, your father is waiting for me outside, we're going home, hoping Luke didn't destroy the whole house. You need to talk to your children. We need to tell Salomé as well. Take some time and think about it. I highly recommend you leave now, and let Adam take care of his mother. It's not your place to be here." My mother is right, but again, when isn't she? Her hippie ways might get on my nerves most of the time, but there is nobody with more wisdom than her.

Turning my back to them, I send one last glance over my shoulder to the life that could have been mine, wondering if I really want to be part of theirs now.

28

NOW - ALANE

"*D*idn't I tell you it would end up the same way as last time?" *Dear God, please give me the strength to forgive those who trespass against me.*

"You should know better than to try to be a Gritt. Seriously, you were never a good match." *Lead me not into temptation but deliver me from evil.*

"I mean, you were that desperate to get him to marry you that you had a kid? Seriously. I thought you were a virgin when you left for your bullshit hockey camp. And almost thirty years later, tadaaaa, you bring a son into the picture after Aaron already rejected you once?" *Forgive me my trespassing.*

"Patricia, shut the fuck up. Seriously! For once, don't speak. Don't be the bitch who wanted my boyfriend so much that she broke us up. Don't be the harpy sharing my private issues with your family, the staff or the whole freaking town or the vixen trying to fuck any Gritt male. Just let me be. I didn't ask for your opinion, and I'm fine by myself. Fuck off."

"Well, I'm sorry, but Aaron asked me here to comfort him. He didn't ask you, but me, so I'm not the one leaving!"

"Patricia, if you don't let me pass, I swear to God, I will publish a list of all the married men you've slept with in this town, and you will be forced to run away. I will also make a list of all the students you've harassed trying to get their father's in bed, and finally, I will knock your teeth out. Let. Me. Pass." I shove her slightly so I can make my way to the restaurant, trying not to make a scene in front of the *Gritt Your Plate*'s staff. I need to talk to Aaron. I won't leave without saying goodbye.

My mother has been admitted to an Alzheimer's residence that my ex found in Phoenix, and even if my relationship with him is done, even if I lost most of my friends.

I've built my life there for years, and my son lives there too, so it's time to go home. I spoke with the principal of the school where I taught for years, and he'll be happy to have me back. I'm taking my mother with me, so I won't feel guilty leaving her behind, but she'd be glad to never have to see me again. Now that her condition has worsened, she's talking to me about the disappointment and embarrassment I was when I got pregnant, as if I was her confidant.

It's not sitting well with me, but it's nothing new.

Adam doesn't know what he wants to do.

He spent some time with the Gritts, but I'm not sure if he spent that time with Aaron, or just Bella and Ridge.

I'm not touching this with a ten-foot pole.

He's an adult, and I won't get between him and Aaron. I'm here today because Aaron helped me find myself again, and even if I'm flying twenty-five hundred miles away, I owe him one last truth. I'm going to miss him, and I'm genuinely sorry for never telling him who he was to Adam.

We had our fun, but if he can't forgive me, then so be it.

And if he actually asked Patricia to console him, then all that I knew about him was wrong, and he's not half the man I thought he was.

"I'm sorry, ma'am, the restaurant is not open yet." A young waiter stops me on my mission.

"I know. I just need to speak to Mr. Gritt. I'll be quick. Can you please tell me where I can find him?"

"Oh, well..." He seems constipated, and I'm not sure if it's because he doesn't know where Aaron is or if it's because he's scared to death of his boss. "Let me see what I can do, Chef Gritt has company, and I'm not sure we can bother him. May I ask your name?"

"Alane Smith." But that might not grant me access. "Just tell him it's important." The waiter disappears behind the kitchen doors, and I take a few minutes to enjoy my surroundings. I was too nervous the first time I came here to really look around, and the darkness of the night didn't do it justice.

The restaurant is located in a twenty-foot high greenhouse, surrounded by plants with outdoor light coming from everywhere. Huge dark tubular heating ducts seem to fall from the sky with thousands of string-lights hanging from them, giving it the impression of being in an enchanted forest about to taste the best meal you'll ever have. The kitchen sits back, closed by two industrial doors that allow Aaron the privacy he needs. It's a beautiful place, and it shows me again that I can't regret keeping Adam as a secret.

He would have never been the man he is today if we had gotten married after knowing I was pregnant. Because the Aaron I know, would have done what was right. He would have found a job and married me. He would have renounced his dream for Adam and me.

. . .

"I demand to see Chef Aaron," Patricia's annoying voice beams behind me. As my nails dig into my palms, I try to remember the names of some of her conquests for the list I promised her I'd write. "Mrs. Smith is not welcome here; you should know that." She continues huffing.

I'm about to punch her in the throat when Aaron appears, followed by his whole family. When I say the whole family, I mean, his parents, Luke, Barn, Salomé and Dex. Thank God his kids are at school and Adam's back on his book tour in New York. He'll be back in two days, and we'll fly together from Burlington. I didn't need the whole tribe there for my apology, but if it's what I have to do, that's what I'll do.

"What are you doing here?" Aaron snarls, looking at me.

"Look, Aar, I'm sorry. I just needed to..."

"I'm not talking to you, Alane." Turning his attention fully to Patricia, he says, "Get the fuck out!"

"But, Aaron, you need me to help you deal with what she's putting you through." Patricia is pointing at me with her red-manicured nail. I want to shove it up her ass. Before I do so, Salomé barks like a seal. I widen my eyes in shock at the same instant as Luke, Barnabas, Dex and Mr. and Mrs. Gritt laugh, clearly all of them are aware of the noises Patricia makes when she comes.

"Patricia," Aaron scowls, "you and I, or Barnabas and you, will never happen. And please don't think of getting anywhere with Adam, Lawson or my Dad. It's pathetic and borderline psychotic. Just leave us alone."

"But, I love you. All I ever did was for you."

"I thought you loved me," Barnabas mocks her.

"Or me," Luke adds.

"Shit, should I be upset you never loved me," Mr. Gritt snickers.

I didn't know the Gritts could be so nasty, but I don't feel sorry for Patricia.

I don't care.

She leaves angry, certainly already plotting her revenge, but I'm pretty sure this time, her brother won't be able to save her reputation at the school.

Some of Aaron's staff members are parents of students, and they seemed happy that the principal has been put in her place. The gossip mill is certainly already going strong, seeing as how they all have their faces on their phones. Aaron clears his throat, and his employees scatter around the restaurant.

Feeling my bravery leaving me, I retreat well aware of the fourteen eyes scrutinizing me.

"I'm sorry, I didn't want to interrupt a family lunch. I'll come back later," I mutter timidly.

"Let me walk you out, Captain. Babe, come with us?" Luke and Dex walk my way.

I glance towards Aaron, but he's already showing me his back, not ready to hear what I came to say. Barnabas winks and shrugs, Mr. and Mrs. Gritt smile softly, and Salomé just stares, as she always did around me.

I sigh, my attempt at saying goodbye and apologizing having failed, I have no other option than to try again tomorrow, if I have the time to.

Once outside, I make my way to my car, not expecting Luke to talk to me. I don't deserve it, after all. He falls into step with me, a smirk on his face.

"Adam is a good kid," Luke says with a smile in his voice.

"He is. Did you talk to him?" I smile.

"Briefly. We ran into him in town and went for coffee." He pauses briefly. "You could have told me, Captain. Maybe you couldn't say anything when we were kids, but you could have told me now." I don't hear reproach in his voice, only facts. He's right, I could have, but I didn't. I stare off into nothing; sadly thinking of the trajectory my story with Aaron has taken. "I wanted to tell Aaron first. Then I would have told Adam. Everything between Aaron and I went too fast and too far since we saw each other again. I don't even know what we had. Maybe we tried to revive too much of what we were and didn't accept who we had become. We skipped steps, fucked hard, found closure without resolution. We both fucked up in our story, I can't carry all the blame." He nods in understanding, walking beside me. Bringing Dex's hand to his mouth, he kisses his boyfriend's knuckles.

"I'm proud of you for not trying to fix it, babe," he tells his beau.

"It was hard, beardy, but I was sure you would have gotten crazy on my ass if I did." Dex looks at him with adoration.

"And since when is that a problem?" Luke chuckles before Dex shoves him with his shoulder, and with a firm look but a sneer on his lips. Fuck, these two are adorable. That's what I almost had with Aaron, what I never got with Mark, what I wish I had for forever. I'm filled with profound melancholy at the idea of leaving Aaron behind and never seeing Luke ever again.

"I'm going back to Phoenix in two days. I came to say goodbye and apologize. I know it's hard to forgive me, but I would prefer not to wait another twenty-five plus years to talk to you again. Maybe I can visit you in LA, or we can meet in Vegas? Anyway, send me a text when you're on the west coast, okay?" Luke is studying me under his lashes like he used to when he was analyzing my every movement on the ice before I was Aaron's girlfriend.

"Do you love him?" he jerks his head in the restaurant's direction.

"I don't think I ever stopped." Luke raises an eyebrow, waiting for me to go on. Dex seems bored out of his mind, waiting patiently for me to pour my heart out. "I could never forget him. When I was looking for peace, he was always my favorite safe haven, still is. He's the one I never got over, and never will, no matter how long it's been."

"He's going to have a hard time forgiving you. You know that, right? I know I would." Luke is nodding, agreeing with Dex.

"I know," I exclaim. "But would he be where is today if he had known? Would he have Hailey and Lawson? Would we still be together? We'll never know.

Nevertheless, I can't regret anything, and he shouldn't either. Luke, I hope you are able to become close with Adam. You're right, he's a good person, and he has your talent for drawing. Once you get to know him, you'll see he's a Gritt through and through. As for Aaron, I'll always love him, but I can't force him to love me or to want me. That's what put us in this whole situation. I'll try to come by tomorrow, but I have to pack my mother's house and get her ready to go to Phoenix, which she doesn't want to do. She's been difficult, and I can't do it alone. Adam said he would help. My ex said he would be there for me. I know it will trigger my anxiety. I can't stay here. I never could without him. I'll try to reach out again, but if I have no time, it means it wasn't meant to be. Maybe we were never meant to end up together."

"Or maybe you will. You need to have faith, Alane," Dex adds, smiling at me. "You need to have faith."

29

NOW - AARON

*N*ostrils flaring, blade in hand, I dice the shit out of an onion after having taken the knife out of the assistant cook's hand. The idiot has no idea what he's doing.

"It's not difficult, for fuck's sake. Cut off the top and discard, slice onion in half vertically, peel off the skin, hold the root and leave it intact while you cut vertical slices, then chop horizontally, discarding the root end. Didn't they teach you anything at school, or the diner you worked at before?"

I throw the knife into the sink, startling half of the staff.

"Is his wife back?" someone whispers behind me.

My vision gets clouded.

My pulse races.

"Whoever said that will be fired. Now go back to work and shut the fuck up!" I storm out of the kitchen and go sit in my office like I've done over the past month now, to deal with paperwork, and try to focus on anything but the picture of Adam's arrival at the Health Center.

His smile, livid-blue eyes, stature, facial traits and expressions; Adam is a carbon copy of me. Totally freaks me out. My mother can't stop going on about it and how he reminds her of me when I was his age. Which is bullshit because when I turned twenty-seven, Jess was pregnant with Hailey. I wasn't an up and coming author enjoying my newfound celebrity status. I was a neurotic father-to-be, working hard to put money aside for financial security and dreaming of opening my restaurant one day. I barely had time to see my wife, and she was letting me know every time she could, that my behavior had to change. I was doing my best to please her, run the Harbor diner and help my parents. I wasn't FaceTiming with my brand-new family, getting to know them or traveling to LA to spend time with my cool uncle. The only one Adam seemed to ignore, is me. Not that I tried to reach out, but seeing how he speaks to my parents once a week and texts Barn and Lawson regularly, I was hoping he would like to get to know me. Feeling my body tensing again, the migraine I expect daily comes back, announcing the end of my workday.

"Chef Gritt, do you have a minute?" My second-in-command peeks his head through the door, testing the waters for my mood. Rubbing my fingers on my temples, I nod my head for him to come in. "What is it?"

"We need to go over the specials for next week. I know you don't want to be bothered, but it can't wait any longer." I nod, closing my eyes, trying to forget about my migraine.

"But first… I wanted to ask you if you needed to talk to me about Jess or someone else? I mean, we've worked together for a long time, Aaron, and you're not quite yourself."

Jacob and I have indeed been working together for a long time, and he has learned to work around my mood. We're not friends, more colleagues who hang out from time-to-time, but he knows how to deal with me. He's married, has two children, and our girls are friends, or they were before a boy got in the middle. We try not to get involved in their on and off friendship. I send him a pointed look, not in the mood to discuss my private life.

"Okay... But please, whatever is happening, be nice, or at least try to be nicer. Two waiters, the commis and the assistant you yelled at today cried this week, and it takes us all a lot of time afterward to calm them down so they can complete their tasks."

I grunt. "Don't make the staff cry. Noted."

"So, for the specials next week, what do you want to do? I was thinking fish tacos and Chinese chicken salad for lunch and for dinner Lollipop lamb and Prince Edward Island mussels. The recipes are here," he dumps a few papers on my desk, "and I need your approval by tonight at the latest."

"Can't you take charge as if I was traveling?" He shakes his head.

"Oh no. Whatever is happening, you're here, so you're in charge. Seeing how anything can trigger your temper, I'm not taking responsibility and having you breathe fire down my neck afterward, or firing me because you were not in the mood to eat freaking mussels."

Rubbing my palms in my eyes, I sigh. "Give me a minute, and I'll look over it. I'm sorry. I just have a lot on my mind and not much patience these days."

"You don't say." He laughs. "It's alright, just try not to be such a dick all the time, or we won't have any staff left soon."

"I know. I'm sorry. I just..."

"Have a lot on your mind. Got it, boss. As for your 'new' son," he mimics the quote to the word son, "text him, and tell him you want to talk to him. Clear this shit up, and you'll see your migraines will disappear. Doctor's order." I smile at my giant of a sous-chef, towering above me. The gossip mill of

Springs Falls has indeed been turning night and day, so I'm not surprised Jacob knows what's on my mind.

"The recipes look good. I trust you."

He nods. "Great, so I'll let you brood or whatever you were doing when I interrupted you, and I'll catch you later." As he opens the door, I stop him.

"Thank you, Jacob. I guess I'll follow your advice." Smiling, my sous-chef walks back toward the kitchen.

"Margaret, bring some ibuprofen and a glass of water to the boss, and do not get on his nerves. Let's move, people! We're opening in one hour!"

After swallowing the ibuprofen, the waiter provided, I reach for my phone. My mother made sure to send me Adam's phone number as soon as he gave it to her. Shaking, my fingers hover above the screen, trying to find the resolve and the courage to start a semblance of a relationship with my son. Breathing in, I bring up his number and call.

"Hello?"

"Hey, Adam, It's Aaron. How are you?"

"I'm fine. I was, in fact, wanting to talk to you about something."

"Yeah?" Hearing so warms my heart. The idea that he would come to me for anything like a son would, makes me happy.

"I'm sorry I didn't reach out to you. I needed a little time to process."

"Yeah. Bella and Mom told me so. Look, I'm just pulling up to the farm. Can we meet tonight?"

"Oh, you're in town. For how long?"

"Don't know yet. I'm not sure it's up to me to invite you for supper, but from what I saw, Bella wouldn't mind."

I chuckle. "No, she wouldn't mind having me for supper. Just tell her I'll be there, and I'll send Lawson and Hailey beforehand. I know you were texting with Law, and I'm sure he'll be happy to officially meet you."

We hang up with the agreement I'll be at my parents in the next two hours once I'm sure Jacob has it all under control.

It's a full house at the farm tonight. I wasn't aware that Luke and Dex were, once again, back in town. As busy as my brother claimed to be for years, he sure finds time to be back much more than he used to.

At this point, they should buy something in the area.

Lawson freaked out when he came face to face with Adam, he couldn't believe his half-brother is the same guy as his favorite graphic novelist. He brought his collection over and had Adam sign anything that he ever drew that Law owns.

It was cute to see my fifteen-year-old nerd so passionate about something. Hailey was more reserved. I had to reassure her our relationship wouldn't change. She was still my favorite sporty girl. Her competitive streak peaked, and I knew she was ready to beat Adam to the finish line or in the nuts. I'm never sure with Hal.

We're now sitting on the porch after supper. Barnabas is explaining to my parents what he wants to do with the farm, how he sees his future. He's sharing his need for adventure and desire to change things around. If I'm following, he wants to make it more of an adventure resort where guests would be challenged. He still wants to host weddings and even proposed new services for bachelor and bachelorette parties, so Sal will still be able to plan it all. Dex looked over all the legal stuff, as the new lawyer of the family. Luke checked the business plan. It's a good plan.

"What about Aaron's restaurant? I mean, don't you have a part of the farm to cultivate the vegetable for *Gritt Your Plate?*"

We all turn to look at Adam. I'm confused by his knowledge of what's happening at the family farm and his concern for my business. The look he sends me reminds me of Alane. He does care. Leaning back in my seat, I go over the myriad of emotions swirling in my brain. I'm surprised, flattered, touched, impressed, pleased, but there is still anger lingering around, even if this anger is not aimed at Adam. When I get out of my head, I now see that they're all looking at me, certainly waiting for my answer.

I hear Luke's laugh and Dex reprimanding him. Turning my attention to Adam, I clear my throat to push away all that I feel and look somewhat normal in front of my family.

"We already spoke about it. I'm fine with just a plot, and I'll pay Barn to take care of it, or I'll hire someone else." I shrug. It doesn't matter to me. Nothing else matters. The conversation picks up back around me, and I slip away again, thinking of all the moments I missed with this kid. How he calls another man Dad, how I wasn't there for any of his firsts. No first smile, words, steps, schooldays, girlfriend, heartbreak, no graduation, puberty, fight, or complications. I had no words to say about anything.

"I know it's not easy," Adam says, offering me a glass of red wine. Looking around, I see Salomé a few steps away, always ready to jump down someone's throat if I need help. Focusing back on Adam, I raise one eyebrow, trying to understand what he means. He sits next to me, a glass of whiskey in his hand. Another great reminder, I wasn't there for his first drink...

"Dex said you like red wine when you're brooding on the porch. Are you in a brooding mood right now?"

"Kind of." I tilt my head, still not sure how to bridge the gap with him, but I don't need to. Of course, Alane's son would know how to talk to me. He would know not to let me drown in my thoughts and to get my head out of my ass.

"I've asked Mom a lot of questions about you in the past month, and she answered as best she could, but there was a lot she didn't know, and I'm curious. I hope it's okay that I'm curious?"

"Of course." I take a sip of my wine.

"She, Mom, she was different here. She was calm, well calmer. She wasn't obsessing with my safety. She wasn't losing herself in the infinity of what-ifs that trigger her panic attacks. Well, she was at the beginning, and then she wasn't. I know you two were seeing each other."

I go to stop him, but he continues, "She didn't tell me. Luke did. I know it's a fucked-up situation. I wasn't happy myself to learn the truth only now, but I know she didn't do it to punish you or me. She did it because she truly believed she was doing the best thing for both of us. I love Mark. I'm sorry if this is hurting you, but I truly love him. He's been a great father to me. He wasn't always a good husband to Mom, but I also know she wasn't always good to him either. She was absent a lot. Not physically. But mentally, she wasn't there. She would be seated with us, he would talk about his day, and she wouldn't be there. Now that I know your story, I'm pretty sure she was wondering what if. She forgave you for breaking her heart. You're going to have to find a way to forgive her because if I get married one day or if I have kids, I would really like to have you around, to get to know you, but I won't if you can't be in the same room as Mom. Because I'll tell you the same thing I told Mark when they divorced, if I have to choose between Mom and you, I'll choose her, always."

Drawing back, I look at Adam. Not as my doppelganger or Alane's kid, but as the man he is. I would be fucking lucky to have him in my life, to be, maybe not his father, but I don't know, his friend. And I for sure want him around for Law and Hal.

"Fuck, you're a great kid."

"Not a kid anymore, but thanks." He winks. He's more outgoing than I am. Nicer too. Once again, we're sitting in the same position, ankle resting on one knee and hand relaxing on the other. Setting my glass of wine aside, I reach for his glass and sniff it, recognizing the scotch my father serves only to me and to Dex. Not even Luke is allowed to drink it. Certainly not Barn, never to Barn. Dad brought out the best for Adam.

"That's a clear indication you're becoming a favorite of Dad's," I say, tilting his glass. "Now, I'm going to fix myself one of those, and then, you're going to tell me everything I missed over the last twenty-six years. It's going to take all night, but I don't give a shit. The only way I can get over all this is to dive right in."

"Let's dive in then."

Standing up, I feel warm, fuzzy and happy to have the opportunity to know this kid and I then realize that my migraine is gone entirely.

Let's dive in indeed.

30

NOW – ALANE

When my mother said she'd die being so far away from my father, I didn't think she literally would.

Since moving back to Phoenix three months ago, she's been deteriorating faster than I could ever imagine. I spoke numerous times with her doctors, wondering what could be done, but it seems there is nothing we can do. She doesn't want to live, and her mind is shutting down her body, one organ after another. Mark has been more present than he ever was during our marriage, mostly because Adam, not being able to be there because of previous commitments in New York, asked him to keep an eye on me.

They both think I'm worried about my mother. My loss of weight, the distance I put between us, and my fatigue are great indicators to them I'm taking my mother is slipping away to heart. They're not wrong, but worry isn't my main problem.

Overthinking my past and trying to convince myself I did the right thing are what's suffocating me. Every breath I take reminds me of Aaron's face when he figured out whom Adam was. Every time I try to close my eyes, I hear the screams of anger from the Gritts.

Every step I take feels like a betrayal.

Add to that a mother blaming me for even being born, a son walking away from me because he has a whole new family to discover, an ex-husband pissed at me for hiding the truth from everybody, a past boyfriend refusing to talk to me before I left, and I'm the shell of myself again.

I'm a zombie with nobody to talk to, nobody on my side, and nobody else to blame but myself. Aaron was right; I was delusional thinking that having him discover the truth would have had a different conclusion than me ending up alone.

Who cares that I gave Adam the same middle name as Aaron? Who cares about my intentions of letting him have the life he deserved? Who cares that keeping Adam from him was my way of loving Aaron and proving it? I was a fool to think it mattered, but I'm even more a fool to think he would care.

"Would you be interested in spending a night at the club, for old time's sake?"

I forgot I was having my bi-weekly coffee with Mark. He's handsome. I wouldn't have spent almost twenty years with him if I didn't find him attractive. His dark features and shiny disposition are the polar opposite of Aaron's. "Are you not missing it? I mean, I miss you. Nobody compares to you and the chemistry we used to have."

Coming back to my senses I realize I missed all the cues of Mark wanting me. He's on my side of the table, his body close to mine, and his arm around my shoulders. He smells good, he looks suave, he feels familiar, but he's not who I want.

"Mark," I push his arm away, "you know that ship has sailed."

He leans away, his eyes trying to avoid mine. "In a way, it's sad that we never had a chance."

"That's not true, Mark. I loved who we were together. I loved what we did. You taught me so much. I became me because of you." I pat his hands.

"You loved who we were together, but you always loved him." Mark is a lot of things but jealous is not in his vocabulary. More than anything, I believe he understands. He always did. We own each other's bodies, but never one another's soul. I always thought it was an unspoken understanding. We never discussed our pasts; we were two broken hearts trying to find comfort in one another. Maybe he did find more comfort in me than I did in him. He kisses my cheek.

"Thank you for keeping me in Adam's life. I know the last few months haven't been easy on you. Why don't you call him?"

"Adam?"

"No silly, Aaron."

"I thought you were pissed at me for keeping a secret about who Adam's father was?"

Mark gives me the saddest smile in the universe. "Alane, I'm not pissed. I'm worried. Adam told me he's never seen you happier than when you were up there. You've been sad since you came back. Are you going to wait around for him forever?"

"He doesn't want to talk to me, Mark. What can I do?"

"The Alane I met didn't wait for me to talk to her to let me know what she was expecting..."

"What are you talking about? You're the one who talked to me first."

Mark laughs. "Not before you eye fucked me for a while,

and I was sure you'd end up in my bed. It still took me one year, but shit if I cared that you had a kid or was inexperienced. You were all I thought about for months. You owned my balls the first time you served me a drink. I used to daydream of you fucking others. I still do." His smile is sad and contagious.

"I'm sorry if I hurt you." I wince, thinking I haven't been the best version of me for a while.

"You didn't. Sometimes it lasts, sometimes it doesn't. We had a great run, and I would like to propose a friendship."

"Why after all this time? We divorced years ago."

"Because you're the only one who knows me? I don't know. I need you, and I know you need a friend too."

"And let me guess, if I find a guy who agrees on a threesome, you should be on speed dial." I tease him. He brings his hand to my hair and wraps my ponytail around, like he used to before kissing me.

"Shit, if it was possible, I would be the first one at your door. I would love to be your friend with benefits, but you already found the guy, you just need him to realize it. He would be a fool to let you get away again. If he's a fool and you need your adventurous life back, you know where to find me, right?" He kisses me at the corner of my lips, but it's more sensual than his last kiss. It's a foreplay kiss. I push him away gently.

"Mark..." I know his body more than anyone else, and the heat coming from him is not innocent. We can't go there. Not again, not ever.

"I know. I need to go, or I'll fuck you here for all to see. Let your mom die. She always broke your spirit. Get your wings back. All I ever wanted was you to be free and happy. Go get him."

"I love you, Mark." He stands up and kisses my forehead.

"I know, but you love him more. Take care of yourself Alane."

Alone in a coffee shop, I come to the realization that my life is nowhere near where I thought it would be, but it wouldn't matter that much if I was in Aaron's arms.

Mark is right, I need to go get him. I tried to walk away, and my world crumbled. Dex told me to have faith, but I also know I need to help fate a little. Hiding in Arizona is not fighting for Aaron. If I hadn't hid the first time, our lives would have been different. It's easy to tell myself I did the right thing, but I also deprived us from each other. I didn't fight enough. Neither did he. We might have just been kids when we fell in love, but we're adults now, and I know I won't find what I felt with Aaron with anyone else. If there is a chance he still has feelings for me, I owe it to him, and to us, to try.

Hope is a funny thing.

You just need a glimmer of light to feel alive again. Would I have preferred for Aaron to come for me? Absolutely. But I know I gave up too easily for him to do so.

As my phone rings, I wish it were Aaron, knowing I just decided to come back to him. I wish our minds were in sync, our hearts talking to each other even so far away. But it's the hospital my mother was admitted to some weeks ago.

Answering it quickly, I throw some bills on the table and hurry back to her side. It's time to say a last goodbye before both of us find our way back home.

We left our hearts in Springs Falls, and it's more than enough time we get it back.

31

NOW - AARON

When I met Alane, my father told me the story of my grandfather, Joseph Gritt, commonly named JG, and his return from the Korean War without a limb.

My father then was five and remembered vividly the pain Grandpa was in because of what we now know was his phantom limb.

He numbed it for years with alcohol, not understanding what was happening, until the day he drove off the road, drunk. My father was ten and the youngest of five. His older brother was twenty, not old enough to be a man, but too young to be a child, and was sent to Vietnam, but that is another story. For my father, missing my mother in the few months they were separated, was like losing a limb back then. I thought I understood what he meant when I flew to Seattle many years ago. I thought I was hurting from a missing limb.

I thought Alane was my phantom limb, until today.

If I had known that losing her a second time would have hurt so much, I'm not sure I would have fucked her on the table of my restaurant. Said table that I asked the staff to destroy, as I didn't need a reminder of her winking at me every time I pushed through the door of my work. I might not have been sure of what Alane and I had when she was here, but I'm damned certain of what my heart is feeling when she's not around. I'm missing a limb, and it hurts like a bitch.

I've done some research, because what else can I do at night while I can't sleep, and there are two kinds of phantom pain: The one before amputation and the residual limb pain. It seems that if you experienced pain before amputation, you're likely to be in pain afterward, as if the brain holds on to the memory of the pain and can't understand that the limb is now missing, continuing to send pain signals over and over again.

My brain remembers Alane is gone every passing second. I wasn't in pain before that. I was in lust, in anger, maybe in love, but not in pain.

The other reason for pain could be caused by a persistent ache in the remaining part of the limb, triggered by an abnormal growth on damaged nerves. This is my case of phantom pain. Seeing Adam, getting closer to him, only reminds me of my failed relationship with his mother and her walking away.

He's my abnormal growth.

As much as I love getting to know him, it hurts. But, because I'm such a glutton for punishment, I keep doing so. In three months, he has become an essential part of the Gritt family. He draws with Law, helps Dad with the farm, goes out looking for girls or hiking—certainly looking for girls as well —with Barn, cooks with Mom, listens to Hailey's boy drama while playing basketball with her, and speaks continuously about designs and comics with Dex and Luke, who are still in

New York State for unknown reasons. He even could break Salomé's coldness, and baked with her a couple of times, something nobody was allowed to do in that kitchen since I left for Seattle.

As for me, I decided to teach him how to skate. He apparently doesn't have either his mother's or my talent, but trying is half the battle. The other half is balance. That's not a given either. Seriously, if he didn't look like me, and if he hadn't so many mannerisms reminding me of his mother, I would doubt he was our son based on his ability to skate. Adam is an excellent subject for whomever wants to write a Ph.D. thesis on the innate or acquired aptitudes of ice-skating and whether athletic performances are determined by genetics.

"What are you doing?" The sweet yet harsh voice of my sister beams in the dark.

"What does it look like I'm doing? Drinking on my porch," I answer in an unsympathetic tone, not willing to deal with the infinite reproach my sister will shed my way for her failed business or love life and anything else she has become.

"Vodka, huh?" I roll my eyes in exasperation. My siblings have this stupid theory that I drink wine when I'm brooding, scotch when I'm happy, and vodka when I'm ready to throw my life through the window and jump off a cliff. I don't drink vodka much. I usually prefer wine.

"I'm fine. Let it be." She sits in the chair next to me, doing the exact opposite of what I just asked her to.

"We used to be close, you know…"

I sigh. "I know, then I left you behind, and you will never forgive me because I was the first one to break your heart. I know your spiel by heart, and any other day I can take it, and take the blame for your failed life, tonight, I can't."

"What I meant is…"

"Grow the fuck up, Sal. You were eight. I was your older brother, and you idolized me. You hated my girlfriend, and you were a fucking brat, but I did everything for you. In one evening, I lost my girlfriend, my friends, and even my siblings refused to say goodbye to me. I got over it, and you don't see me holding that over your heads repeatedly. I'm sorry I left and went away, but I fucking came back, and the only one that was there for me then was Barn. So not tonight, Sal, not tonight."

"You're hurting. I know hurting. All I wanted to say was that I'm here if you need me."

I snort "You're here if I want to talk to you about Alane? That's grand," I scoff loudly.

"Yes, I am. Because I believe knowing how I used to dislike her that if I tell you that you're being an asshole and you should fight for her, you'll listen to me. I talked a lot with Luke, and it helped me understand a lot of things. As you said, I was eight. You were the only brother who talked to me, played with me, and didn't tease me. I thought my big brother was my everything, and she stole you away, but I always thought you would marry her. So, once you were gone, I accepted it. I accepted the fact you left because I thought you'd find your way back to her.

"When you came back with Jess, that's when I realized you were just like every other guy, blinded by pussy and beauty. You were such a terrible match. I couldn't understand how you didn't see it. But I couldn't say anything without being the jealous little sister. That's what you all saw for years. I'm the little sister idolizing her older brother. The fact that Jess was clearly using you just to have children, that she didn't respect you or your career, that you were marrying her when you were still in love with Alane didn't matter. My opinion never mattered.

"I'm stuck between being six and eight years old to all of you. You could get over Barn pissing on your bed, but you will never see the woman I've become. I'm a thirty-five-year-old woman who has loved and has been hurt, so I will tell you this. You, my dear brother, are an asshole. You refused to listen to the woman you always loved because of pride. So, she hurt your ego by giving a father who wasn't you to your child. But didn't she say you were with someone else? Didn't you make her believe you were choosing Seattle over her? Didn't she try to tell you but thought you'd moved on? Which you did. You moved on first. You can't be mad at her for doing the same."

I go to interrupt her, but she doesn't let me.

"Now you're going to tell me she had every opportunity to tell you when she ran into you again. But again, she said she tried. You know she's prone to anxiety. You know she wanted to tell you something before Adam strolled in. You know she's not malicious. Jess was, certainly still is. Did you know she told Alane she was your fiancée after being with you for only six months? Tell me, Aaron, were you really engaged with Jess when Adam was born? Did all these details compute in that empty brain of yours, or are you too hurt to see your ex-wife is surely the one responsible for you not knowing you had a son?"

I look at my sister dumbfounded by the speech she just delivered. She's right, she did grow up, and I didn't see it coming. As for her Alane tirade, she's dead-on once again, I am an asshole.

"How do you know all of this?"

"You all think I don't talk much because I don't like people. I distance myself for a reason. I prefer to observe. You are in love with Alane, you always will be. It's easy to see. Also, Dex and Luke are the biggest gossips I know, and they talk to Alane a lot."

I shrug, feigning indifference. "What did she have to say?" Salomé laughs.

"Do you really want to know? Because from what I heard, you didn't answer her phone calls, blocked her number, and maybe didn't even read her email…"

"I didn't erase it." I reach for my phone in my pocket "It's still in here…" I say, showing her my phone. Salomé takes it from my hand.

"Would you like me to read it to you?" She puts my code in to unlock my device.

"How do you know my code?"

"As I said, I observe, and I remember. It's not that difficult. So, want me to read it to you, or do you have the balls to read it alone?" Throwing the rest of my vodka on my front landing, I nod for her to proceed. She clears her throat before sitting straight.

"Dear Aaron,
I'm sorry I didn't fight for us when we were kids. I'm
sorry I never told you about Adam.
I'm sorry I married someone who wasn't you and gave
our son the family he deserved.
I'm sorry I love you, and I'm sorry I can't be there
with you.
My mother is dying, but as soon as she passes, I'll be

back. I'll fight for you, for us, and I won't let you
walk away this time.
Always yours,
Alane."

Putting my glass down, I wipe the tears forming on the side of my eyes.

It reminds me of the letter I wrote all those years ago, the one I thought she didn't want to read because I let her down, the one I know now she never received because she was already gone.

The letter said how sorry I was to love her so much I had to leave.

I apologized for not having fought for us, not being enough for her, and I was begging her to wait for me because I would fight for her once I was back. She was only doing what I had done.

She had let me have my dream while not following hers, except she had made one mistake.

My dream was a life with her, not becoming a chef.

I stand, deciding like the fool I am that I need to talk to my Sweets. Taking my phone from Salomé's hands, I kiss her forehead.

"Thank you, sis. I'm sorry for never treating you like the woman you are." She smiles at me like she used to as a kid, with all the adoration of the world in her eyes.

"Dex is still my favorite brother now, but you come in a close second."

"Fuck, Dex is my favorite brother too." I laugh, walking away to find the privacy of my bedroom.

"Where are you going?"

"To pour myself a glass of scotch and call the woman I've been madly in love with for thirty years." I don't turn back to see my sister's shy smile, because I know it's there. I know what I need to do to be the brother she once loved so much. I need to finally have the balls to go after whom I really want.

"About time you make that right, bro, about time..." she yells in the night. And she's right, it's just the right time.

My pain is dulling, I found the way to my lost limb.

I'm on the waiting list for a transplant now, just hoping it's not too late.

NOW – ALANE

*a*aron Gritt.

His name illuminates my screen as my phone blares the first notes of *Nothing Compares to You*.

My first thought goes to Adam. He's not supposed to be at the farm, is he?

"Aaron?" I pace my living room, picking up a few things I need to put away.

"Hey, Sweets." His voice is calm, steady, not worried. My heartbeat calms down instantly. That's the effect Aaron has on me, even apart.

"Hey… Is everything alright?"

"You tell me…" Silence falls. If it were about Adam, he would have told me already. I let out the breath I was holding.

"What's up, Aar?" I smile into the phone.

"I was wondering if I could ask you something?"

"Ask away." I sit, beaming at my phone.

"Did you ever receive the letter I sent you when I arrived in Seattle?"

"No... What did it say?"

"More or less what your email said. I asked you to wait for me and told you I'd be back for you. When it came back to me unopened and unread, I thought it was your way of telling me we were over. That's why I jumped into a relationship with Jess. I thought we were over." My throat chokes up by all the different emotions I feel.

"And that's why I didn't tell you about Adam, I thought you'd moved on." We both sigh in unison.

"Listen, I know you said you'd be back here once your mom passes, but I need to see you, to touch you, to talk to you. I can't wait any longer, I want to apologize but in person. I can't pour my heart out over the phone."

"You never could. But I need a little more time. Now that I've decided to come back to Springs Falls, it seems like she's taking her sweet time. Oh my God, I'm sorry, I'm awful for saying that." He chuckles.

"No, you're not, Al. You're anything but awful."

"What am I then, Aar?"

"You're perfect."

I laugh. "You're such a tool."

"Are you alone?"

"Yes. Why?"

"Open the door, Sweets."

"What do you mean?" I walk toward the door and open it, without any doubt that Aaron is behind it. That's the kind of things he did, and seeing as he's standing before me, still does. He's wearing a light blue V-neck T-shirt, which shows a few grey hairs of his chest and paired with a pair of jeans. All blue. All Aaron. Looking deep into his eyes, I see forgiveness, love, and acceptance. He steps closer, still holding his phone to his ear.

"Hey."

"Hey." Our noses almost touch. He tucks a piece of hair behind my ear, taking my phone from my hand and ending both of our calls. "I wanted to call you last night, but I decided to come this morning instead," he grins.

"You took the red-eye?"

"I asked Dex for a favor..."

"I asked Chris for my old job back and to be the coach of the hockey team once I'm back home..."

"Home... I like to think we have the same definition of home now."

"How much is this favor of yours going to cost you?" I ask Aaron, smirking.

"Proclaiming he's my favorite brother at the next family supper..." He laughs nervously. "You?"

"A meal at your restaurant." I shrug.

"Chris is an asshole, he always eats for free at my place," he scoffs. "I spoke with Sal last night... She's, in fact, a big fan of yours." I frown. "Don't seem so taken aback." He chuckles. "Anyway, we talked, and she might have made me see the light..."

"Mm-hmm." I bite my lower lip, trying to repress my smile.

"So, I wanted to ask you if you wanted to go out sometime." He rubs his thumb in the palm of my hand, sending chills down my arms.

"I think we're past going out sometime..." I tease. Resting his forehead on mine, Aaron kisses my nose before pulling back.

"I don't agree, Sweets. I want to date you. I want to know who you have become.

I want to be with you. We fucked, and it was amazing, but I want to know adult Alane as much as I knew teenage Al. I want to know what makes you tick, what makes you smile, and what makes you happy. I want to love you the way you deserve to be loved, and I want to show you my end game was always you. Not to become a chef, to have the best restaurant in the state, to expand my kingdom, but to be yours." I swallow and blink rapidly to chase away the wave of repressed emotions emerging after so long.

"So, what do you say?" I nod, not trusting my words.

"I'm saying I want you. But don't worry, we won't date like when we were teenagers. My body is yours to explore, Sweets." His fingertips brush my ass, sending a jolt of pleasure inside me. Bringing his mouth to my face, he kisses one cheek.

"I'm sorry I didn't fight for us." He kisses the other.

"I'm sorry I was mad." He kisses just below my lips.

"I'm sorry I was an asshole to you." He kisses my neck.

"I'm sorry I moved on." He kisses under my ear. I'm on fire, needing him to fuck me, but I don't want him to stop what we're doing.

"Most of all, I'm sorry I never made love to you," he whispers, his tongue licking my earlobe. "Did anybody ever make love to you, Sweets?"

"No." My voice is raspy and reflects the pool of desire I feel between my legs. His fingers are on every inch of my skin. All my senses are alert. His lips find mine, and just the feeling of his beard on my pulsing lips could make me climax.

"I'll take it slow, Sweets, a good missionary style like I've imagined taking you for the first time a million years ago. Where is your bed?" I jerk my head in the general direction of the guest bedroom Adam let me use. "Come on, let me love you like nobody ever has."

There is no rush in any of his movements. Aaron takes his

time undressing me, his hands gliding on my body like a promise. Peeling off my oversized T-shirt from my shoulders, his fingers caress my breasts, hardening my nipples even more. I shudder, feeling his breath on my navel. As his hands work on unbuttoning my jeans, I feel his gaze on me. I blush like the girl I was before.

"If it makes you feel better, Al, I've never made love to anybody either until tonight." I capitulate at his words, letting him guide me to the unknown pleasure of being cherished by someone I love. Shimmying my jeans off, he drags his fingers all along my legs before kissing his way back up, alternating each leg. My ankle, my calf, the hollow of my knee, above my other knee, the middle of my thigh, my groin.

"You smell so good, love," he mumbles, dragging his nose over my soaked panties. Kissing my core through the cotton, he nibbles his way to my hip before resuming his shower of kisses. My hip, my navel, my rib, underneath my bra. By the time his lips are around my nipple, I'm ready to combust

"Please, Aaron, I need you inside me" My voice shakes as much as my body. He smirks before bringing his lips back to my breasts, his tongue playing with my hard pebbles. "Aaron," I moan impatiently, waiting for him to take me. Lifting his head from my breasts and reaching behind his neck while holding his body with one arm above me, he pulls off his T-shirt. Removing his jeans, he pushes them down onto the floor, still putting his weight on his forearm. The movement is defining his muscles like I've never seen them before. I tilt my head to kiss the inside of his arm. Sliding his hand under my back, he unhooks my bra and frees me. Both in our underwear, feeling his skin on mine and the heat coming from him is like a caress to my soul. Chills spread over my body, sending it into quivers.

"Are you okay, Al? Is it anxiety?" As I look at him, I see all the worries of the world on his shoulders.

"No, no crisis since you last calmed me down." I stroke my hand through his hair.

"Not even after what happened between us?" he asks, giving me a peck on the mouth.

"No. I thought being here alone would send me spinning back, but nothing. Don't get me wrong, I was miserable, but no anxiety attack."

"Hmm." He kisses my lips again. "We'll talk about it later. Right now, I would really like to continue what I was doing." His hand is going back down my torso, taking the same trail his lips just followed. I push my hips for him to understand how much I need him, and when his fingers push my panties down, I shiver. His fingers enter me at the same time his tongue finds its way inside my mouth, and it seems impossible for me to take it slow. But Aaron doesn't thrust as if he's about to lose his mind, he pulls in and out slowly, letting me feel every callous on his fingers and every dent on his skin, while his tongue follows the same pace. I feel like I'm burning inside and freezing outside. I feel my mind lost in desire and found in love. I feel my core clenching and my body relaxing, and with a touch to my clit, I come.

Pulling down his underwear, Aaron hovers over me, placing the tip of his shaft at my still clenching entrance. I feel myself wetting his dick, and as my hand caresses his back, he pushes in and comes fully back out a couple of times, still at an excruciating slowness, sending me back right away into another climax.

"Look at me." And when I do, I see more desire in his look than I ever saw in my many partners.

Thrusting deeper inside me, he accelerates his cadence

until he comes, while kissing me, holding me tight and rubbing my clit for me to reach my peak again.

Sprawled on me, our bodies intertwined with his dick lodged in me, we fall asleep, knowing our bodies, our hearts and our souls reunited tonight, and we do not need more confirmation than that to know what we feel for one another.

THEN – AARON

"One day, I'll marry you," I said confidently.

Alane snuck out tonight after her parents fell asleep so we could celebrate our second anniversary under the stars. I made a picnic, laid down a blanket in the bed of my truck, and lit candles all around us. We're cuddling, my hand slowly stroking her hair.

"I know you will," she says, nuzzling her nose in the crook of my neck.

"We'll have the wedding at the farm, we'll be surrounded by my family and yours and only the people we love. I'm sure my mother will insist you look like a hippie bride. She'll have you in a flowy dress with your blonde hair down in big curls and a flower crown on top of your head, but you'll be beautiful, nonetheless.

"Or my mother will put her foot down and insist we get married at the church and then might allow us to have the reception at the farm..."

"And your dad will marry us... that's terrifying." I kiss the top of her head. I can't not touch her tonight.

"That's what you get for wanting to marry the pastor's daughter." She chuckles, and it pierces my heart like cupid's arrow. I keep falling in love with this girl.

"Tell me more about our life together," she adds in a sleepy voice.

"We'll have three children. Two boys and a girl. I would like the girl in the middle." Her hand grips my shirt.

"I already have their names in my head..." she whispers.

"Yeah?" I feel her nod against my chest.

"Want to share?"

"No, it will jinx it." I pinch her slightly.

"Come on, Sweets, it's me. You know you can tell me anything."

"I discussed baby names with your mom last time I was there." She continues telling me about names and how she wants to name our hypothetical children, but I can't listen because images of Alane being pregnant are invading my brain. Babies means sex. Pregnant means bigger tits. As much as we're spending a sweet and romantic moment, I'm hard, and I need to calm down. "Wouldn't that be great?" Alane asks full of hope.

"Yes, amazing." I close my eyes, trying to picture her friend Patricia, so my boner goes down. It does.

"Where would we live?"

"Next to the farm? Or wherever your professional career takes us. We'll have to time those kids right, so it doesn't ruin your chance for an Olympic medal. Or you'll wait until you retire. I mean, we can have children in our thirties, I don't mind."

"I would like to live close to your family and have Luke nearby. I hope he finds a great guy to love."

"I think he's hooking up with Chris," I say only for her to

hear as if it's a dirty secret. I'm not ashamed my brother and best friend are gay. I'm just trying to understand what they are to each other. Especially because I know Chris also has sex with girls.

"I knew they spent a lot of time together, but…"

"I almost walked in on them behind the barn last week. I was shoveling fertilizer when I heard two guys moaning and grunting. Thank God, I recognized their laugh, so I walked away before burning my retinas." She swats at my arm.

"Come on… I'm sure it was hot."

"Maybe for you, but really, seeing my brother with my best friend, no thanks."

"Well, I hope they are as happy as I am."

"That's sweet of you. By the way, you can't tell Patricia."

"And break her heart because her brother went where she never could… of course not."

"I think she moved on and is trying to get me now."

Alane scoffs. "You're ridiculous. Soon you're going to tell me she wants to be with Barnabas." She laughs. "She's not that desperate to be part of your family, you know. She's pretty active and has a lot of guys running after her."

"Believe me, we know. If Chris is not around in the locker room, that's all we hear about. As for Barn, he loves you too much to ever fall in love with someone else."

"He's so cute… I hope our son is as cute as he is."

"Maybe less rambunctious? He can also be extremely mean to Sal…"

"Sal is not as innocent as she seems, Aaron."

"I know…" I kiss the top of her head again.

"So, two sons, a daughter, can we have a dog as well? I always wanted one, but my parents always said no."

"Whatever you want, Sweets."

"We'll call him Garfield. He needs to be orange though."

"An orange dog called Garfield. You got it. I'll find a way to make that dream come true. I'll marry you as soon as I can."

"Is that an official proposal?"

"No, it's a promise, Sweets, one day, I'll marry you."

"*W*elcome to the first annual Gritt Hockey Tournament." Ridge screams in the megaphone.

"Dad!" Barn screams back "We already told you it's a game. We can't have a tournament with only two teams!"

"It's a game for the moment, Barnabas Topher. Think further, and one day, they'll be more of you, and you'll each have your family, and it can be a tournament. Well, except for Dex and Luke, they'll be referees by then as they don't want children…"

"Bella…" Dex scolds Aaron's mom for what she just said.

"Sorry, Son, I know, no baby talk, I promise."

"Can I start my announcement again?" Ridge screams.

"Yes!" We all answer back.

"Welcome to the first annual Gritt Hockey Tournament. As we all skate, well, more or less" all eyes turn to poor Adam, "and as we're all family, well, more or less" now we all turn to Chris, "no violence of any kind will be tolerated. You also need to have at least one woman on your team."

"Are you implying girls don't skate as well as boys, Coach?" I tease Ridge.

"Yeah, Grandpa, what do you mean?" Hailey shouts, crossing her arms.

"Stop busting my balls, ladies! Now, please, line up for this year's captains to make their team." Everybody lines up except for Aaron and me.

"Ready, Gritt?"

"Bring it on, Smith!"

"As the oldest player on the ice, I will flip the coin. Aaron being a gentleman decided to let Alane choose Heads or Tails."

"She's going to choose head," Luke shouts behind me.

"Of course she'll choose head." Aaron laughs. Adam, Lawson, and Hailey grunt their disapproval at their innuendos.

"Tails, for now, head for later," I say, winking at Aaron. Ridge flips the coin up in the air, and, of course, it falls on Heads.

"Yeah!" Aaron says raising his fist in the air.

"You want to play like that, Gritt?"

"You know I love you, Smith, but there is no love on the ice..."

I skate around him, slightly pushing him.

"Shit, Mom, I didn't know you could be so competitive." Adam laughs behind me.

"Aaron, you can pick first," Ridge says.

"Chris," he calls, his hand ready for a high five his buddy has in the air.

"Ridge," I scream.

"Dex," Aaron calls.

"Luke," I yell.

"Barn."

"Sal."

"Law."

"Hailey."

"Mom," Aaron calls Bella, leaving Adam the last player to be picked.

"Oh, come on, Aaron. If I get Adam, you need to give me Chris or Dex. He's a huge handicap on a team."

"Well, thanks, Mom," Adam pouts.

"No, Sweets, I don't have to give you shit. It's your fault our son didn't know how to play hockey until I came into his life." I love hearing him call Adam "our son". Since I came back to Spring Falls, Adam spends most of his free time with us, and even if it was a little rocky at the beginning, the five of us together found a great dynamic.

"Seriously? He can barely stand on skates. You're a shit teacher..."

"No trash talking, Smith!" Ridge shouts from behind me. Aaron seems too pleased with himself. I need to win and wipe that smirk off his face

"Who's in your net?" he asks smugly. I look at my team, and Sal raises her stick.

"You go, sister!" I shout at her. "I guess you're taking the net, Gritt? And your buddy is your captain?" Chris and Aaron nod. "So predictable," I scoff.

"Because you being captain is not predictable, Captain," Aaron sneers back at me.

"I'm going to kick your ass, Aar... You might even orgasm from it!" I reply, getting a high five from Luke for my come back.

"Take your positions," Ridge screams for all to hear. He drops the puck between Chris and I, and quickly skates back in defense. We play six on six. Aaron and Salomé are goalies. Ridge and Adam are my defensemen, Lawson and

Bella are Aaron's, and our offense is composed of Luke, Hal and myself in the center facing Dex, Chris, and Barn. Our skates swoosh and our sticks battle for thirty minutes. Adam falls only a few times, the stick helping him with his balance. Goals enter left and right. I love scoring against Aaron. Every time, Luke, Hal, Ridge, and I do a little dance while Adam stays put, afraid to fall. And every time Aaron swears. Sal is a wonderful goalie, but Chris, Dex, and Barn are a powerhouse that nothing can stop.

It's four-three for Aaron's team, and when I feel Luke coming from behind, I pass him the puck for him to take a shot at the net. It's a beautiful shot, clean and precise but unfortunately, Aaron stops it and sends the puck directly back into play. Awkwardly for him, he makes a mistake and slides it my way behind the blue line. Nobody is in front of me, and I don't think twice, seeing clearly where I need to shoot to score, I raise my arms and go for a slap shot, the puck flying towards Aaron in a straight trajectory.

"Noooooo," the whole family screams behind me. Keeping my head in the game, I skate as fast as possible toward Aaron in case of a rebound, not seeing any of my teammates moving fast enough. Aaron stretches to the corner and throws his whole body on the puck. "What the fuck, Al!" he screams, tossing his gloves on the ice.

"Why are you stopping the game?" I hit my stick on the ice. "Come on, play!"

"I told you she wouldn't see it." Luke laughs from the sidelines.

"Why are you not playing?" I turn around dumbfounded by my team.

"After forty, you can't see if something is square or round,"

Ridge's voice beams in the silent rink. I look at them, irritated by their contented smiles and loving expressions.

"Sweets." Aaron laughs, "You just took a slapshot with your engagement ring." I turn toward him, raising my eyebrows to my hairline, to see him on one knee, a crushed box in his hand. Opening it slowly, he releases a breath when he peeks inside.

"She didn't destroy it!" he screams to the sidelines.

"Are you? What is this?" I tear up.

"Alane, it's on this rink exactly thirty years ago that I fell in love with you. You were lying down on the bench, raised on your elbows with your head tilted back, your hair falling like a golden waterfall. After being impressed by your talent, I was mesmerized by your beauty. That day I knew you would be my wife. Alane Nora Smith, will you marry me?" I look at the destroyed box in his hand to see a round ice blue sapphire ring on a rose gold band. I can't take my eyes off it.

"So, the game was rigged?" Aaron shakes his head. "But they all knew." He nods. "Are we going to continue playing after this?" He nods again. Extending my hand for him to get up, I skate to him and kiss him softly. "Of course, Aaron Jax Gritt. I'll be lucky to have you as my husband."

"And when we get home, there is an orange dog named Garfield waiting for you..."

"We're getting a dog?" Lawson and Hailey scream behind us at the same time I hear Adam say, "Aaron's middle name is Jax? Shit, I love my Mom."

Kissing Aaron quickly, I remove my glove to shove the diamond ring on my finger before I turn around to face the family. Bringing my fingers to my mouth, I whistle loudly.

"Back to your positions, peeps, and let's play. I'm not going to allow my fiancé to win!

Head in the game, Gritts, head in the game!"

. . .

THE END.

Pre-order Forsaken, book 2 in the Gritt Family Series now on Amazon.

Join my Facebook Group: Get Twisted with Gab for news and shenanigans

MERCI, ETC.

I wrote this story in three weeks. Aaron and Alane were naturals, and they were talking to me so fast, I didn't have much to do. Then I tried to think about Barnabas and Salomé, and they were much more complicated to write. You would think the broodiest of the siblings would be the hardest to write. He wasn't... He was direct, to the point and knew what he wanted.

And how fun it was to see Luke young! If you haven't read Often & Suddenly yet, do it. Luke is just the best, and Dex... Shit, I already miss him, but if you've read all of my books, you know Dex is never far...

For this book, I particularly want to thank my husband and Jen. From "Can you lose your aim when you ejaculate on a woman?" to "Does the proposal make sense?"I consulted them more than usual.

Thank you, Shaun, Pam, Tracy, Darlene, and Athena for all the work ensuring that the manuscript was spotless, and of course, my Twistees, always supporting and advising me.

But most of all, an enormous thank you to Cleo for listening when I was lost and for giving Heartbroken the most beautiful cover when I didn't know what I wanted... (Do I ever?). C, thank O and L for me... Their help and input are more than appreciated. Always.

If you wonder how Alane got pregnant, it's called a splash pregnancy, and women who suffer from vaginism use this method to get pregnant. The things I learn while writing books. Google it.

Next in the Gritt Series, Forsaken. We travel to New York for a brother's best friend romance like no other. Salomé and Chris might finally get a chance to be happy. Might... Please don't hate me...

But first Trouble, the second book in the Darling Devils, and his love story with Naomi. 2020 is going to be a hell of a ride!

As usual, bear with me, the road is long and bumpy, but we'll get there together;

Live long with the Force, Hakuna Namaste!

—

Join my Facebook Group: Get Twisted with Gab for news and shenanigans

ALSO BY GABRIELLE G.

ANGELS AND SUNSHINE SERIES

(LA Stories)

Always & Only (Hollywood romance)

Never & Forever (Enemies to lovers)

Often & Suddenly (M/M)

THE GRITT FAMILY STORIES

Heartbroken

Forsaken - A brother's best friend story like no other – 2020
Pre-order now.

Untamed - A single mom, a town Casanova and a little girl dreaming
of a daddy. - 2021

DARLING DEVILS

Darling - A rockstar romance with swoons, laughter and
heartbreaking truths.

Trouble - A friends-to-lovers romance to the beat of the Darling
Devils – May 2020 – Pre-order now

Sweet - 2020

Follow me on Amazon to keep up to date with my latest release.

ABOUT THE AUTHOR

Gabrielle G will do anything for a hot cup of tea, still celebrates her half birthdays and feels everyone has an inner temptuous voice.

Born in France and having lived in Switzerland, Gabrielle currently resides in Montreal with her husband, three devilish children and an extremely moody cat.

After spending years contemplating a career in writing, she finally jumped off the deep end and took the plunge into the literary world. Writing consumed her and she independently published her work.

Gabrielle's style is fiercely raw and driven by pure emotion. Her love stories leave you out of breath, yearning for more, while at the same time wiping away tears.

Join Get Twisted with Gab for exclusive content and shenanigans and shop for merch on TeePublic

Made in the USA
Monee, IL
13 August 2020